THE HOT WIFE CHRONICLES 7

DARREN BAKER

CHAPTER ONE

1

"The guy that turned up at the wedding," I said. "The guy from Anissa's past, Gareth. I recognised him. I've met him before. He was married to Tara. Anissa was fucking her own sister's husband years ago."

Gareth shrugged. "Yeah, I know."

I felt my world implode even further.

"She told me."

I'd begged her for years to tell me. Years!

"I said it didn't bother me." Gareth pulled out his mobile. "You've tried calling her?"

"No."

"What?"

"I want her to come to me, Gareth... Or I want to give her space... I don't know." I slid the ring off my finger. "Does this even mean anything?"

He had his phone to his ear.

"Who are you calling?" I asked.

"Anissa."

2

My wife was with another man. And another man was calling her. A man she'd been intimate with only hours earlier.

This hadn't started with swinging. This had started earlier.

I remembered our first Christmas together.

I should've seen the signs.

6 years ago, and I'd been so naïve...

CHAPTER TWO

1

I coughed, the electric fire my only source of heat in the living room. The radiators were working, but the oil from our fuel tank had been stolen. Christmas lights lined the window. Snow was falling on the driveway outside our terraced house. Or Anissa's house, as it was at the time. We'd been together nine months, and I'd yet to move in with her.

I tapped the end of my cigarette over the ashtray on the coffee table, and reached for a tin of *Carlsberg*.

My eyes refused to settle, returning their gaze to the clock on the mantelpiece. It was nearly eight o'clock in the evening. Why wasn't Anissa home?

I shook my head, insisting I behaved. She was on her Christmas dinner with her work colleagues, most of whom she barely even liked. Yes, there would be drinks. Sociable drinks. She wouldn't get drunk. She wouldn't do anything stupid. She wouldn't...

She was beautiful.

My doubts were disgraceful.

She was irresistible.

I'd no reason to distrust her.

She wasn't the one I was worried about.

I stood, and rubbed my hands together. I heard singing from the neighbours' house. I didn't know the family. A married couple with young children. She was a looker. A sophisticated, always impeccably dressed lady in her mid-30s. He a bit of a boring bastard. They joined their kids in a rendition of *Silent Night*.

I caught my reflection in the mirror. Perhaps my only problem was my jealousy.

I just wished Anissa was home.

2

Music played softly through the walls from our neighbours' house. I recognised Dean Martin crooning *Let It Snow*.

What was keeping Anissa? She'd told me she'd be home about half seven. It was now after nine.

My heart beat a little faster, and I swallowed. Swallowed the miserable, miserly fact that I'd some issue. Some low-down, distasteful issue with trust. With self-esteem. With worth.

I pinched myself.

Anissa was the most stunning girl I'd ever met in my life. What she saw in me was beyond my comprehension.

I shook my head.

Whatever she saw, she saw it in me. Anissa's eyes were for me. For me alone. She would never stray.

I ignored what I'd witnessed the night we met.

3

The tyres of the taxi crunched the gravel outside. I heard the flirtatious laughter of my girlfriend. A muffled "Merry Christmas." The slamming of the taxi door. Her stiletto heels clicking on the driveway. I discreetly closed the blinds and curtains. Anissa hadn't noticed I was watching her.

The front door opened. The living room door followed.

My jaw dropped. My tongue fell forwards. My cock stood in my trousers.

Anissa stumbled then stood, propped against the frame of the door, in a fine, sexy pair of black knee-high boots, fishnet tights and a figure-hugging black dress under a fluffy white coat. She pouted.

"Hi, gorgeous," she said, her look completed by a Santa hat she didn't appear to realise was on her head.

"Hi, Anissa."

She hiccuped.

"You're..." How could I shroud my tone in anything but an accusation? "... Late."

Anissa was twirling, her hands on her hips. "How do I look?" she asked, taking an accidental additional step as she stopped.

I stood up from the sofa. "You..." I moved towards her. "Look..." I reached out, slipping one hand to her waist. "Absolutely..." The other around the back of her head. "Amazing." I pulled her lips to mine, and tasted vodka.

Anissa broke the kiss, and stepped back. "What are you going to do to me?" she asked, pressing her forefinger on my chest.

I breathed and heaved against her touch.

"Come on, baby." Anissa altered her stance, so her legs were farther parted. "I've been drinking, and I'm feeling *very* horny."

I swallowed. "What would you like me to do to you?"

Anissa closed her eyes. "You really are so young, sometimes, Mark."

I seized her finger in my palm, turned it and forced it down to her belly, further to her groin and finally under her dress.

Anissa wriggled her digit free.

I worried not, and pressed my own hand into her crotch. I could feel the white linen of her panties over her fishnets. "I like these," I said, smiling.

Anissa bit her lip, then threw her hair back on her shoulders. "Go on, baby," she teased. "Show me why I made the right decision when I agreed to go out with you... A younger man."

The fingertip of my middle finger found the underside of her lips, clad under the linen.

"When I set aside the fact you were *so* inexperienced..."

My thumb pushed on the hood of her clit.

Anissa elicited a sensual gasp. "... Compared to me."

I snaked her tongue into my mouth, as the first of my fingers sneaked between a gap in her fishnets.

"Mark..."

So did a second.

"Shit... Let me-"

My front teeth caught the tip of her tongue.

"Mmmmmm."

I reached inside the lining of her panties, and pulled them to the side of her pussy.

Anissa's white coat fell to the floor, and her pupils blazed and enlarged.

I slowly released her from my teeth, rolling my tongue against hers as I did. My eyes implored her to relax. To relent. To rely.

On this.

"Jesus!" Anissa cried.

I hammered my fingers into her cunt.

Anissa gripped the elbow of my ravishing arm for support. Her eyes fell backwards in her head.

"That's it, isn't it, Anissa?" I said, tightening my grasp in her vagina. "That's the spot that shuts your mouth."

She nodded sheepishly, flicking the pom-pom of her Santa hat from side-to-side.

I wrestled her insides more roughly, ripping her fishnets. Anissa released an illustrious howl, and I decided to lower her onto the sofa. I wrenched her legs wide apart, forcing her dress to her waist, and twitched on her internal sponge.

"Fuck, Mark, baby, do that harder! My pussy loves fingers! Give them to me!"

I swore I could hear *Nat King Cole* rhyme off the opening lines of *Chestnuts Roasting on an Open Fire*. The bloody neighbours. I finger-fucked Anissa's cunt, causing her face to contort.

"Oh shit, baby, I love it when I get a man's fingers inside me."

A man?

Her legs flopped to either side of my rib cage. "Easy, Mark."

I laughed, slacking my fingers inside her, and concentrated slow, circular motions with my thumb on her hood.

"Oh God," Anissa cried, and stuffed her forefinger between her front teeth.

I reached my free hand to the black patent material of her right boot, and unzipped her. I removed both boots. Her skin was unusually olive, owing to a rare visit the previous evening to a local tanning studio. Anissa had been determined to look her best for her Christmas dinner, and not to be outshone by any of the other girls in the company's employ.

I leaned down, and flicked the edge of my tongue on her clit.

Her hands roamed the sofa, seeking sanctuary from my pleasure. "Oh shit, baby."

I snapped my tongue away. "Yes?" I asked, innocently.

She grabbed my head. "Don't stop doing that, Mark, please." Her hips gyrated, propelling her sex against my chin and lips.

I lapped my tongue lasciviously against her clit.

Anissa reached out to the coffee table and found a remote. She tapped on several keys, until a rock ballads CD pounded *Alannah Myles' Black Velvet* from the surround speakers. "I couldn't take anymore of Jack frigging Frost," she panted.

I was locked on her labia.

"Fuck!"

I sniffed her juices. Sucked her lips. Probed her insides.

Anissa brought her knees to my shoulders, then suddenly pushed me away.

"What is it?" I said. "What's wrong?"

"Nothing," she said, and sat up. "I don't think so." She pulled her panties over her pussy lips. "At least I hope not."

4

"What?" I snapped.

"I'm not sure, Mark." Anissa threw her head to one side, swinging the pom-pom.

"Is there something I should know?" I asked. "You were late home from dinner. Did something happen?" Coherence momentarily misfired in my mind. "Something that shouldn't have?"

Anissa unbuckled my belt, yanked it free and put it in my hand. "I want you to take that, baby, because I *do* have something to tell you." She unzipped my fly.

My heart thudded faster.

"I've checked the internet history on my laptop." Anissa squeezed my erection. "I know what you want to do to me." She rolled her palm on my foreskin, freeing the head. "You want to punish me. You want to *beat* me."

I said nothing.

She started to wank me.

"Yeah," I groaned.

Anissa tightened her grip.

"Fuck, sweetheart, what is it... What is it you have to tell me?"

Anissa smiled around my member. Her eyes flashed upwards. Her mouth snaked downwards. She swallowed my cock to the base.

I placed my belt on the top of the sofa, against the wall.

Anissa pried her lips from my shaft. "You taste wonderful, Mark. And you look so young... So naïve."

There was only two years between us. "I'm not a kid, Anissa."

"My inexperienced, little lover," she taunted.

Anger raged inside, and I reached for the back of her head. "I'll show you, Anissa!" I rammed my cock down her throat.

"Mmmf!"

My pubes enveloped her nostrils.

Her eyes bloated.

I shoved myself further inside her.

Her hands patted at my stomach.

I swept them away.

Her fingernails caught my arms, and sliced tiny marks in my flesh.

I held her for several more seconds, pulsating between her lips, then I finally released her.

She was coughing, striving for a breath, and wiping running mascara from her cheeks. "Shit. Fuck." Her eyes met mine, staring. "Where the hell did that come from, baby? That was so fucking hot."

What?

She watched me, her chest rising and falling in rapid succession.

"I don't like being mocked, Anissa."

Anissa pursed her lips. "Or... Maybe you do."

The song faded out.

"To get that reaction... To stoke your fires... To *truly* turn you on."

I wanted a cigarette.

5

I stubbed out my cigarette in the ashtray, and looked at Anissa. She'd removed her fishnets.

"Baby," she began, tugging at my trousers.

I lifted my ass, and she stripped me from the waist down.

"Your cock is gorgeous, Mark." Anissa stared at my erection for several seconds. "Will you let me sit on it?"

"Oh yes, babe."

Her eyelashes fluttered. Her lips uncurled. Her smile faded.

"What is it? What's wrong?"

Her chest heaved under her black dress. "I don't want you to be mad." Anissa grabbed my cock, pulling me into a sensual wank.

"Mad?"

She nodded.

"How could I be mad, Anissa? You're the most beautiful girl in the world. You want to sit on my cock. Nothing could ruin that."

She increased her pace.

"Oh fuck, sweetheart, that's it."

Anissa bit her lower lip. "There is something, Mark. Something I *have* to tell you. I don't want to make you mad. Can you promise me you won't get mad?"

I humped her hand, hesitating only in speech.

"Please promise me, Mark. I don't want secrets between us."

"Okay... I promise."

Anissa thumbed the straps of her dress in turn, lowering it off her shoulders. Her body was petite and svelte. Her blonde hair long and flowing out from under her hat. "Do you like?"

I nodded.

Anissa tugged tighter on my cock, squeezing precum over her thumb. Her dress dropped under her bra.

I cupped her groin through her panties.

"No." Her free hand pushed mine away from her crotch. "Just sit back and enjoy what I have to do to you, Mark." She shifted herself onto her knees on the floor. "I drank too much wine with my Christmas dinner, baby."

"I... Can... Tell."

"*Please* don't be angry, baby. I want to tell you this." She pulled her hand from the base of my cock to the head, then paused. "In my wildest dreams, you might *like* what happened... Maybe even encourage me to..."

"To...?"

Anissa snagged her mouth suddenly around my member, sucking up my precum. She broke away. "I don't know how you went for years with nothing more than masturbation to relieve yourself, Mark."

My cheeks reddened.

"I could never go without sex. I think if I was ever single again..."

Why was she thinking along those lines?

"... I'd have to seek out one night stands, see if I could be provided a succession of cocks for my pleasure."

What on earth had happened at the Christmas dinner?

"You understand, Mark, don't you?" She squeezed my cock, forcing out more precum. "My pussy will always need attention."

I nodded.

"I don't know how much I had to drink tonight. The other girls kept filling up each other's glasses. The boss sent more and more bottles down to our end. I got carried away. I let my hair down, so to speak, Mark. I know I had too much. I can feel it now. My head's spinning." Her smooth palm massaged my balls, releasing my cock for temporary respite. "But not just from the alcohol. I got another buzz."

My heart panged.

"All us girls were getting pissed. We downed our dinner, and that steadied the effects. But not for long."

I stared at her.

"Please don't be angry, Mark." Anissa returned her hand to my cock.

"You cheated on me, didn't you?" I said.

She watched me.

She wanked me.

She wanted me.

"Anissa, please, I can't take this. If you were with someone else, just tell me."

She grinned. "Yet your cock is so hard in my hand, baby."

"What-"

"Tell me you love it, Mark. *Please*, try to enjoy it."

"I can't-"

"Embrace your fears, Mark," she interrupted. "Ignore your instincts. Trust your desires. Feel your cock throb in my hand, and release yourself to your primal urges." She grabbed suddenly on my testicles with her free hand. "Trust your balls in my palm, Mark. Feel them wanting to hear what happened at the dinner... What I got up to... What I did behind your back-"

My hips bucked involuntarily, and I rammed my cock violently into her touch.

"Woah there, Mister!" Anissa cried, and released my genitals.

Wind whispered through snowflakes and rattled the walls of the house.

I grabbed my cock, and wanked it furiously before her.

Anissa swiped at my hands. "No, baby, wait. Wait!"

I couldn't stop.

She backhanded my wrist. "Stop!"

Somehow I let go, and panted aloud.

"Take it easy, Mark," she said, and rubbed a vein which led to my balls. "I want you to relax and last the distance."

"I can last, Anissa. Please don't stop wanking me. I need it."

"You *need* it, baby?"

I nodded.

She laughed. "May I continue my story?"

My every inherent thought dictated she should not continue. That promiscuity, however small, should be discouraged... Or punished. "And if I choose to, I can beat your beautiful ass with my belt?"

Anissa shivered, though her eyes sparkled. "Yes, baby, for being a naughty girl." She reached behind her back and unclasped her bra, revealing stunning, pert breasts.

"I want to suck them, Anissa."

"Later, baby." She jerked my cock harder again. "But I have to tell you what happened after the dinner. The boss must've been encouraged-"

I jolted forward. "Did he touch you?"

Anissa shook her head. "He just kept sending down more wine. The labourers were laughing, watching us and telling us to get drunk and get our tits out for them."

My cock stood harder in her hand.

Anissa bit her thumbnail. "I think you like the thought of me straying, Marky baby."

"Don't call me Marky, Anissa."

She laughed.

"Anissa, tell me what you fucking did behind my back or I'll beat the shit out of you with that belt."

"Promises... Promises."

I seized her blonde hair in my hand. "Trust me, sweetheart, you won't be able to sit down for a week."

6

Anissa slipped her free hand into her panties. "Fuck, Mark, I'm soaking... At the thought of it."

"What?"

"I..." She may have slid a finger between her lips. "I want you to treat me badly. I want to be punished for being..."

I waited for several seconds. "For being what?"

Anissa shook her head. "You'll be angry, Mark. I don't want you to be angry... Not for real."

"For crying out loud, Anissa, just spit it out. What did you do?"

She rolled her forefinger and thumb around the edge of my foreskin and stared at the slit. "I danced... With several of the labourers."

Jealousy juxtapositioned fear and wonder. "Drunk dancing?" I demanded.

"We were all drunk, Mark." She stuffed my cock into her mouth.

"Oh, fuck... Shit, Anissa."

"Mmmmmm," she gargled.

I had to fight my fingers into her hair, dragging her back from the base of my member. "I'm gonna explode, if you keep that up, honey!"

She snarled. "I want your cock, Mark. I *need* it!"

Holy shit. Something had sparked fireworks in her. Something... Or... Some*one*. "Tell me more, Anissa." I wrapped my hand around my cock.

Anissa's glance fell on my masturbation. "Oh, baby, look at the way you stroke yourself. You *really* do know how to pleasure yourself, don't you?"

"Yes."

She smiled. "Years of practice, right?"

I hesitated.

"You masturbated for years when you were single."

I nodded, embarrassed yet aroused.

"You don't mind that I'm more experienced than you, do you?"

Where was she going with this? I reluctantly shook my head. "You're just so beautiful, Anissa. I'm thankful I have you. I know how lucky I am." Something about her past – or what I knew coupled with what I imagined of it – tore arousal through my apprehension.

"I know a thing or two about how to turn a man on, yeah?"

I nodded more vehemently.

"I did that tonight, baby." Anissa's hand moved to my thigh, stroking my hairs, then onto my balls. She leaned her mouth forward, and took a testicle between her lips. Her fingers pried at mine, freeing my cock from my clasp.

Our digits entangled.

"Let me, baby," she mumbled, muffling her voice with my bloated balls.

I surrendered.

Anissa pulled her mouth away. "Some of the dancing was just fun. A group of us girls got up first. The labourers were watching us. Nici thought it'd be a laugh to start busting a move. She was grinding herself against Tracey. Sharon grabbed me. We must've read each other's minds."

The tip of my cock twitched in her hand. "What did you do?"

"We were running our hands over each other, spinning around and gyrating our asses together. The men were going nuts. It wasn't that smutty. Or maybe it was. Shit, Mark, I have to work with these people... What have I done?"

I humped her hand. "I don't know. Is that it? You put on a show for the labourers, and they loved it?"

"The boss was watching... So was his son."

"His son?" I asked. Anissa had mentioned him before. "Sean?"

Anissa nodded.

The next-door neighbours' Christmas carol contest restarted with *Hark! The Herald Angels Sing*.

"He always thought he could have me, baby. He thought he could click his fingers and I'd come running. The spoilt brat thought his daddy's money could buy him my affections. But I was never interested in him. What I look for in a man... Baby, money is nothing compared to what I find in you." Anissa climbed up my body, and licked quick, circular motions around my lips until finally she twisted her tongue over mine.

I melted under her. My hands found her cheeks, her hair and finally her Santa hat, throwing it beside me on the sofa.

Anissa broke the kiss all too abruptly. Her hand was milking precum from my penis.

"Anissa," I muttered hoarsely. "Be careful... If you keep that up... I'll cum... And I need to fuck you." She slowed, as I gathered precum on my forefinger and placed it on her lower lip.

"I love that," Anissa said, licking it off. "Just like I loved the attention earlier. Nici and Tracey were nothing compared to Sharon and I. We even pecked each other on the lips. I think Sharon wanted to go further, to really wind the guys up, but I didn't do it. I might've if the boss hadn't been watching."

My suspicions were solidifying. "What about Sean?"

"He watched." She wrestled my cock from tip to base. "Some of the labourers got up. Tracey and Nici cooled their dancing..."

"What about you and Sharon?"

"Sharon wanted to keep dancing with me."

I twirled a strand of her hair in my forefinger. "And you, Anissa?"

She bit her lip. "Please, don't be angry, baby."

Arousal anchored my cock in her palm. What was so suddenly stimulating about her potential treachery? I was confused, my excitement compounded by imaginings of her acting out adulterous intent. "I won't be," I said. "I won't get mad at you."

"You sure?"

I almost told her I promised.

"Well, I could see all the men staring at me. One of them even rubbed his crotch as he watched. No one else noticed-"

"Did you fancy him?" I asked.

Anissa shook her head, and weakened her wanking. "It wasn't about him. Or any of them. It was the attention. Their eyes. Their cocks. They all seemed to want me. I was twirling my ass to them. Sharon warned me it was only a matter of time before one of them broke in-"

"Broke in?"

"One of the bigger of the labourers... Jim."

"What's he like?" I asked, trying to visualise it.

Anissa's grip became a tight grasp. "He's in his mid-40s, married, grown-up kids and he's really big. A real man. He just cut in between us and grabbed his hand behind my back, pulling me into him. All the lads were cheering him on. I couldn't look at the boss. I was embarrassed. Then I caught Sean's eye. He was looking... He was looking angry. He couldn't believe I'd given myself to Jim-"

"Given?" My cock surged out of her hand.

Anissa caught me, rolling her fingers around my shaft, and giggled. "Oh, baby, don't be too jealous, I was only doing it to wind Sean up."

"Doing... What?"

"I let Jim run his hand over my back. My waist too... And he copped a good grope of my ass."

"You just let him?"

Anissa bit her lip, mocking innocence. "I *encouraged* him."

7

My balls threatened to explode and my head spun. What was so amazing about the realisation of my worst fears? "Tell me what you did, Anissa."

"I pushed my ass against his hand, Mark. Then when the music changed, I pushed it into his crotch."

"Was he hard?"

"*He* wasn't... But the next guy was."

"The next guy?"

"I danced with almost all of them. Oh, baby, don't be annoyed. It was harmless, *really*. They all appreciated their Christmas treat. The more drink they had, the more they wanted to push it. But they were nothing I couldn't handle. I've been around the block. I knew what I was doing... Well, most of the time. I can blame the alcohol for the rest."

The rest?

Anissa seemed to notice my suspicion, and strengthened her tug on my cock. "Most of them were really nice about it. They said I'd made their night. Tracey and Nici seemed a bit pissed off, like I'd stolen their thunder or something. While Sharon was more than happy to lap up the attention of my sloppy seconds."

My torso was rigid. My mind shaking inside.

"Some of the guys were keeping Sean going, telling him to lighten up and enjoy himself. They wanted to know when he was going to have his turn with me."

"Turn?" I snapped. "Jesus, Anissa, you make it sound like you were their slut to be passed from guy to guy."

She shook her head. "I was just letting my hair down, baby-"

"You said you felt one of their erections!"

Anissa wrenched my cock forcefully up and down. "I never said those words, Mark. I said I felt the second guy to dance with me was hard." The heel of her hand hit my balls. "He wasn't the only one. It was nice to have them like that, and know I was the cause." She licked her upper lip. "But they'll be more embarrassed than me come Monday morning, trust me."

Trust. What I thought had been the epitome of our relationship seemed suddenly no more than an epitaph of what had been.

Anissa eyed me with suspicion.

My struggles were within. My issues with trust a prior engagement to her confession. Anissa was amazing. I had to realise that. Yet I'd doubted her fidelity regardless of her actions. I undervalued myself. And next to a woman so beautiful and alluring, what man would be any different? "I'm so lucky, Anissa."

Her smile lit up her whole face. "Really? You're okay?"

I nodded. "I'm the man you come home to."

She rubbed my balls. "Keep this spunk for me," she commanded, then released my cock and sat back on the coffee table, spreading her legs.

"I'm gonna fuck you so hard, Anissa."

The Christmas carol next-door finally came to an end.

"Not yet, Mark." She pulled her white linen panties to one side, revealing her moist pussy lips. "I'm not finished."

I overcame instinct, suppressing my accusatory tone. "So, did Sean get his turn to dance with you?"

"No." Anissa rubbed her clitoris between a small mound of pubic hair. "He stormed off in a rage as soon as his dad decided to call it a night."

"What?"

"Wait. Are you okay, Mark?"

"Yes," I insisted.

She looked at my erection. "I can see you're aroused, but you're definitely okay with what I've told you?"

I ploughed through my hesitation. "Yes, tell me more. I..." Did I dare explain it? "I think I like it."

"Like what?"

I breathed a deep exhalation. "I think I like the thoughts of you dancing all sexy and steamy with other men... Behind my back."

Anissa groaned as she slipped two fingers into her pussy. "What about that part? The part about it being behind your back. How does that make you feel?"

"Angry-"

"Oh."

"And aroused."

Anissa's eyes flamed. "Oh my God, baby, you're what I've always wanted." She rammed her fingers inside herself. Her breasts bounced as her momentum grew.

I wanked slowly, mesmerized by her self-mauling. "You said there was more?" My voice grew more authoritative. "Tell me what happened."

She squirmed.

"Tell me what the fuck you did." I reached behind my head for my belt. "Then I can beat the living hell out of you for it."

Anissa lost herself in her lust, sliding her fingers into her wetness with delirious force.

The leather of my belt crashed hard on the coffee table beside her.

Anissa jumped. "Fuck!"

"Don't forget about me, Anissa." I whipped the belt back beside me. "Tell me what happened."

Her eyes wandered my length, as her tongue ran the ridges of her mouth.

"Tell me," I said. "You can play with yourself." I grabbed my cock. "And I'll play with myself. You'd better tell me everything you did in detail, Anissa. If I suspect you're hiding the truth, I'll smack you across your thighs with this belt. You won't be able to wear your short skirts again until you're healed."

Moistness oozed from her opening. "I danced with the labourers. I felt one or two erections against my ass–"

"How many?" I shouted, and released my cock to seize my belt.

"Two, baby, two. I'm sorry. I got carried away."

I held the leather taut in my hand. "Are you sure?"

She nodded, her breathing swift. "I'm sure."

"Not three hard cocks against you?"

Anissa shook her head, her hips gyrated and her fingers slipped inside her pussy once more. "No, I only felt two hard cocks."

"What size were they?"

"They were big, baby."

"And did you feel them for long?"

Her voice fell to a whimper. "Not long enough."

I was in awe, at one second convinced she was exaggerating, the next fearful she was holding back. What if she mistook my encouragement for complacency? For weakness? For permission?

"It was *so* flattering, baby. They all wanted me. But they were only bold in the heat of the moment, and because they were egging each other on. I knew who *really* wanted a piece of me in that function room, and he was terrified to make a move."

I let go of the belt. "Sean," I said.

Anissa watched me stand. Her fingers froze in her pussy.

I left the living room in silence.

8

I dried my hands in the bathroom, and looked at myself in the mirror. My cock was somewhat deflated. Somewhat, but not quite. I scrutinized my eyes. What was wrong with me? As angry as I was with Anissa, I was consumed by her words. The whites of my eyes stared back. She was lying. There was no truth in her tale. The Sean element moved my pupils. Something *had* happened. Something *was* happening.

"Baby?" she called.

"Yes?"

"Are you okay?"

"I'm coming down now," I said.

Anissa was silent.

I looked again in the mirror, and wondered what part of her promiscuous behaviour was responsible for my sudden erection.

9

I threw open the living room door, and stared at Anissa, sat now completely naked on the coffee table. She turned to me, showing my belt clenched between her teeth.

I walked to her, seized my belt and sat on the sofa. "Talk."

"Anything else?"

"Can you suck my cock and talk at the same time?"

Anissa bit her thumbnail. "No."

"I didn't think so." I pointed to her crotch. "Spread your legs. Play with your pussy. And tell me *everything*. I think there's more chance of getting the truth out of you if you're aroused."

"Oh, I am aroused, Mark," Anissa said, parting her legs. "I'd had my fun on the dance floor, but Sean's dad had seen enough. He's not a big drinker, and he announced the night was coming to an end. I spied Sean pushing one of the workers out of the way."

"One of the workers?"

"One of the labourers, Mark. One of the guys who'd thrust his cock up and down the crack of my ass."

"What?"

Anissa smiled, gliding her fingers over her clit. "The second guy with the hard-on had been a little more adventurous than the others. He wasn't shy to show off what he was doing."

Anger disembowelled my desire. "Keep talking!" I barked.

"He was more physical than the others. He wasn't malicious. He just seemed more up for a laugh. But then I realised he was hard. And I... I encouraged him. He'd only grazed against me once, perhaps accidentally, but I made sure it happened several times. The music changed and I performed some routine... I don't know... I was copying Sharon. We bent over quickly, and grabbed our ankles. It was only supposed to be for a split-second. Tracey and Nici were doing the same. But this guy-"

"What was his fucking name, Anissa?" I'd my cock in one hand, and the belt in the other.

"George."

I heard my pulse pound in my head.

"He's about 35. Tall and tattooed, with a beer belly. The moment I bent over, he rushed behind me and pretended to dry hump me... Except he wasn't pretending. His cock was between my cheeks. He held me down like that for a few seconds. I felt his cock against my pussy, Mark. It was embarrassing. Everyone was cheering him on. Well, nearly everyone."

My imminent orgasm stagnated. "They were laughing at you," I said.

Anissa pleasured her pussy lips in a V-like shape.

"Laughing at *me*."

She shook her head. "It wasn't like that, baby. Only the boss might've thought it was getting out of hand, and he called time on it before anything else happened."

"Really, Anissa?"

Her fingers folded together, and entered her opening. "Fuck!" she cried. "Well... Nearly anything. Sean stormed out after I stopped dancing, and I had a little thrill in my knickers."

"A thrill?"

"Yes, I was leaking, knowing I'd got the better of him." Anissa's eyes locked on mine. "Jesus, Mark, do you think it's possible to want to fuck someone you don't even like?"

10

Anissa shut her eyes, melting in malevolent memory. "I don't know, maybe I just liked having power over someone who thought they could buy me."

"So you stopped dancing and," I glanced to the clock, "obviously didn't go clubbing."

"No, baby... I followed Sean outside."

I wanked, trapped between trepidation and the thrill of treachery.

"I wanted a cigarette, and I knew he'd have one." Anissa dragged her digits from her pussy to her swollen hood.

"You could've got a cigarette from anyone, Anissa."

"I know." She nodded, smiling through her shame. "I wanted to see Sean. I wanted to see what my teasing-"

"Your torture."

"Yes." She brought her second hand to her sex, manipulating her cunt and clit in unison. "I did. I tortured him. I embarrassed him. The labourers told Sharon he'd said months ago he was going to nail me. And he never got anywhere... Well, not before."

I felt a depth-charge in my abdomen.

"I was so wet, Mark." She looked at my cock. "Are you angry?"

"I don't know."

"Can you take more?"

I nodded.

"Tell me, baby!"

I pumped furiously at my hard cock. "Yes, tell me more, Anissa. Tell me what happened outside with him."

"With Sean," she said, deliberately rolling her tongue around his name. "It was freezing outside. The wind gusted against my legs, making my juices suddenly cold."

"Did he..." I groaned under the red rawness of my length. "Do the decent thing? Did he give you a coat?"

"No, the fucker." The fact seemed to enhance her pleasure, and she threw her torso back on the table and her legs wider apart. "The fucker!" Anissa ploughed her fingers into herself, and unleashed an expulsion of sexual secretion. "I'm fucking gushing, baby!"

I leapt from the sofa, driving my mouth to her vulva and downing her juices. Her body shook. She instinctively pulled away. I found her hips in my hands, and dragged her pussy to my lips.

Do you think it's possible to want to fuck someone you don't even like?

Precum seeped from my erection.

Do you think it's possible to want to fuck someone you don't even like?

My tongue buried between her velvet mounds.

Do you think it's possible to want to fuck someone you don't even like?

"Jesus Christ," she moaned, and pulled my head higher to her clit. "Lick it like you've never fucking licked it before."

I obeyed, lapping at her.

"I went outside, baby. Oh shit, it was cold." Anissa's fingernails scraped my skin. "He called me a slut, Mark."

"What?"

"Sean." She clamped my mouth to her clit. "Oh yes, that's it. Lick it, baby, and don't stop no matter what I say. You'll have your turn when I'm finished."

I moaned approval to her audacity.

"Sean called me a slut, Mark, and my pussy throbbed against my panties. The linen felt so sexy on my lips. They were tight and moist, and the cold wind was doing nothing to cool my wild desires. I grabbed the cigarette out of his hand, and he just stared me up and down. My breasts were rising with every deep breath I took. He was mentally undressing me. I felt he was going to stick his hand under my dress. He wanted to. Oh God, I know he wanted to. If he hadn't been scared of his dad catching him I think he'd have made a move on me there and then and... Oh... My cunt was so alive." She pushed her clit against my front teeth.

I gently nibbled.

Do you think it's possible to want to fuck someone you don't even like?

I tugged a little forcefully.

"Fuck!"

I probed against her.

"He just kept muttering the word slut as he looked at me. But he wasn't looking in disgust, Mark. He was looking like the spoilt bastard who wanted the one thing in the room he seemed to believe everybody else had a shot of having. The dickhead didn't have a clue. Oh shit, yes!"

Do you think it's possible to want to fuck someone you don't even like?

"Mark, I was standing with my legs as far apart as my dress would permit. My juices were soaking my legs. He called me a slut. A filthy, fucking slut."

I rotated my hand on my cock. I was dangerously close. But I had to contain myself. To constrain and conduct the flow of her story. Her confession had to continue.

"Sean's words were overwhelming, baby. I wanted him to keep calling me it. You know how rarely I smoke. How I *really* enjoy the drag, knowing my lipstick is wrapped around the tip and leaving a print. I passed it back to him. His breath was ragged, lighting up under the moon. It was like he wanted to take me against my fucking will."

I hesitated my facial humping.

"But it's only rape if you don't consent."

I parted from her pussy.

Anissa's hands snapped at the back of my head, pulling me to her again. "Don't stop. Oh God, please don't stop... He took the cigarette, and came forward. He could've told me I was sexy. Or that I looked good. Any complement at all. I'm sorry, Mark, my pussy had a mind of her own... Again. All it would've taken was an effort. Instead, he eyed all parts of my body. Then he pointed above my head to mistletoe... He took another step forward... He grabbed my chin... He was rough and his fingers stank of... Him... His sweat... His drink... Shit, Mark, I think I smelt his piss..."

Fury furrowed my brow. Drenched my dread in disgust. And anchored my arousal in sickening, twisted depravity.

"He brought his face to mine... I was shivering in the cold, Mark... It was so fucking cold... He dropped his cigarette... The wind blew again between my legs... I wished for my panties... To... Just... Disappear... My pussy *needed* to breath...”

I greedily chewed on the lips of her sex.

“He pressed his mouth to mine... Our lips touched... My heart melted... My pussy was on fire, Mark. I fucking hate the prick and... We were practically kissing. But we weren't. It was barely a peck. Our lips were just *there* together... *Locked* together... Our eyes open... Staring at each other... Wondering... Who would make the first *real* move. I knew it wouldn't be me. I wanted to slap him... To belt him... To send him flying the moment someone else came out of the bar.”

I tongued her clitoris with deliberate freneticism.

“He touched me...”

My mouth smacked her skin as I left her. “Where?” I demanded.

“He pressed his fingers into my belly. He wasn't rough. He wasn't gentle. I almost laughed. He didn't have a clue what to do. Poor rich boy... He would've needed his daddy to put it in.”

Anissa pulled at my neck, and placed my lips on her soaking labia.

“He tried to put his arm 'round my waist. He breathed into my mouth. He caught it. He wheezed... If I could've felt his cock... Oh, if only I could've... I *know* it would've been hard... Fuck... It... Would've... Been... Huge!”

“Slut,” I said into her sex.

“Yes!” Anissa cried, and ejaculated her hot, sweet juices into my gaping mouth.

I lovingly lapping up her liquid.

Her body rocked violently, unleashing fresh dispenses.

“Slut!” I bellowed, spilling moisture on the floor.

“Eat it!” she ordered, and clutched my cranium. She clamped her legs to my shoulders, and ferociously fucked my face.

“Sl-” I was muffled. “-ut!”

“Ah-ah fuck! Oh-oh... Yes!” More juice squirted from her.

I ignored instincts she'd taught me were due to my inexperience, and hungrily swallowed the warm fluid.

“Fuck, yes! Eat me, Ma-ah-at!” Anissa's body flailed in sporadic convulsions. Her pussy prodded further. Her hips huddled closer. Her abdomen tensed. A final, climatic crescendo exploded from her insides, coating my mouth, my hand, and my thighs below. “Oh my

God! Oh my God! Oh my God! Mark, baby, you eat my pussy so good."

I slurped from the edge of her anus, along the reddened, moist crack of her cunt and to her hood.

"Mmmmmm," Anissa muttered, lying back and allowing her head to fall away from the other edge of the coffee table.

"Slut," I said, massaging her cooling juices into my crotch.

She reached for my cigarettes across the table.

I leaned back from her, gazing in amazement and in pride. She was a beauty. A debauched beauty. My fingers found the leather of my belt.

11

"So," I began, gently tickling the inside of one of her thighs with my hand and the inside of her other with my belt, "you seem to like that word... *Slut*."

Anissa sucked seductively on the cigarette, then fixed her eyes on the belt. "What are you going to do with that?"

"I'm going to beat you, Anissa." I was still kneeling before her, knees parted and erection standing.

"But..." She bit her lower lip, and tapped ash on the table. "... Why?"

"I'll tell you, sweetheart, one smack across your hole at a time." I snatched the cigarette from her, and stuffed it in my mouth. "Stand."

Anissa dropped her bare feet on the floor, and stood. Her pussy lips were hidden between her thighs and under a slight mound of pubic hair.

"Open," I said, and pushed the steel buckle of the belt between her knees.

Anissa retreated from the cold metal, but parted her thighs.

I steadied her in place, then ran the buckle up her soaking skin. "I'm going to..." I pushed the metal hook of the buckle between her pussy lips.

Anissa shuddered, inadvertently hiding her sex deeper between her crevice.

"Clasp your hands behind your back." I prodded her entrance

further with the slim hook.

"Mark," she gasped. "It's so cold."

I eased it in and out of her. "Then warm it, slut."

She nodded, as goosebumps dotted around the shaven edges of her pussy lips. "Oooooh, baby."

"Do you have any idea what I'm going to do to you, Anissa?"

"I've seen the sites you looked at on my laptop."

"But you haven't seen the browsing history on *my* laptop," I said, then pushed the hook all the way inside her until the rest of the cold metal buckle caressed her lips.

"Mark, oooooh God, it's so cold."

I grinned, stubbing out the cigarette. "You like it, though."

She curled her toes.

"You *don't* like it?" I pushed the heel of my hand against the buckle, sealing it to her skin.

Anissa winced. "No, Mark."

I rotated my hand on her. "But you seem to enjoy things you don't like, right?"

Anissa closed her eyes.

"Like Sean's lips on yours. His insults. The way he looks at you like you're a piece of meat..." I pushed my finger through the buckle to the hook and dragged it upwards against the rough insides of her sex. "A *cheap* piece of meat, Anissa. He can't call you anything but a slut now for how you behaved tonight. *I* can't call you anything but a slut. The way you had hard cocks against you." I yanked the belt from her.

Anissa recoiled, stumbling. She threw her hands up as I stood. "No, Mark, please. I've changed my mind. I don't want you to beat me."

I seized her waist, twisted her around and pushed her down on the coffee table. "Too late, slut."

12

She grabbed at the wood, seeking to pull herself away.

I slapped my hand on her ass cheeks, pinning her to the table.

Anissa squirmed, flailing her blonde hair wildly. "No!"

"Slut," I muttered, moving my palm to the small of her back.

"Don't-"

The leather of the belt swished through the air, and smacked harshly against her pert, round cheeks.

"Aaaaah-ooooow-oooooh," she cried, then stilled suddenly.

I blew gently across her ass, and released her. "Don't fucking move, slut."

Anissa lay exposed.

I walked around the rectangular table, eyeing my prey. I folded the belt, and slapped it against my palm.

Anissa grimaced. "Please don't hurt me, Mark."

"I'll hurt you no more... Than you hurt me." How I longed for cuffs to restrain her. For rope to bind her. To hold her. To fix her in place.

Anissa nibbled her lip, as I walked around her again to the sofa.

I gently lowered the belt onto her buttocks. "You didn't finish your story, Anissa." I dragged the leather slowly over her curves. "The last thing you told me was you wanted to feel his cock... His *huge* cock, you said."

Her body physically tensed under my scrutiny.

"What happened next?"

"Nothing."

I slapped the belt on her left cheek, leaving a beautiful mark. "Aoooow."

I watched her skin redden. "Something happened, Anissa." Her right cheek looked delightful. "You didn't just miraculously appear home."

Her silence would prove her undoing.

"I don't believe you... Slut." I unleashed the belt, slamming down on her right cheek. I pulled it away, folded it again and slapped it across her entire ass.

Anissa squirmed away.

I flung the belt down, missing most of her buttocks, and slapped the small of her back.

She cried out, whimpering.

"Hold still, you fucking slut!"

The room stopped suddenly. The walls appeared to close in. Smaller. Tighter. A cell more confined to my composure. My direction. My command.

I leaned down to her ear. "The next time you try to pull away from your punishment, I won't be responsible for what I do to you, Anissa." I breathed on her, watching her beautiful blue eyes blink. "Tell me you understand."

Her breasts heaved as she sighed deeply.

I grabbed at her ass. "Last chance, Anissa."

She defied my decree.

"I... *Hope*... That you're secretly going to enjoy this." I masked the growing momentum of a chuckle. "I know I will."

"Wa-"

I cracked the belt against her behind.

Anissa screamed out.

I struck her again. Again. Again. I was building more power in each strike.

"Stop! Stop! Stop!"

I whipped a final sting across the bottom of both cheeks.

Anissa sucked in hysterical breaths, turning her head towards me. Her eyes pleaded in submissive silence. Her mouth rounded in dramatic O's. Her body ragged and stilled.

"Talk," I said, motioning my foreskin back and forth above her. "Or I'll gag you with this until you choke."

"Okay, okay, Mark. Just please don't hit me again." A stream of mascara careered down her face. "I'll tell you what happened."

I lovingly stroked the red welts on her backside. "Sean breathed into your mouth. He was holding your waist. You wanted to touch his cock... Continue."

"He... Oh, Mark, please don't hit me-"

"Tell me what fucking happened!" I shouted, and smacked my palm against her cheeks.

"Aaaaah-ooooow!" Anissa wriggled, scuffing her knees on the wood.

I stepped up, and placed the sole of my foot on the small of her back. "Last chance to confess... And if you leave out a single detail, Anissa, and I ever find out, this beating will be nothing compared to the one you receive then."

"He..." She was gasping for breath. "He-"

"Call him by his fucking name, slut!" I mauled her ass, slipping my middle finger between her crack and into the soft, wet opening of her pussy.

"Sean!" she cried. "Sean! Sean! Sean! He tightened his grip on my side, like he wanted to pull me into him... I... I... Oh shit, I wanted him to pull me into him. I wanted to surrender to him. His size. His money. His tongue... His fucking possessiveness... But he wouldn't take it. He wasn't man enough to have me. He did... Nothing."

I yanked my finger from her cunt. "You tell me now, Anissa." I placed the underside of my fingertip over the puckered knot of her anus. "Or else."

"He opened the tiniest part of his mouth, Mark. He pushed the smallest tip of his tongue towards me. Oh God, it was gross. It was like he'd never kissed anyone in his life before."

"And what did you do, slut? Did you kiss him back?"

She hesitated. "No."

"I don't believe you."

She heard the buckle of the belt skirt across the wood as I lifted it. "No, Mark, no! I swear to you! I didn't kiss him! I just stood there, one second aroused, the next embarrassed. I was embarrassed *for* him. He wanted me so much, and he didn't have a fucking clue what to do with me. I'd no longer any interest in him... Other than to laugh at him."

I lowered the belt gently over her ass, until the metal buckle cooled her reddest, sorest spots.

"But I didn't... I lost my need to laugh."

Agitation irked my erection.

"I saw it, Mark."

My heart thumped. "You saw *what*, Anissa?"

"His fly was open."

13

"I could see into his trousers," Anissa whispered.

Curiosity became a necessity. "What did you see?"

She paused. "I saw *it*."

I was mute.

"Sean's dad came out the front door a split-second later. Sean turned quickly away from me. But then I could *really* see it through his fly. It was hard and pushing against the material." Anissa tucked a blonde strand of hair behind her ear. "His cock was thick, Mark.

I've no idea what length he was, or what the shape was really like...
But now I know he has a thick cock." She shifted her legs together.
"Oh God, I wanted to reach out and touch his dick. I wanted to
stroke it. Fuck, I'd danced with those other guys. I'd made him
jealous. I'd made him angry. I'd driven him to make the closest thing
he could to a move on me, and it was me who was stood beside him
with my legs parted, my thighs soaking and my eyes stuck to the
barest glimpse of his cock. I just wanted a feel, Mark."

I struggled for breath.

Anissa unlocked the fingers of her left hand, and glided them
down her body. "Just a few seconds. I wanted to slip my fingers
inside, and touch him. I thought of the smell of his fingers..." Her
back arched. "His piss..." She raised her ass. "And..." Her hand
slipped under her groin. "Oh God, Mark, I wanted it... I wanted
every sordid part of that fucker."

My erection withered, and I dropped the belt on the floor.

"Oh yes," Anissa moaned. "His dad told him to hurry up. He
gave me a look as well. Sean was shy. He couldn't look at me. Fuck,
I couldn't tear my eyes from his thick, fucking cock. The light was
just hitting it at the right angle." Anissa's hips ground her cunt into
her fingers. "Oh God, Mark, the way his father looked at me, it was
so hard to read. He finds me so polite compared to the other girls. He
always has a smile for me. And I for him. Sean gave him a look. A
fuck off look. His dad walked away to his car. Sean half-turned to
me. Fuck, my pussy was on fire, flaming and craving for this
ignorant prick I can't stand. Oh, Mark, I'm sorry, I couldn't take my
eyes off his fucking cock. His thick, fucking cock."

I was jacking myself again, confused by my fascination with her
philandering.

"I wanted to reach inside... And give him a wank."

My cock stiffened in my palm.

"He asked me if I needed a lift." Anissa's naked body was
writhing on the coffee table. "He couldn't look at me, and I couldn't
look away." Her lust was flummoxing. "I said no." She seized a
breast in her free hand. "Did I want to go clubbing? I said no again."
She pinched a nipple. "He looked gutted." Anissa smiled, sheepishly
yet shamelessly. "I didn't want to *go* anywhere with him."

"Slut," I whispered, unheard under her commotion.

"He said something about us all going out for drinks another night... And the word *maybe* slipped out of my mouth."

I watched her, as I masturbated. Hungrily. Happily. Inexplicably.

"I wanted to make him cum in his trousers, then smell his filthy, fucking cum and piss on my fingers." Familiar fires seized and tensed her torso. "Oh fuck, Mark, grab me."

"What?"

"Pull me off this table! I need to sit on you! I need to sit on your fucking cock!"

14

I seized her, and dragged her off the table.

"Oh shit!" Anissa cried. "Treat me rough, baby! Yes! I deserve it!"

"Come here," I commanded, and mauled the red marks on her hips as I pulled her onto the sofa.

Her legs splayed to either side of mine. "I need this."

"You're going to get fucked..." I positioned my cock at the entrance to her cunt. "*Hard...*" I guided her soaking lips downwards. "Little girl."

Anissa slapped my chest. "What the fuck are you doing, you fucking idiot?"

I was speechless.

"How dare you!"

I bucked angrily up against her.

"Fuck!" she screamed. "You fucker!"

I seized her chin, and forced her to look down at me.

"You fucker, Mark, what are you doing to me?" She was shrieking, arching her back and shoving her cunt aggressively onto me. She slapped my chest again, leaving a reddening palm print.

"What?" I was clenching my teeth.

Anissa threw her hands around my neck, slid forward and swallowed my tongue. "You..." She was insatiable, biting and licking. "Know how I feel..." She sucked swiftly on my lips. "About letting you fuck me..." She pulled my skull back, and devoured my neck. "Without a condom!"

I clasped her breasts, massaging each areola simultaneously, then pinched her nipples gently, fearful of another rebuke. "Yet you'd have loved that bastard Sean fucking you without a condom."

"Oh God!" Anissa cried, shutting her eyes.

I suckled on her tits, ramming my cock up inside her.

"You fucker! Fucking me without a condom! No! No! No! You dirty fucker!"

I drove deeper into her.

"Give me it, baby." Anissa's fingernails scraped my shoulders. "Give me your inexperienced cock. Show me what I've shown you!"

I held her down, and fucked forcefully up into her. "Slut!"

"Shit, Mark."

"What are you thinking?"

Her body stretched, her pert breasts pointing upwards.

"Answer me, slut!"

Her throat gargled. "Sean," she managed hoarsely. Her clitoris hit my groin, and her juices exploded suddenly, saturating my pubic hair in a mix of our moistures.

I stood, lifting Anissa with me.

Her torso was a turbulence of orgasmic destruction. "Fuck, fuck, fuck!"

I placed her on the coffee table, spreading her arms and legs. I stared down on her. "You don't know who you are," I said, then fucked violently into her.

"Oh my God!" she screamed, as my balls slapped against her thighs. Sounds of sweat and love juice grinding together coursed the room. Anissa was powerless but to proceed in the direction dictated by her climax. Her eyes rolled back in her head. "Jesus, Mark, give me it harder! Give me it! Treat me like a slut!"

"You are a slut!" I bellowed, and shoved her back on the table.

Her head smacked off the wood. "Fuck!"

I humped into her, almost using her body as nothing more than a hole to grind my cock in and out of. My kisses and caresses never came. My words of comfort and complement never arrived. I was fucking my girlfriend as a bull fucks a cow. A stallion fucks a horse. A stud fucks his bitch.

Anissa's cooling juices swirled around my cock, then dribbled onto the table. Her body stuttered. Her eyes stared up. Her fingers, at one second fighting the table for a grip she never found, stilled.

I fucked without recourse into her.

Her clitoris glistened, and her cunt ejaculated another round of warm, wet fluid onto my abdomen. "Fuck!" she cried, facing the ceiling with a look of abandonment. "Oh God, Mark, I'm cumming again!"

"Yes, you are, my slut," I said, and rammed my cock deeper.

Anissa screamed, pushing pathetically at my chest for freedom. I pulled suddenly out of her.

"Thank you," she whispered, shivering.

I watched her lips pulse around her gaping hole. "Turn around," I said.

15

Anissa blew her fringe from her forehead. "Baby, please, I'm done."

I pulled at her waist, and her ass slid on her abundant juices on the surface of the table. "I want you on all fours, Anissa."

She narrowed her eyes.

"I *demand* it."

She licked her lips.

"Think of me... As your boss."

Anissa's stare stagnated. "His son," she said quietly.

My chest heaved.

Anissa pushed herself up on the heel of one hand. "Sean." She collapsed on the elbow of the other. "Fuck, baby, I'm worn out."

I flipped her onto her tummy with one hand. "I'm going to cum inside you, Anissa," I snapped, and hauled her hole back to me.

"No, you're- Fuck!" she cried out, feeling her pussy impaled on my erection.

"Six fucking months you've made me wait." I grabbed her blonde locks in a bunch. "There's no way you made your ex wait as long."

Anissa fell predictably silent, as she always did when he was mentioned.

I fucked into her soft, perfect opening and smacked my palm across her ass.

She was bent impossibly over before me. "Oh my God!" she screamed, sure to disturb the neighbours. "That's it. Give it to me!"

I hammered at her hole.

Anissa struggled to balance herself on one arm, then threw her free hand over her shoulder to my mouth. "Suck my fingers, baby, suck them!"

I greedily tasted her insides upon them.

"God, baby, I'm gonna hate myself in the morning when I wake up and realise what I've done tonight."

I spread her cheeks wide as I fucked her, and scrutinized her tight asshole. Perspiration pooled at her opening, lubricating that most sensitive of orifices. "Tell me what you did." Easing, tantalising and teasing it for my consideration.

"I felt their cocks. I danced my ass against them. I was doing it to make Sean jealous. Then I saw a glimpse of his thick cock in his trousers... And I wanted to wank him off so fucking much."

My testicles were tensing.

"I came home, and taunted my boyfriend about his inexperience."

My blood pumped wildly. My breathing grew ragged. And my motions quickened inside her.

"And how my temptations turned to other men. In particular to one other. A guy I can't stand. And yet somehow I want to crumble before him, and let him violate me. Treat me like shit... Cum... Piss... Cum... Oh my God... I want *his* cum... *His*... *Pi-*"

I came horrendously inside her. "Fucking slut!"

"You filthy bastard!" she yelled, bucking her hips back. "Cumming inside me without a condom!"

I flung my cock further inside her velvet temple, unloading multiple volleys of sperm.

"If you make me pregnant-"

I fell forward, and bit her exposed shoulder.

"Aoooow, Mark!"

I clasped her waist, drilled my dick finally inside her, and erupted one last, momentous spurt, as I grunted, sweated and stifled revulsion at her revelations. The point of pleasure was passing. Realisation was riotously dawning upon me.

"Jesus, Mark."

I pulled out of her. My girlfriend had been touched by other men. My girlfriend had *enjoyed* being touched by other men. "Slut," I said aloud, as Sean had said before me, and I slid to my feet. I walked around the coffee table.

Anissa fell flat on her breasts. "I do love *your* cock," she whispered, as my semen seeped from her used hole. She reached out for my rod, and stuffed it eagerly into her mouth.

I thought suddenly of losing her to someone else. My heart was compounded by terror, and my mind spiralled into an abyss of abhorrence.

What if I couldn't accept her behaviour so far?

What if her pussy was already more promiscuous than she'd dared hint?

What if she wanted to push her limits further?

Her blonde hair bobbed back and forth, her lips engorging my length. "I love sucking cock," she confessed.

What limits?

CHAPTER THREE

1

I awoke sometime around 4:30am. Anissa's mouth was wrapped around a pillow, her torso splayed out on the mattress and the duvet draped tantalisingly between the naked cheeks of her ass. I was restless, and erect, and felt unable to resist the temptation to sneak downstairs for a wank.

I dropped my boxers to my ankles, shivered in the cold and grabbed my cock in my hand. The lager had worn off, but my mind was clouded by doubts of her loyalty. And intrigued by thoughts of her adultery.

I mauled my love muscle, throwing my closed eyes into conjured images of Anissa's dress barely covering her backside, roaming against the erections of the men she'd danced with. The labourers she described as *real men*. The watchful stares of the others, waiting their turn. And Sean. Sean, waiting, watching and wanting. His frustration turning to anger. One word in his head billowing and bellowing inside.

"Slut."

Anissa's refusal to revoke any attempt he made upon her.

Her desire for him to touch her.

Her want for him to touch her.

Her *need* for him to touch her.

His cum.

His...

I came violently into my palm, streaming spunk between my fingers onto the floor below.

I leaned back, taking a few seconds for respite. I'd find the tissues soon enough. Clean up. Hide the evidence.

Anissa'd never know the true arousal I found in her behaviour.

2

"You filthy fucker!"

I heard her somewhere on the peripheral edges of a dream I was having about scoring a goal against Spain in the World Cup.

Anissa picked the nearest newspaper from the coffee table and smacked it against my naked knees.

I jolted upright, realising my boxers were still around my ankles and my spent cock shrivelled between my thighs. "Shit." I looked to the mantelpiece. It was almost 10am.

"Who's a right little wanker?" she teased, showing no signs of the hangover I'd anticipated.

"You got me," I muttered, then reached down to my ankles for my underwear.

"No, no, no." Anissa walked quickly forward, and placed the heel of her foot on my boxers. "You don't get out of it that easily, mister."

I looked up to her in awe. Her figure was tightly wrapped in a pink satin nightdress, hid over the shoulders by the wool of my unfastened dressing gown.

"What did you masturbate to?" she demanded.

My face scorched with further embarrassment.

"It was me." Her heel hit the floor, trapping my boxer shorts in between. "Wasn't it?"

"Of... Of course." My chest heaved beneath a deep sigh. "It's always you, Anissa."

She laughed. "Tell me more."

"That's what happens to a guy when he goes out with the most stunning girl in the world." I smiled hopefully up to her. "He fantasises about her even when he's not with her."

Anissa grinned. "You're sweet, Mark, but that's not what I meant." She reached down, and peeled back the bottom of her nightdress. "I want to know *what* you were fantasising about... About *me* in particular... As you wanked yourself off in the middle of the night."

I stared at her beautiful thighs, until she dropped the satin.

She raised her foot from my boxers. "Don't pull them up, Mark."

I gulped, and nodded as her foot travelled higher between my legs.

"What did you wank over me doing?" Her nightdress rode higher on her legs.

I felt my body slowly sink into the sofa. "I relived last night," I said. "All of it."

Her toes tussled with my todger. "Good."

"Until I came."

Her big toe pressed on the fullest part of my cock, pushing it between my hairy thighs into the sofa. "What did you cum to, Mark?"

I hesitated.

"Tell me."

"What you did with Sean... And, even more so, all the vile, disgusting things you said you wanted from him."

Anissa took a sharp intake of breath. "I *was* a filthy bitch with you last night," she said, scrutinizing my naked form from the waist down. "I may have exaggerated some things."

A wave of relief wrestled my thoughts away from my disappointments.

"I *may* have exaggerated, Mark."

I locked my eyes on hers.

"I may just be telling you that so you don't get angry with me."

My cock stirred under her footing.

"Ba-by," she teased, failing to miss the fact.

3

Anissa was lying back on a three-seater recliner in the conservatory when I brought her her first cup of tea of the morning. Her blonde hair was dishevelled, yet cascaded beautifully over her neck and shoulders. A strap of her nightdress had fallen, revealing more of her sensational skin. Her nipples pushed against the material. Her legs were crossed, the satin stopping halfway down her thighs. Her knees were red, perhaps marked from the scrapes of the coffee table the night before.

"Thank you, baby," Anissa said, taking the cup and looking ahead to the Christmas tree on the other side of the room.

"You should put socks on," I insisted, sitting next to her and massaging her toes. "You'll catch your death in here."

"I'll be fine, Mark. I already put the central heating on. This room should heat up in no time." She broke a foot free and fondled my cock through my boxers, finding a path inside the opening at the front.

"Anissa..."

She sipped her tea, smiled and uncrossed her legs, delicately parting her knees.

I could see a hint of her pussy in the darkness under her nightdress. "Anissa, you're not making this easy."

The underside of her big toe pushed my cock back from my balls. "I haven't the slightest inkling of what you're talking about, Mark."

I sighed, grinning against my own wishes. "We need to talk, Anissa."

"All I want to hear is how long it took you to cum when you wanked."

"Not long."

"What part in particular made you cum, Mark?" Her foot was rubbing me to a full erection.

"When... When you talked about Sean's cum..." My cock burst through the gap in my boxers. "*And* his piss."

Anissa brought her other foot forward, positioning my cock between the soles of both. "You liked that?" She started to masturbate me with her feet. "You liked the idea of me being tempted by someone else... Someone I can't stand... Someone I find physically repulsive."

My teeth were clamped together. My gums retreating. Seething. "I think so," I said.

She increased her pace on my penis. "Are you jealous?"

"Yes," I answered quickly, hoping to suffocate any suggestion I no longer cared or craved her.

"How jealous?"

"I'm okay, I'm coping."

She brought the heel of one foot to my balls, and pressed gently. "Coping?"

"I'm embarrassed."

Anissa said nothing.

I felt obliged to continue. "You let yourself go around the guys. You danced with them."

She smiled.

"You weren't the only girl dancing... But... I know they would've all been looking at you-"

"They tried to touch me too."

I shot my stare to her eyes.

"They *did* touch me... A bit."

I tried to ease myself backwards on the recliner. "I don't know how I'll feel if I bump into them, Anissa. They'll all talk about you. And then there's the Sean thing. I'm angry..."

Anissa drove her foot deeper into my balls.

"... But it turns me on so fucking much at the same time. What's wrong with me?"

"You're a pervert," she whispered.

"Am I?" I snapped.

Anissa was all smiles. "Mmmmmm... Baby, I wish I'd my six-inch spiked heels on. Can you imagine what I'd do to your balls then?"

My erection soared between her soles.

She purred. "Would you mind getting them for me?"

I cringed. "Where are they?"

"Under the stairs, baby." She released my cock. "Go. Now."

I reluctantly stood, then walked into the kitchen.

Anissa wolf-whistled after me.

I found her black patent heels. "Holy shit," I muttered, inspecting every lethal last inch.

Anissa shivered, as I re-entered the conservatory.

"Are you sure it's warm enough for you in here?" I asked.

"I'm fine," she insisted, and clicked her fingers. "I want you to put my heels on me, Mark."

I glanced to the conservatory's double-doors, lined with Christmas decorations, then slipped my cock back inside my boxer shorts.

"Hey," Anissa said. "Get that out again."

"But what if one of the neighbours-"

"I don't care, Mark." Her finger was pointing at my crotch. "Do what you're told. The neighbours shouldn't be looking over our fence. If I catch anyone staring at my man's cock, they'll have *me* to answer to. Now... Fix my heels to my feet."

I did as I was instructed, lavishing the skin of Anissa's beautiful ankles in kisses. "I love you," I said, tightening the strap of one shoe.

"Good."

My cock grew a little longer.

Anissa lifted her leg high in the air, inspecting my handiwork.

Her nightdress rode higher.

I glanced to her pussy.

Her fingers snapped again. "Eyes on my feet, Mark. You had my pussy last night. I haven't even washed her yet."

I fell into subservience, shedding the instincts I'd learned in training, and glanced momentarily from her feet to her face, then finally again to her pussy. I knew her sex was where I was destined to lose all my inhibitions.

"You love having me as your girlfriend, don't you, Mark?"

"Yes, sweetheart."

"You were very jealous at the beginning of our relationship, though... When I told you how many ex-boyfriends there'd been."

I'd felt inadequate.

"And about the one-night stands too."

They'd been more difficult to accept. That she'd released herself spontaneously to men who hadn't earned their right to be with her.

"The amount of cocks I'd had inside me before you." Anissa eased her legs gently apart. "I *know* you found it hard. To be honest, Mark, I thought you were going to find it impossible to accept. I even considered breaking up with you early on-"

"What?" I'd just finished attaching the strap of the second heel to her foot.

She pushed a spiked heel into my chest, encouraging me back on the recliner. Her second heel snagged my boxers. "Pull these down to your ankles. I want to see your naked cock in all its glory."

I was hesitant at first, then obeyed her. "You really considered breaking up with me, Anissa?"

"Yes." She rested her heel on my thigh, and rubbed the bare skin at the side of her foot against my cock. "I started to think we were too different." Her other foot fell from my chest to my crotch, sandwiching my member. "I'd done so much. You'd done so little. But..."

"Aow," I said involuntarily. "Go easy, Anissa, those spikes hurt."

"... You'd such a nice dick... And a heart of gold. Once you stopped quizzing me twenty-four seven about my past, and accepted me for who I am, I soon forgot about Cameron. I learned to relax. And before I knew it..." She rotated her right foot, digging her heel into my scrotum. "I'd fallen in love with you."

"Fuck," I cried, fighting for grip on the recliner.

"It's not my fault I've been trussed up by a number of men before you, is it?"

4

I was panting, drawing breath I hoped would dull the pain.

"Is it?" Anissa demanded, and scraped her heel on my balls.

I yelled out.

Anissa reeled her feet away from my crotch. "Shit, Mark, are you okay?"

My fingers were white. "I..." I dabbed my testicles.

Anissa was staring at me. "Baby?"

I shook my head. "Do that again," I said, and placed the heel of her foot carefully on my balls. "But be gentle. No sudden movements, or you'll tear a hole in my sack."

Anissa tried to move stealthily, but the sensations she caused were still sharp.

I placed my hand on my cock. "Slip off the dressing gown," I said.

"It's too cold, Mark," she replied.

"Do it!"

Her brow furrowed. "Who d'you think you're talking-"

I smacked my free palm against her upper leg, reddening her flesh. "Do what you're fucking told, Anissa. I said this room wasn't warm enough. We could've moved. *You* didn't want to. Now, take off my fucking dressing gown."

"Bu..." She thought better of it, and slipped the gown from her shoulders.

I backed away from her spiked heel, and furiously wanked my cock. "You are fucking beautiful, Anissa."

She smiled, rather sheepishly, and fixed a strand of hair behind her ear.

"A beautiful... Fucking... Slut."

Her heel struck my scrotum.

I focused, allowing the agony to envelope my senses, and tried to adopt the pain as my stimulant. "Every man who's ever had you must've thought he was the luckiest bastard alive."

"They didn't." Anissa blinked. "Trust me."

"They should've." I watched her breasts move as she breathed. "You're fucking gorgeous."

"Here," Anissa said, and pulled her tits over the top of her satin nightdress. She pinched each nipple.

"What's going to happen when you see him again?" I croaked.

"Who?"

"Sean... We have to talk about it."

"What is there to say?" Anissa parted her knees to either extreme of the recliner. "He'll never get *this,*" she said, and nodded down to her pussy, exuding as much class as she did corruption.

I felt a spate of delight in my chest, easing my anxiety. "You sure?"

Anissa laughed. "Oh, baby, of course I'm sure. If I was going to have sex with anyone other than you, I'd like to think I could do better than Sean."

"But you *will* have to see him... Everyday."

Anissa coaxed anguish into my testicles, sliding her spike ceremoniously along my scrotum. "Oh, baby, don't be jealous. You've nothing to worry about... I *promise.*"

How could I be sure?

"Wank harder for me," she said firmly. "Wank at the thoughts of him having me. At me betraying you. Imagine Sean sending Sharon out for lunch. Picture him closing the door to the office. His dad being off, and all the labourers out on site. Can you see me sitting innocently at my desk, Mark? Can you see Sean standing next to me, watching me and remembering last night?"

I was intoxicated by her. My every instinct dictated her behaviour was wrong, yet the charges which fired through my torso craved every last word.

"Imagine him simply saying... *Slut*... And all my inhibitions would disappear. He could unzip his fly, guide my mouth down to him and I'd have no choice but to swallow his thick, fucking cock."

My eyes feasted on her pussy. She'd been wet for him. She'd wanted *him.*

"It wouldn't matter if he'd washed it or not, I'd take every inch of him, and make sure he enjoyed it. My pussy's needs wouldn't matter, Mark. Something about Sean being in power above me'd melt me."

I wrenched my hand over my member.

"How demeaning. How wrong. To bow before someone I despise, and serve their sexual whims on a plate. You wouldn't be on my mind, Mark. *He'd* be my concern. *His* pleasure my priority. I'd probably forget all about you, to be honest."

My cock was rigid, surging with blood.

"I'd be so much better with him than anyone he's ever had before, Mark. Fuck, can you imagine if I started having an affair with him? I could come home, and tell you all the sordid details."

My balls bulged with semen.

"That's it, Mark, cum for me! Cum all over my patent shoes!"

5

I pulled Anissa down the recliner, until her pussy was gaping under me. She looked into my eyes, and exhaled. I yanked her satin nightdress over her ass, grabbed the small of her back and forced my cock into her.

"Fuck, baby!" she cried.

I ravished her, using her hole to assist my impending explosion.

"Oh my God, Mark, you're so hard!" She snagged her knees around my back, and aimed her spiked heels inward. "Like I bet Sean would be."

"Ugh!"

"You bad bastard," Anissa scratched my shoulders with her fingernails, "fucking me again without a condom."

I hammered into her.

"Can you imagine Sean doing this to me? Can you imagine him bare-backing me in the office?"

My back grazed her stilettos. "Jesus!"

"Oh yes, Mark! Give it to me like I deserve it! For being such a filthy bitch... For wanting another man's big, thick dick in my pussy."

I was losing control inside her, pinning her torso to the recliner.

"For wanting Sean's cock in my cunt."

I pummelled her.

"For giving you the constant worry that when the dust settles... That it might *really* happen..."

I crashed into her filthy cunt.

"... Behind your back."

"Fuck!" I yelled, digging my fingers involuntarily under her arms.

"Are you going to cum in me again?"

"Yes!"

"Oh my God, this is *so* not what I want from you, you filthy bastard!"

I grabbed her chin, forcing her to face me. "You *do* want it, Anissa."

She nodded.

"Say it."

She shook her head.

"Say it, Anissa!"

Her blue eyes stared back.

"Fuck!" I clenched my teeth, as her spiked heels scraped agonisingly against my skin. "Fucking whore!" I yelled, and my first shot of spunk erupted insider her.

"Yes, baby, yes!" Her heels dangled over my ribs. "Oh God, yes, that's so hot when I feel it inside me!"

My testicles emptied remorselessly into her vulva. "I can't resist you, Anissa," I said, and slumped over her, my body saturated in sweat.

"Good boy," Anissa said, gently tracing my hips with her heels. "You fucked me good, Mark. All that pent-up frustration about my dancing with the labourers and what I did with... Sean. It works a treat, doesn't it?"

I nodded.

"Pardon, baby?"

"Yes, Anissa."

I felt her cheek next to mine stretch into a wide smile. "Good boy, because I really did enjoy last night, and even more so reliving it with you, taking the fantasy to another level."

I felt my testicles tense as another little load seeped into her.

"Mmmmmm." Anissa planted a kiss on my cheek.

I was too lost in my loins to return the favour.

"I love you, Mark."

My breathing was still ragged, my attention snagged on her adulterous fantasies.

"Nothing like that will ever happen in the office," she insisted.

"I was just saying it to get you off... I promise."

I pulled slowly out of her, and grabbed my cock. I squeezed the head until another drop of spunk fell on the fucked lips of her pussy. "How can you be sure, Anissa?"

"Because we don't drink at work, Mark," she snapped.

"Not usually, sweetheart." I leaned back from her, caressing her legs as I moved. "But what about the Christmas party on Friday? You told me your boss is having a party for the staff... *In* the office."

Anissa's eyes widened. "Oh shit."

6

Anissa and I'd been silent to each other since that morning. She'd quietly crossed her legs over me, swivelled off the recliner and headed upstairs to the bathroom to wash. I'd pulled up my boxers, sat in front of the TV and searched for something to watch which didn't include cookery or celebrity gossip.

When Anissa reappeared, she avoided eye contact. I suspected a guilty conscience, and held my tongue, my concentration taken by the tights jeans which hugged her ass and the knee-high boots she wore over them. She completed the look with a pink sweater, hooped earrings and her blonde hair tied back in a ponytail.

I scratched my balls as she prepared lunch, clattering cutlery, tussling with towels and planting plate after plate noisily on top of each other.

"Anissa," I said, standing in the doorway.

"What?" she snapped, slicing the crust from a sandwich.

I paused.

"I'm waiting for it." She looked over her shoulder. "Whatever it is you have to throw in my face, just do it. I probably deserve it."

"Sweetheart," I cupped her magnificent ass through denim, "I'm not going to do that."

Anissa turned to face me.

"Fuck it, Anissa, let's be honest. Okay?"

She gnawed on her lower lip. "Yeah."

"You want to know if I'm pissed off about last night?"

"I *need* to know, Mark."

I drank in the desperation in her eyes. "The truth is, Anissa, I don't think you did yourself any favours with your work colleagues. I hope they saw the funny side of it, I do. But I know what lads are like. Of all ages. There'll probably be banter, jokes. Hopefully most of them saw it as a bit of harmless fun."

"That's right," she said, crossing one booted heel in front of the other.

My eyes darted to the denim around her pussy. So tight. So wonderful. "Sean *will* be different, though. He stuck his lips on you. He called you a slut... That *is* true, right?"

"I'm sorry, Mark." She nodded. "It's true."

"But he doesn't know you saw his cock?"

"Not unless he noticed his fly undone later and suspected it, but I doubt it. He's a big oaf, only in that job because of his dad."

I leaned back against the wall. "But he'll not talk to anyone. He's not one of the lads, is he?"

"No, baby, there's no love lost between Sean and the labourers."

Did I imagine her pupils blossom when she said his name? "And if he was to brag to any of them... Well, he's nothing to brag about really, right? He tried it on with you, and he got nowhere. But if he did decide to brag-"

"They wouldn't believe him, Mark." She brushed a lock of hair behind her ear. Her hooped earring swung.

"Okay... But somehow I still feel Sean got the best of you last night."

"Of course he didn't, Mark!"

"Yes, Anissa, I think he did. Or at least he'll think he did. He watched you dance with the other guys. He watched them paw over you, and you didn't let any one of them push you into a kiss... Or even close to it, did you?"

"No."

"But Sean will feel he did. That you didn't stop him. That you might've even let him go further if his dad hadn't interrupted."

Anissa didn't answer.

I glanced at the outline of her breasts under her pink sweater. "Would you have?"

She traced her front teeth with her tongue.

"Sweetheart?"

Anissa's breasts rose as she breathed. "Things at work will be fine, Mark. It *won't* be mentioned."

"I'm going to be on edge about it, sweetheart, if I'm honest. But I trust you. And I don't think he has the balls to do anything when he's sober."

"He barely has balls when he's drunk," Anissa insisted.

"I'm coming to your office party on Friday afternoon," I said.

Anissa's jaw dropped. "What?"

"I can't stand the thought of Sean or any of them plying you with drink, trying to take advantage."

Anissa shook her head. "You can't, Mark. It's staff only. No one ever brings their partners along."

"I don't care. I'm going."

"Baby, it'll be so obvious why you're there-"

"How?"

She sighed. "Because they'll know. They'll read between the lines."

"I'm going, Anissa."

"No, Mark, please. I'll be humiliated. They'll work out I came home last night and told you what happened. They'll assume you were so angry you insisted you come along to chaperone me. You'll really set their chins wagging."

"Anissa," I began, reaching out and taking her hands in mine, "we'll just say we're going out for a meal afterwards, and I'm there to pick you up."

She was almost shaking. "You don't trust me," she said.

I kissed her gently on her lips. "I love you, Anissa. It's Sean I don't trust. I don't like that he might think he has one over on me, or you. I want him to see us together."

"You're just insecure."

"No, Anissa. Listen to me. If he got jealous of you dancing with other men last night, we're sure as hell going to make him jealous when he sees my arms around you on Friday." I leaned into her ear. "When he sees me kissing you."

"Baby," she whispered, "I *don't* want you there. If people see your hands all over me, they'll know you're mad. They'll think you're possessive."

I pulled my hands away from her. "And so what, Anissa? I've every right to be. You paraded yourself around like a piece of meat last night! You'd hard cocks rubbed against your ass, never mind the kiss... *And* it made you wet!"

Anissa's eyes were fixed on mine. Water welled, but never flowed. "*You* liked it."

Shame strangled my arousal. "This is not up for discussion, Anissa. I'm going to your staff party whether you like it or not."

"You're making something out of nothing, Mark."

"I'll be there."

"But I could get fired."

"Don't be fucking ridiculous, Anissa."

"Sean's dad might think you're there to cause trouble."

I shook my head. "I won't have him around you when there's drink involved. You can try to talk me out of it all you want, Anissa, but it won't do any good. I'm going."

Anissa wiped under her eye. "This is a trust issue, Mark."

"It's got fuck all to do with trust... I'm going."

7

Do you think it's possible to want to fuck someone you don't even like?

Anissa's words played havoc with my head throughout the week. I sat at bus stops, plagued by thoughts of what she and Sean could be doing at work. I bought newspapers, tantalised by the Page 3 Girls each day, wondering if Anissa's breasts were bare before Sean's eyes. I walked through the park, saw two lovers holding hands, and wondered if Sean had talked Anissa into taking a stroll on their lunch break. I flicked through the TV channels, found Kylie Minogue's perfect ass on her *Spinning Around* video and imagined the labourers making for a swift grab of Anissa's.

The thoughts were as arousing as they were worrying. I tried to calm myself, insisting Anissa was only flirtatious under the influence of alcohol. Nothing untoward would happen within the sober doldrums of her daily work life.

Kylie's ass twirled.

I saw the labourers dancing with Anissa.

Kylie's cheeks squeezed through her gold hot pants.

Jim and George's cocks ground against Anissa's ass.

My cock stretched painfully in my jeans.

Anissa's legs parted, her pussy soaking as she stared through

Sean's fly to his cock.

Kylie gyrated, revealing more flesh.

To his *thick* cock.

Do you think it's possible to want to fuck someone you don't even like?

I unbuttoned my jeans, and yanked my hard cock out of my boxers.

This had happened every single day.

I masturbated furiously, ignoring the open curtains and blinds, and recalled Anissa's fantasies of her and Sean being alone in the office. I saw her swallow his dick. She liked what she'd seen. She *liked* what she'd fucking seen.

Do you think it's possible to want to fuck someone you don't even like?

What if she was jacking his cock at that same moment I was jacking mine? I was delirious, excited and sickened at once. I wanted her to come home. I wanted her to confess she'd let something happen. Fuck, that she'd *made* something happen.

I jerked harder, in delightful delinquency.

My free hand found my phone, and I typed out a text. "How's Sean with you?" I hit send before humility could rouse regret.

Each passing minute became an image etched in my mind.

My girlfriend bent over her desk.

My girlfriend hitching up her skirt.

My girlfriend pulling her g-string to one side, and turning her head to nod to Sean.

"Ugh!" I spurted violently across the floor. "Fuck!" Twin jets landed on the coffee table. "Shit." My senses staggered from the sexual to the rational.

Anyone could've approached the front door, looked in the window and seen me.

My mobile beeped beside me.

It was from Anissa. "Sean's avoiding me. He has done all week. Please don't come to the Xmas party on Friday. It's not necessary."

My doubts raced into imaginative overdrive. "I'm going."

8

Anissa marched through the living room. It was Thursday evening, and her pre-party nervousness concerned only the selection of her outfit. She glided by, fresh from a bath, in only a purple thong and fluffy slippers. Her nipples were erect, each areola swollen, and her skin covered in goosebumps.

I reached out from the sofa, and grabbed at her ass.

Anissa swatted my hands away. "Don't, Mark, I'm freezing!" She stepped into the kitchen. "I can't find the skirt I wanted to wear."

"What's it look like?"

"Red, with a black belt and a gold buckle."

My eyes were on the *Channel 4 News*, read by Jon Snow. "I've never seen it before," I said, shrugging my shoulders.

Moments later, Anissa stood in the doorway with her arms folded under her breasts. A daring, short red miniskirt stopped barely below her crotch. "This is the one."

I leaned forward, and gazed up her long, naked legs. Without much effort, I could crane my neck for a glimpse of her underwear. "You look amazing, Anissa."

She smiled. "You sure?"

I nodded. I was in awe. I swallowed. "Yes, but..."

She dropped her hands to her hips, revealing her flat, perfect stomach. "But *what*?"

"It's a little short... Which is great. Sexy. You do look fantastic." I smiled. "But is it wise?"

Anissa's face contorted.

Oh shit.

"*Wise*, Mark?" Her feminine forces were scrambling.

"Just... With..."

Her wilds and ways mobilizing.

"What happened with Sean."

She stood, topless and dominant, staring silently downwards.

"You," I paused, "don't want to encourage him."

"No man will tell me what to wear, Mark," she snapped. "And no man will *ever* stop me wearing what I want. Sean might think he got one over on me, but I'm determined to even the score."

Panic pulled perspiration from my forehead. "How are you going to do that?"

She revelled in a devilish smile. "I haven't decided yet."

I doubted her.

Anissa walked forward, placed her palms on my knees, and kissed my lips.

I opened my mouth, slipping my tongue to hers.

Anissa moaned, meeting my passion.

I reached up, cupping her cool breasts. "You're beautiful," I said, as she broke the kiss.

"Would you do anything for me?" she asked.

I was surprised by the question, but nodded nevertheless.

"Please don't come to the staff party tomorrow."

I glanced at my girlfriend's excuse for a skirt. "There's no way I'm letting you go on your own, Anissa."

"What if I drive to work?" she suggested, sitting on the edge of the coffee table. "I won't be able to have a drink then. Nothing could possibly happen if I'm sober."

I sighed. "Anissa, you don't realise where I'm coming from with this. It's not *you* I'm worried about. It's the others. I wouldn't trust Jim, George, Sean, *any* of them... What are you doing?"

Anissa kneaded her naked nipples.

"Anissa..."

Her legs were spread, her purple thong exposed under her miniskirt. "You know what I want, Mark. I'm pleading with you." She stretched her back, pointing her pert, prominent nipples upwards. "*Please* don't come to the office tomorrow."

Suspicion ransacked my synapses.

"Come on, Mark, let me do something for you." Her painted red fingernail touched the outline of her underwear. "I'll give you the most amazing sexual pleasure you desire. I'll put on *any*thing you want me to wear... In exchange for your absence." She breathed over me. "I'll do anything *with* you... *For* you... *On* you."

My cock grazed erect against the denim of my jeans. If I could just reach inside and relieve myself I could resist her temptation.

"What would you like me to dress up as for you, Mark?" Anissa slipped her fingers under her skirt, hooked her thong and pulled it down her bare legs. She crumpled it in her palm, and placed it on my forehead.

The thin strap rested over my sinus, and I scented the sweet smell of her anus.

Anissa kicked off her fluffy slippers. "Not very sexy, are they?" She spread her legs further, edged herself forward on the wooden table and began to circle her clit. "Wouldn't you like me in a pair of heels? Big stiletto heels. Five inches, Mark? Six? Or what about boots? Oh, baby," Anissa slipped a finger into her pussy, "wouldn't you like to fuck me in a pair of knee-high boots? Oh, Mark, look at your cock in your jeans. It looks huge. Feed me it, baby. Just say you'll stay away tomorrow. Or, wait, wouldn't you like to bend me over the kitchen sink in a pair of ankle boots? You know the ones. Navy blue with silver studs up the side." Anissa gasped as she inserted a second finger. "Oh fuck, Mark, I know what you'll want. How about I fish out that old pair of thigh-highs my sister Tara used to own? The ones I told you she used to wear over her tight leggings in the early-90s. The ones you came over the thoughts of. Oh, you dirty bastard, I have them in the attic. Just give me the word, Mark, I'll get them. I'll wear them... *Only* them... And you can fuck me in the outhouse. I'll be so naked, so cold, so vulnerable, and you can just fuck me like a selfish bastard."

My exhalation was deafening.

"Imagine the neighbours overhearing. That arrogant prick, Sebastian, wouldn't you love to get one over on him? Have him hear the sounds of me getting fucked? Or what about his wife, the one you called the MILF?"

"Sophie," I said quietly, having learnt her name only a day earlier when their post was wrongly delivered to Anissa's address.

Anissa smiled, then smothered her pussy in three of her fingers. "Yeah," she whispered. "Sophie. She's very beautiful, isn't she? About 35, sophisticated... Way out of your league." Anissa's tongue rolled between her lips. "Wouldn't you love to fuck me in the thigh-high boots while she listens? Can you imagine her doing to herself what I'm doing now?" Anissa rammed her fingers faster inside herself. "Picture it, Mark."

I studied Anissa's lips puffing with each additional stroke of her palm.

"You're resisting." She smiled. "Maybe there's an outfit you won't be able to turn down. I *do* have such a collection, after all. All the men I've been... It's mounted up. Take your cock out, Mark."

I unzipped my fly.

"Go on. Don't be shy, baby."

"I'm not shy," I insisted, and seized my length.

"You're going to fuck me with that, right?"

I nodded.

"And that means you're not going tomorrow." She lifted her hips, sliding her skirt to her waist, and hammered her cunt into her fingers, taking a fourth digit. "Wouldn't you like me to go upstairs and slip into..."

My eyes widened in anticipation.

"A maid's outfit? Mmmmmm, you'd like that. But which kind, Mark? I've more than one. You want me frilly? See-through? Crotchless? Oh, I know. You like your kinks, baby, don't you? How about I dress up as your filthy, latex, rubber-encased maid? Your slave? Just tell me what I need to hear."

My interested garnered.

"I'll beckon to your every need."

My resolve was compromised.

"I'll obey your every command."

I yanked my cock as she watched.

"What about something I wore for someone else?"

I was becoming putty.

"Something I wore *specifically* for someone else?"

9

Anissa pried her fingers from her pussy and placed them, one-by-one, in her mouth. "Fuck, baby, I love my own taste."

"Go on," I said, capitulating to corruption.

"Tell me to stop before you get jealous." Her middle-finger plopped from her mouth, slipped down her chest and her abdomen to her groin. "I'll name no names."

I wanted to know who.

"You'll just have to wonder."

I wanted to know where.

"You'll just have to guess."

I wanted to know when.

"Unless you fuck me, Mark. Then I'll tell you everything about each outfit, each time you fuck me in one of them."

I was silent, slapping my cock vigorously as she watched.

Anissa's torso knotted, as her fingers fought deeper in her snatch. "I could dress up as a nurse, or in a wet look catsuit. What about my fishnet body suit? I'll even tell you how the crotch got ripped all the way to my lower back."

I persevered at my pulsating penis.

"Maybe you want the really kinky, Mark. Wouldn't you love to tussle me up in leather ankle cuffs, joined by a chain across my back to another set of cuffs on my wrists? You could fuck me in any place you want, and I mean *any* place, Mark... All you have to do is agree not to come tomorrow."

"I'm going," I said, between clenched teeth.

"Oh God," Anissa began, panting, "the memories these bring back. I could fuck one of my dildos for hours... Just reliving the past."

"I'm going as your chaperone."

"Backless rubber panties, baby." She fixed her stare on mine. "You know what hole that'd expose?"

I dreamed of drilling her anus, and felt my balls tensing as my palm bashed above.

"What about my lingerie?"

My indeliberate contortions proved ever more impossible to hide.

"I must have close to a thousand different pairs of stockings in this house."

I would concede to her dominance if she discovered how close I was to cumming.

"Sheer, seamed, criss-crossed..."

I'd fall for her seduction.

"Demi-toe, lace-topped, satin-bowed..."

I'd agree to avoid her party in exchange for a night of sexual debauchery.

"Striped, opaque, black, white, red, grey..." Anissa's body encountered, then embraced her spasms. "Oh God, Mark, I'll even unlock my biggest secret." Her hand fastened insider her. "A complete second skin body suit that covers me head to toe. Someone..." Her fingers blurred in and out of her cunt. "Someone I'll never even admit to seeing... He used to make me wear it for him!"

I was losing my will, wishing horrendously to relive her delinquent past. With her. On her. In her.

"Fuck!" Anissa screamed, her orgasm erupting on the soft, smooth skin of her hand. "I was his property." She wailed wildly, flailing her fingers thunderously into her cunt. "His possession." Her first ejaculation hit my jeans. "He owned my body." She smothered the second in her free palm. "He owned my pussy." Several more splashed on the floor. "It was *his*..." Anissa's face grimaced, as her fingers commanded her sordid cravings. "His *cunt*."

Who was he?

Anissa flung herself off the table.

"Shit!" I yelled, driving my cock into her mouth.

Anissa swallowed to the base, muffling her menacing moans.

My balls bloated below her. They tensed temporarily. "Ugh!" Then unleashed shot after tremendous shot of sperm into her throat.

Anissa gargled, stifling a gag.

"Fuck! Shit! Fuck, Anissa!"

Anissa wrapped her lips tight around me.

"Jesus!" Dreams of digestion drove a renewed supply into her mouth.

She swallowed, her breasts bouncing as she rocked back and forth on my girth.

My eyes rolled back in my head. I was a concoction of dizziness, delusion and dismay.

Who was he?

Anissa winked one eye over my dick.

Who was she?

I spasmodically emptied more inside her.

Who was I?

CHAPTER FOUR

1

The winter wind whipped against my ankles, as I crossed the forecourt of the industrial estate. Snow was shovelled to the sides, out of the path of vehicles. I shivered, holding my coat tight at the front, and marched onwards.

I pulled out my mobile, and checked the time. Four o'clock. Anissa said the first drinks tended to come out any time between the end of lunch and 3pm. She was adamant she wouldn't be drinking much, and certainly not in the early afternoon.

I stepped in a puddle, cursed, and stopped to shake my shoe dry.

I'd left my entrance deliberately late. Sharon, Nici and Tracey would've already seen to Anissa's plans to stay sober. I wanted the labourers to liquor up too. To loosen up. I wanted Sean to make an appearance. To dare make a comment. One line – hell, one word – out of place. I wanted every single one of them to be irretrievably drunker than I. Perhaps I'd even catch Anissa out. She'd been so determined to stop me from showing up. Was I right to assume there was something else going on?

I slipped my mobile back into my pocket, and hoped I hadn't left it too late.

2

The reception desk was empty. I leaned forward to push the glass front door. What if it was locked? I thought of Anissa up there, downing alcohol. Downing their cocks. His cock. *Do you think it's possible to want to fuck someone you don't even like?* Sean's thick cock.

The door opened easily, and I stumbled into the reception area, my shoes clumping on the floor and echoing all around. My wet foot slid, and I flew forward, waving my arms hysterically.

"Fucking hell!" I cursed loudly.

I caught the arm of an errant chair. A chair on wheels! I slid ridiculously onwards, careering into a bin and falling head over feet onto the floor.

Unforgiving seconds ticked swiftly by.

"Hello?" came a girl's voice.

I pulled at the bin for leverage, succeeding only in dragging more rubbish to the floor.

Heels clicked, as they scurried towards me. "Are you okay?"

I kicked the bin in frustration, and pushed myself to my feet.

"Can I help you?" she asked.

"I'm here for the party," I snapped.

She was red-haired, slim, attractive and around the age of thirty. "The party?"

I nodded, then pulled a used tissue from my elbow. "That's right. The staff party. Is it upstairs?"

Her eyes narrowed. "Are you staff?" She scrutinized me from my shoes to my forehead. "I don't recognise you."

I threw out my hand. "I'm Mark."

She reluctantly took it in hers. Her skin was cool as we shook. "I'm Tracey."

"Tracey, yes." I charged positivity into my voice. "I've heard all about you. You work the reception, right?"

She seemed unfazed by my enthusiasm.

I released my grip. "I'm Mark."

"Yes." Tracey sniffed, revealing one nostril blocked. "You said."

"Aren't you expecting me?"

She looked from the bin to the front door. "No... Wasn't that locked?"

I uprighted the bin. "I'm with Anissa."

Tracey's face whitened. "Anissa?" she gasped, her eyes darting to the steps which led to the next floor.

"Yes." Suspicion lanced at my resolve. "I'm her boyfriend... Mark."

"Anissa's *boyfriend?* I didn't know she-"

"She didn't mention I'd be coming?" I demanded, paranoia purloining my pride.

Tracey didn't budge, her arms folded, her fingers drumming the insides of her elbows. "She didn't mention you even existed, honey." Her disclosure stirred jealousy in my loins. "Are you sure you're supposed to be here?"

For God's sake, yes, woman! "She's expecting me," I insisted.

Tracey balanced on one heel, pointing the toe of her other foot to the door.

This was preposterous. My girlfriend was somewhere in the building. Who was Tracey to barricade me out? "Can you take me to her... *Please?*"

Her chest expanded in slow motion.

Was something going on?

Her chest deflated.

Was she covering for Anissa?

Tracey's eyelids blinked in one foul swoop.

Do you think it's possible to want to fuck someone you don't even like?

"Okay, Mark." Tracey smiled, and slipped an arm around my back, rubbing between my shoulder blades. "Come with me." She led me across the floor. "The party's just upstairs where the other girls work. Some of the labourers went for a few beers at lunchtime, so forgive them if they seem a bit rowdy to you."

I swallowed a lecherous lump in my throat.

3

There was raucous laughter. Male laughter.

My feet fell on the steel steps and my palm on the icy cold handrail. Tracey was behind me. I heard the first notions of music. Festive music.

The office door swung open up ahead. *Last Christmas* played gently out, drowned by a series of wolf-whistles and cheers.

If I found Anissa putting herself on display for the labourers again...

Tracey offered a weak, disingenuous smile.

I stepped up to the higher level. A bulky individual was leaning his head into a dry wall, holding a mobile phone to his ear.

"Ally," he called, his tone beyond tipsy, "is that fucking you?"

Tracey rolled her eyes.

"Put your mother on the fucking phone!"

Tracey nodded towards the office door.

I hesitated, then squeezed past the pisshead.

I felt their eyes burn upon me the second I entered. The music continued, drowned under the attempts of a girl I soon learned to be Sharon at singing along. The male members of the workforce, I approximated a total of around twenty-five, were scrutinizing the intruder in their midst. Who was I? What did I want? And why was I staring at the blonde stunner in the red miniskirt and black lacy top? She was looking up into the eyes of a tall, bulky builder-type. There was measuring tape strapped to his belt, paint splattered on his trousers, and a tin of beer in his hand. Anissa was laughing, touching his arm, and telling him to stop.

"All right?" asked one of the younger labourers.

"Yes," I replied.

"This is Mark," Tracey said. "Mark, meet the apprentice."

The apprentice extended his hand. "Good to meet you, Mark."

"He's Anissa's boyfriend," Tracey added, twirling a finger on the thin ends of her red hair extensions.

The apprentice failed to hide his surprise. "Oh right." His handshake weakened.

I released him.

Anissa looked over, a plastic cup in one hand, the muscle of her labourer friend's arm in the other. Her fingertips stroked his tattoo for a split-second longer than I was comfortable with, then snapped to her side. Her face grimaced, then she feigned a smile.

"Who's he?" I heard a male voice snivel from under a set of flashing Christmas lights.

"Fuck knows," came the whispered response.

I sensed Tracey shush them behind my back.

I broke between desks, side-stepped stacks of paper, and narrowly avoided tripping over an unplugged printer.

Anissa fixed her hair behind her ear. She looked stunning as I approached.

"Hi, sweetheart," I said, the music seeming to dim in the background.

"Hi," she replied.

I embraced her, and her face fell deliberately to one side of mine, pulling me into a hug rather than a kiss. I felt every eye in the office upon us. They'd watched her dance the week before. Hell, some had had their turn with her. How many of their erect cocks had grazed against her?

"This is Jim," Anissa said, tapping the back of her hand against the tattooed man's chest. "Jim, this is Mark."

Jim, one of the men she'd willingly encouraged.

We shook hands.

"Good to meet you... Mark."

She'd claimed he hadn't been hard as they danced. "I'm Anissa's boyfriend," I stated.

Jim's expression noticeably changed, then he channelled his surprise to a smile and a wink. "You're a lucky lad, mate." He looked down to Anissa.

Her face was coy.

"Make sure you look after her."

"I will," I insisted.

There was silence between songs. Nobody in the room was speaking. The apprentice fiddled forcefully with the sound system. *Numb/Encore*, a mash-up hit by *Jay-Z* and *Linkin Park*, exploded suddenly. Younger waists twisted above younger hips. Older hands found older ears. The apprentice's hand swiftly turned the volume to a more acceptable level.

"Someone get this man a beer," Jim shouted.

A number of cheers, claps and a nervous smile from Anissa ensued. Within seconds, a tin of *Harp Lager* was in my hand.

4

There was the usual, predictable small talk, which I'd have happily avoided at the best of times, never mind while under an overwhelming sense of suspicion. The labourers talked. Talked extensively and nonsensically, switching subject swiftly and without warning. The girls Anissa worked with – Tracey, Sharon and Nici – transpired to be much more sober than the previous week, and were full of questions rather than answers. I was pushed from person to person, involved in everything from conversation to chatter and finally to uninterrupted rant. In the fact nobody was saying anything of substance I became certain they were hiding something.

I met another labourer, George, and realised he was the one who'd dry-humped Anissa on the dance floor. He was huge, a menacing presence, and made my place in the hierarchy clear when he, just like everyone else, expressed his surprise that Anissa even had a boyfriend.

"Yes," I insisted. "We've been going out for a few months now."

George rolled his eyes, as if the seriousness of the relationship existed only in my mind.

"Nine months, to be precise."

Nici whispered in Anissa's ear.

"Well," George said, glancing between Anissa's cleavage and miniskirt, "she's let on round here she's still single."

A couple of the guys behind us laughed.

I stood awkwardly, and downed more beer.

U2's Vertigo shook the stereo.

I was dragged into a conversation about the Dharma Initiative by two of the smaller, skinnier lads, who were in turn mocked by the others, led by George and Jim. Each of the boys were insistent on their theories of the *Lost* island. I made a comment about star Evangeline Lilly, detailing what I'd do to her in a doggy-style position, and my escape from their clutches was secured.

Nici asked how Anissa and I had met. I told her a clean version of the truth.

"She never said a word," Nici replied.

Sharon's dressing down came in a similar fashion, resulting finally in, "We thought she was out every weekend playing the field!"

"She can play in my field," shouted one of the guys.

My anger was rising as *The Darkness' Christmas Time (Don't Let the Bells End)* threatened all-out ruination. Fingers drummed. Feet fell in unison. Whether consciously or not, the room was giving its permission for further Christmas tunes.

"Bah-humbug," I muttered, as Tracey placed a Santa hat on my head.

Nici and Sharon were giggling.

The first labourer to fall was a man on the edge of retirement. A taxi was subsequently called.

I tapped Anissa's elbow as she hung on every word of a tall workman named Billy. His eyes were feasting vicariously on her. She ignored my second tap, and pushed her pert breasts skyward to him.

Billy's tongue escaped his foaming mouth.

"Anissa," I said, and seized her elbow.

"What?" she said back, suppressing a snap only because of the watchful eyes around us.

"Can I have a word?"

She sighed, fixing her hair as she looked up to Billy.

5

Anissa's heels clicked on every steel step as we descended from the office party to the reception. My hand was on her lower back, encouraging her to continue until we hit the ground floor.

"What is it?" she asked, shivering as a cool draft blew in from under the front door.

"You tell me," I said.

"Out of my way, Mark. I can't be bothered with this shit. This is my Christmas party. I just want to enjoy myself before we break for the holidays."

I had my hands on the bottom of her ribs, holding her in place through the fabric of her thin, black lacy top. "Kiss me."

She sighed, relinquished a thin smile and placed a peck on my cheek. "There."

I pulled Anissa's head to mine, and placed my lips on hers. *Smack!* We kissed.

I let go of her. "Was that so difficult?" I asked.

"No." Anissa gently edged my hand from her ribcage. "Can we go back upstairs now?"

I released a ridiculous excuse for a chuckle. "What's the point, Anissa? Nobody knows who I am. Not one person up there even knew you *had* a boyfriend. You don't want me here. You're obviously ashamed of me. I might as well just leave now and let you have your fun with your rough."

She stared, stretching on for seconds.

I could feel a vein swell by my forehead. Anger was turning to rage. And rage to resentment.

"I'm..." Her perfume was beautiful and intoxicating. "Not..." Her gold hooped earrings swivelled. "Ashamed..." Her talons scratched at my back. "Of..." She raised one leg from the floor and pushed her groin against my thigh. "You." Her tongue traced the length of mine in my mouth.

I broke the kiss, and looked at her. Anissa's eyes were bulging, and gorgeous. Her mouth parted, almost panting in need. I seized her lower back and pulled her in for another kiss.

"Fuck," she whispered into my mouth. "The taste of beer on your mouth is so sexy, baby."

"Why does no one know about me, Anissa?"

She bit her lower lip. "Mark, it wasn't the way you think it is."

"Anissa, we've been together for months now and the people you see everyday thought you were single. The men seemed to think you were available. It looks like that's the way you've wanted to portray yourself."

"No."

I scratched the back of my head, steering my eyes away from her.

"Baby..." Her legs were together. "Can I explain?"

Anxiety exhaled my breath. "I hope so."

"Mark, since I've worked here every relationship I've tried to start has ended miserably. You've no idea what that does to someone's self-esteem. To think every man you meet is attracted enough to you physically, but can't stand you once they get to know you... How do you think that feels? All those rejections. All those failures. And then there's my reputation to boot. I didn't tell anyone here about you because I was scared."

"Scared?"

Anissa nodded. "Yes, baby." She folded her arms and pressed her cleavage higher. "You're a couple of years younger than me. I can't help but feel you'll tire of me and want someone else."

I laughed. "Anissa, you're stunning. You're beautiful." I leaned forward. "You're fucking irresistible."

A door upstairs opened momentarily. Some *Britney Spears* shite escaped. The door slammed shut.

"That's it, Mark... All you see when you look at me is my looks. It takes more than looks to hold onto a man, especially a good one... Like you." She looked up, above my eyes, and bit her lip.

"What is it?"

"Your hat." Anissa shook her head. "Baby, you look ridiculous."

I caught the pom-pom in my hand.

"No!" She swiped my hand away. "Leave it on. Please."

I sighed. "Okay."

"Shall we go back up?" she asked, reaching her hand out and taking mine. "I want you to. I'm *not* ashamed of you, Mark. Baby, please, believe me. I'm just not as secure as you seem to think... Or expect me to be."

I smiled. "I don't *expect* anything of you, Anissa. I'm just glad you're..." I squeezed her hand. "*Mine.*"

"Yours," she whispered.

I turned towards the steel steps. "Come on."

"Wait." Anissa kissed my mouth again. "Do you have any cigarettes on you?"

"Yes."

She pulled my hand in the direction of the front door. "Come with me for a quick smoke... Then we'll go up. *Then* I can show you off as my boyfriend."

6

Anissa huddled close to my chest, slipping her arms inside my coat and around my waist. Her breasts pressed against my torso.

"We'll just share a smoke," she said, as her warm breath lit up in the darkness.

"Okay." I lit a cigarette over her soft shoulder. She felt amazing against my body and I couldn't wait to take her home after the party. "I'm gonna fuck you senseless when we get home, Anissa."

"Mmmmmm, that'd be nice, baby." Her hands locked around my lower back. "And will you punish me for keeping you a secret from my colleagues?"

"Yes, Anissa, your behaviour more than warrants another spanking."

"In this weather, baby?"

I smiled, toking on the cigarette. "Your ass was built for my belt, sweetheart."

Anissa swapped the cigarette from my mouth to hers. "So tell me, baby, are you going to cum on my face tonight?"

"Top o' the mornin' to you!" shouted a boisterous voice, feigning a Southern Irish accent.

I turned.

A tall, rotund guy of my age or younger was jumping between puddles and palming falling snowflakes away from his face. "Hello there!" he called.

Anissa's hands left the inside of my coat.

The big guy shook his jacket, sweeping snow from his shoulders as he ducked under the extended exterior roofing of the building for shelter.

Anissa's boots retreated from between my shoes. She gave me back the cigarette.

"I suppose you thought I wasn't going to show up," he said to Anissa, his gaze falling to her legs.

I wondered if I was going to have to introduce myself.

"This," began Anissa, the back of her hand grazing my chest, "is-"

"Mark," he interrupted, and offered his hand.

"Hello," I replied, impressed and yet dubious as to how he knew my name when everybody else hadn't a clue.

His handshake was firm. Certain. Confident. "I'm Sean."

I felt the colour drain from my skin. His demeanour was so different from how she'd described him. He *was* overweight and far from good-looking, but it was his stature which threatened me. He towered over us both, smiling down and slithering invisibly yet intimately between us.

"I've heard about you," he added.

How? When? From Anissa? "It's good to meet you, Sean," I said.

Anissa was staring at him.

He looked at me as if to suggest he knew I knew what'd happened between them.

Anissa was nibbling her lower lip.

"How's the party?" Sean asked, pulling a cigarette from his inside pocket.

Anissa leaned forward, holding a lighter to his tip.

Sean's lips curled. So smug. "Thank you, Anissa."

"It's okay," I said finally, when it was apparent Anissa was too lost in her attention to answer his question.

"Fecking shite then," he said, laughing.

It roused Anissa from her silence, mimicking his giggles. I traced her line of vision to his mouth. She was staring at it. Did she want to kiss him? I looked back at her. Her eyes had shifted. Down. To his crotch. I glanced to her once more. Anissa's tongue was rounding her upper lip.

"The music isn't really my thing, Sean," I said. "I'm more of a heavy rock person."

"Me too, Mark." He was looking past me, down to Anissa's cleavage.

I took a deep inhalation of smoke, held my breath as I seethed, then released it through my nostrils.

Anissa's left hand found my right, entwining. "Can I have another drag please, baby?"

Sean popped open his packet in one swift motion. "Help yourself, Anissa."

She shook her head, and took my cigarette from my mouth. "No thanks, Sean. Honestly, I just want another drag. I'm not a big smoker-"

"Only when you drink," he interrupted.

Something glinted in Anissa's eyes.

He watched her.

She watched him.

Were they daring each other to go further?

A window from the office opened above us. The music was immediately louder.

"It must be getting warm up there," Sean said, his eyes circling her breasts.

I thought of her job. I focused on her pay. What would happen if I punched out the boss' son?

Anissa tossed away the end of the cigarette. "Yes," she replied. "*Very* warm."

Sean sucked deeply on his cigarette. "Is my old man up there?"

"No." Anissa moved one boot apart from the other. "He took one glance at the guys coming in from the pub after lunch and told Sharon she was in charge."

Sean laughed.

Anissa laughed.

What'd happened in the seven days between the Christmas dinner and the staff party? There was no awkwardness between them. No animosity. No inkling of the word *slut* on his tongue.

"Shall we go upstairs?" Sean suggested, flicking his cigarette across the tarmac.

"After you," I said, reaching for the door and opening it for him.

"After me it is," he replied, rolling his tongue around each syllable.

Anissa pulled at my hand as I followed, turning me around. Her mouth was on mine as the door closed behind Sean.

I broke the kiss. "What's going on?" I demanded, as Sean stepped onto the stairs in the reception.

"I want your fingers inside me, baby."

I was perplexed. "No, sweetheart, I mean with you and Sean."

"What?"

"The tension between you two is off the chart. It's... It's not what I expected... There's chemistry there... I'm worried about it."

Anissa squeezed my cock through my trousers. "You're my chemistry, baby. Trust me."

I shook my head. "I saw the way you looked at him, Anissa."

Her mascara was flawless. "I'm playing with him-"

"You're playing with fire, Anissa."

The cold air clasped at her throat, and she coughed. "You..." She kissed my neck. "Can trust..." She mauled my Adam's apple. "Me."

"Your job could be on the line, Anissa. You shouldn't underestimate the power he has."

Her eyes lit up at the word power.

I imagined her pussy, moistness coasting her lips, matting her surrounding pubic hair, pulling every muscle to the centre of her sex.

There was boisterous laughter from the window above. Sean had entered. Someone had given the crowd something to laugh about. My paranoia insisted it was at my expense.

"It won't get out of hand, baby. I'm just having a bit of fun. I need to establish who's *really* in control between me and him."

My eyebrows practically crisscrossed. "How come he knew about me, Anissa? I thought you hadn't told anyone."

"Oh, baby, I had to tell Sean."

"Why?"

"So the fucker could know I'm off limits. I feel he got the upper hand on me last week. I want to even the score, Mark."

"You... Do?"

"And you're going to make that happen."

The alcohol flowed in the office. The laughter roared. Harmless wolf-whistles evolved into dares for the women to dance in the middle of the room where desks had been moved aside. Nici and Tracey were the first to accept. Sharon was tapping her feet, holding her hands on her hips and occasionally swaying her buttocks. Few eyes noticed. The rest were roaming Anissa's figure.

Her hand clenched mine as she downed yet another cup of white wine.

"Go on, Anissa, get up there and show them how it's done," shouted Billy.

There were claps and cheers.

Jim and George smiled. Crudely.

My heart pounded as I swigged from another tin of *Harp*.

Sean worked his way around the crowd.

"Fuck it," Sharon said, and pulled the apprentice onto the dance floor as *Kylie Minogue's Can't Get You Out of My Head* pumped out of the stereo.

Shouts of "Dark horse!" and "Go on, son!" echoed across the room.

Anissa poured more wine into her polystyrene cup.

Sean crossed the dance floor. He stopped behind Nici, unbeknownst to her, and mocked a provocative dance, rotating his groin in unison with her hips. The labourers laughed. Tracey rolled her eyes and Nici was a split-second from realisation when Sean cut his routine short and walked away.

"Do you fancy heading home soon?" I said to Anissa.

Her breasts heaved as she sighed. "Aw, baby, can we not stay longer?"

I nodded. "Anything you want, Anissa."

She smiled. "*Any*thing?" Her eyes returned to the dance floor.

Was I paranoid or perceptive? She was looking at Sharon and the young guy. As they twirled out of her sight, however, her eyes remained ahead. Her mouth opened, allowing her tongue to circumnavigate her lips. Sean caught her gaze, nodded to her, and returned his attention to a labourer.

"Anissa," came a deep male voice from behind.

She released my hand, spun and confronted Jim. "Yes, sweetie?"

Jealous cogs twisted in my loins.

"Too bad you're not getting up there yourself, or I might've asked you for a dance," Jim said, no doubt recalling a memory he assumed I'd no knowledge of.

George was standing nearby, watching and grinning.

"It *could* happen," Anissa said, pointing the toe of her boot to him.

Jim's eyes were transfixed on her thighs below her miniskirt. "I'm afraid not for me. My wife's outside. She's picking me up." He looked to me, laughing. "I have to be good."

I nodded, then scratched my head under the Santa hat.

"Aw, sweetie," Anissa said, placing her palm on the side of his face and drumming her fingertips on his skin.

Jim's face immediately reddened.

I felt anger and anxiety bite and spit ferociously at my inner arousal.

Sean fixed his genitals in his trousers.

"Merry Christmas, Jim," Anissa said, then stood on her tip toes and kissed him gently on his cheek. "And a happy new year."

"Yes, yes." He was in seventh heaven. "Yes, you too."

My cock responded to her behaviour. What was so exciting about watching her behave mildly promiscuously in front of all these men?

"Oh my God," Anissa declared suddenly, as *Beyonce's Naughty Girl* broke out. "Hold this."

Her cup of wine was placed in my free palm.

She raced to join the others.

The apprentice made to bolt away for his escape. Sharon snagged his arm in hers. His fate was sealed.

My eyes darted between Sean and George, readying myself for the consequences if either made a beeline for my girlfriend. I knew her mood. I knew her alcohol intake.

Sharon spun the apprentice, shoving him gently towards Anissa. My girlfriend laughed, then danced around him, moving her body in motion with the music.

The labourers heckled him, mocking his timidness.

Anissa just smiled. Smiled, swayed her ass and sashayed across the floor. Her blonde hair swung in several directions. Her boot heels scratched the surface of the floor. Her waist bent. Her back arched. Her ass danced dangerously closer to the edge of her skirt. She snapped suddenly into a vertical position, winked at me and continued, shaking her booty simultaneously with Tracey's.

I watched George. He whispered something in the ear of another labourer. Laughter ensued. He noticed my attention, and lifted another tin of *Harp* for himself from the floor.

I looked across to the other side of the room. Sean was different to George. He wasn't looking for the kicks of his peers. He wanted Anissa on his own. Alone. Vulnerable.

I was overcome with the urge to escort her out of the building. She was surrounded by men who were downing more drink with each passing minute. She was dancing provocatively. The boss wasn't around. All the behaviour of the previous week was looking likelier to repeat with each motion her torso twirled.

Sean stared at her, his hand over his crotch.

Anissa's lithe shape careered in one direction, squeezing her cleavage together, then snapped to another, rotating her ass as sweat poured from every male member of the crowd.

There was a sudden squeak and a shrill. Tracey was a blur of red hair as she crashed to the floor. Sharon discarded of the apprentice, sending him spinning into a printer covered in tinsel. She and Nici raced to Tracey's side.

I set Anissa's wine and my beer on the nearest desk, then went over to help.

"I'm okay," Tracey was insisting, slurring her words. "Honestly."

"Check her head, Nici," Sharon barked.

Christmas lights flashed above us, reflecting on Tracey's face. Her eyes were hazy. Several of the men rushed over to assist. Some stumbled. Some argued. Their opinions were ignored.

Tracey was pulled to her feet, staggering slightly and whimpering. Billy and another labourer offered to carry her.

Nici and Sharon were adamant they'd be the ones to help her.

The crowd quickly dispersed, and the *Beyonce* song faded to silence.

I turned to where Anissa had been dancing.

She was gone.

I looked to where we'd stood together.

She wasn't there either.

George was supping his beer, surveying the terror that'd crossed my face.

I swivelled 180 degrees.

Sean had disappeared too.

<h1 style="text-align:center">8</h1>

"And so we've ordered the box sets of the first three seasons of *24* for Christmas..."

I couldn't concentrate on the young labourer's voice.

"We're going to watch them over the holidays."

"Have you seen Anissa?" I said finally.

"I'm bleeding!" Tracey wailed in the background.

He looked around. "She was just here, dancing, last I checked."

My eyes searched the office for her. I couldn't see her anywhere. For crying out loud, she was trampling over my trust!

George drummed his fingers on his tin of beer. His eyes flicked from me to where Anissa had been dancing in the middle of the floor. Back to me. His lips curled into a grin. His eyes strayed once more. Across the floor. Between the crowd. And to where Sean had last stood in conversation with his colleagues. His absence was as defining as Anissa's.

Do you think it's possible to want to fuck someone you don't even like?

I had to find her. And fast.

Tracey cried over the music, shaking as if she'd barely survived an assassination attempt.

I was slapped suddenly on my back. "Are you all right there, Mark?" asked Billy, cradling a tin of lager against his chest. "Can I get you another drink?"

I shook my head. "Have you seen Anissa?"

Billy looked around. "I didn't realise she wasn't here, mate. She must've slipped outside for a smoke."

Of course! And who else had cigarettes? Sean.

"You sure you won't have another drink?"

"No, really-"

"Have another drink," Billy insisted. "Dave, grab Mark another beer!"

Dave nodded, and tugged a tin free from one of the dozens of six-pack rings.

"Biff Tannen!" someone shouted loudly to a response of hysterical laugher and applause.

Dave tossed Billy the beer.

Tracey's tears and torment roared behind us.

Billy caught the beer in hand, ripped open the ring pull and slapped it into my palm. "There you go, kid, get that down your neck."

Their laughter. Their smiles. The festive spirit was lost upon me, and I felt their falseness fester.

"What do you think of our party then, Mark?" Billy asked.

Could there be a conspiracy to their camaraderie?

I shrugged my shoulders. "It's not bad." I downed more beer.

Could they really all be working together to conceal whatever was occurring between Sean and Anissa?

Billy was shaking his head, then his eyes were drawn to Nici's swaying ass as she walked past with a cup of water for Tracey.

"I like a pint," I said, realising my ridiculous attempt at small-talk the moment my mouth opened. I decided to plough on regardless. "I mean, in my local."

Billy nodded.

"Even if it is a dying trade," I continued, as Dave and the apprentice lassoed themselves into our conversation. "Sometimes there's nowhere I'd rather be than sat on a barstool talking to a stranger about everything and nothing in the world-"

"I spent half my life doing that, mate," Billy interrupted, cringing over the sound of Tracey's howls. "I'd bang the world to rights, I'd solve the Middle East, the economy, the war, poverty, hunger, Australia..."

The apprentice and I glanced at each other. Down Under?

"... Then I'd go outside and I couldn't find my car in the car park."

Dave and the apprentice laughed.

I slid half the contents of the *Harp* down my throat, and recalled Anissa's description of Sean's mouth on her lips.

"It happened all the time."

How her pussy had soaked her thighs.

"But I learnt in the end."

How her legs had parted.

"You know what I did?" Billy asked.

Wishing for his fingers.

"What?"

For his cock.

"I started sharing taxis."

She was with him. She was throwing herself to her temptation. To her desire. To her need for degradation with someone she couldn't stand.

"Hahahahaha, Billy!"

Enough was enough.

"Good one!"

I slammed down my beer on the nearest desk, and stomped across the floor in the middle of the office.

Alarm bells echoed in my head.

Voices and faces blurred into insignificance as I passed.

My eyes caught a glimpse of my reflection in a window. The red Santa hat was still sat ridiculously on my head. I wrenched it from my scalp, and hurled it to the nearest bin.

9

My shoes thundered on the steps which led from the office to the reception.

Hear me, Anissa, I thought, *hear me and spare me the humiliation of catching you in his arms.*

I hit the floor, and charged out of the building and onto the tarmac ground, swivelling and surveying the area. Accusations, orders and rebukes charged from my abdomen to my throat, and fell dormant upon discovery of their absence.

"Anissa?" I called finally, and wearily.

The still air of the evening returned silence.

"Anissa?"

Nothing.

"Anissa?"

I slammed the front door, shaking half the building.

No heads twisted in and out of sight, stealing a glance.

No mouths shared clandestine whispers within earshot.

Wherever they were hiding, it seemed I wouldn't find them.

10

"You find Anissa?"

I shook my head.

He was a labourer I hadn't even spoken to yet. The fact he knew she was missing made me even more suspicious.

I glanced around the office. Nici and Sharon were dancing to *The Jackson 5's* rendition of *Frosty The Snowman*. Tracey was slumped on a swivel chair, salivating on her own blouse. Billy and several others were laughing together and swigging more beers. The apprentice was the butt of their jokes, taking them in good jest. And then there was George, laughing louder than all the rest and flicking his eyes ever so occasionally to mine.

He *knew*.

I was certain.

If Sean's tongue was in Anissa's mouth, he *knew*. If his hands were on her ass, he *knew*. Her breasts, he *knew*. Her ass...

Oh God.

Anissa's pussy.

I swallowed.

His fingers... Ploughing into her... Frustrating her at one second... Pleasuring her the next... She would be gasping... Gagging... Gargling... Oh fuck!

"Give me your thick, fucking cock, Sean."

I could hear her.

In my mind, I could actually hear her.

11

Sean entered the office, slipping smoothly between drinkers and avoiding my eye. Sweat matted his hair to his forehead. I was certain it was sweat.

Sharon grazed her crotch against Nici's ass, their bodies swaying in time to *Christina Aguilera's Dirrty*. Whoever was in charge of the music couldn't have picked a more appropriate tune, as I waited for

Anissa.

12

"You left me up here on my *fucking* own, Anissa." I was speaking through clenched teeth, forcing the volume of my voice under the music.

Billy was watching, as Anissa's body language betrayed the false smile on her face.

"You must've bolted out the door hand-in-hand with Sean when everyone was distracted by Tracey going down as if she was shot."

George tapped the arm of another labourer, then pointed past a water dispenser draped in tinsel to us both.

Anissa was shaking her head, crossing her arms and, I noticed, rubbing the inside of one leg against the other. Her pussy was alive.

"What the fuck did you do while you were away with him?" I demanded, hiding my face behind a tin of *Harp*.

Anissa's breasts heaved under her lacy black top as she breathed. "Who?" she asked, her lips deep red, clad in a new layer of lipstick.

"You know who."

Anissa stared ahead.

"You were with Sean."

"I didn't tell you that."

"You were with him, Anissa. You were gone for ten minutes. Do you think I'm a fool?"

She twisted her head to face mine. "Baby, I don't think you're a fool. Please, don't talk like that. I'm just..."

"What, Anissa? What are you *just*?"

She grinned. "I'm just having a little fun."

My blood boiled. "A little fun? Jesus, Anissa. What do you mean?"

"Look at me, Mark," she said calmly.

My vision was vexed, fixed on Sean.

"Please, baby, don't be mad." Anissa tucked her blonde hair behind her ear. "You've no reason to be angry. You know you're the man I'm in love with."

Did I?

"I've searched all my life for you. I don't want to lose you. Can you *please* just look at me, Mark?"

My eyes wallowed in the wealth of her beauty. The sexy stance. The manner in which her brown leather boots shaped her legs. How her red miniskirt barely covered the bottom of her ass cheeks. The way her black belt tightened her waist and her tight top accentuated off every perfect inch of her chest. How could I ever walk away from that?

"Baby," she began, teasing her tongue across her top lip, "I want you to answer me honestly."

The atmosphere of the office changed as *My Heart Will Go On* started slowly. Somebody was taking the fucking piss.

"Have you ever kissed another girl in the time we've been together?"

"No!"

Sharon and Nici were the final refugees to flee the makeshift dance floor.

"Are you sure?" She placed her palms firmly on her hips.

"Yes!"

Sean performed an about turn and marched over to the stereo.

"Shit," Anissa said.

"What is it?" I asked.

Sean switched off the music.

"Well then, Mark..."

He fed the lead of a microphone to the apprentice, who promptly plugged it into the stereo. The high-pitched feedback was instantaneous.

"I guess you've my permission..."

Sean stood forward, and the unfortunate output was cut.

"Next time you think you've a chance-"

My coherence was crumbling.

"Can I have everyone's attention please?" Sean asked, his voice booming over the speakers.

13

The labourers and ladies turned to Sean.

"What's happening?" I asked. "What's he doing now?"

"I..." Fear flushed her face. "I don't know."

My mind parachuted into a panic.

Anissa sealed her legs together.

"Ladies, gentlemen," Sean started, stretching the microphone lead away from the stereo, "I've a very important announcement to make."

Anissa was breathing heavily.

In desperation, I reached instinctively for her palm. Instead, I crushed my hand into a fist. I wouldn't be holding hers in the second Sean shamed us.

"First of all, my family would like to wish you all a Merry Christmas-"

"Get on with it, Seany boy!" George heckled to the laughter and applause of his peers.

Sean sighed, amplified over the speakers. "Thanks for that." He pointed to the remaining tins of *Harp*. "No more for him."

The raptures of laughter returned for another round.

"Anyway, have a Merry Christmas, a Happy New Year and all that feckin' bollocks. My da's left you's all a Christmas bonus." Sean produced a collection of red envelopes and placed them on the nearest desk. "Don't forget to lift them on the way out. And, George..."

George looked up.

"Just feckin' lift your own this year, okay?"

There was more laughter.

George raised his middle-finger.

Sean returned the gesture. "'Tis the season to be jolly, and all that."

Sweat saturated the small of my back.

Anissa's red thumbnail was nervously rotating the tip of each finger in one hand. She inhaled, held her chin high and pushed out her breasts. Her ass jutted magnificently against her miniskirt.

"All right, now those formalities are aside, I can make my announcement." Sean tilted his head to one side, his eyes lingering momentarily on Anissa's legs. "Today is officially my last day with the company."

Tracey gasped.

Dave cheered, expecting his peers to follow suit. He fell swiftly silent when they didn't.

"Thanks, Dave." Sean looked to the labourers. "Guys, it's been a pleasure working with you. I've never met harder workers in my life."

"Cheeky fucker!" Billy shouted.

Sean winked, smiling. "It's time for me to move on."

"Where are you going?"

The colour drained from my face as every attending employee turned to Anissa.

"I'm leaving the country, Anissa," Sean said coolly.

"Where?" she said, her voice barely audible.

My heart pounded in my chest, jealousy and angst coagulating as one.

"I start in January. I won't be back here. So... I guess it's goodbye."

"Where..." Anissa's whisper fell to silence, lost in the sudden commotion of George and the others volleying a dozen different questions to the centre of the room.

Sean handed his microphone to the apprentice, as *U2's Beautiful Day* pumped out from the speakers.

"This is my last chance," Anissa stated quietly, then sipped more white wine. "To gain the upper hand on him, I mean."

I watched her. Her eyes narrowed as she studied Sean, her boots parted again.

Do you think it's possible to want to fuck someone you don't even like?

14

"Anissa, what the hell's going on here?" I asked, quietly, feigning calmness.

"Things are falling into place, baby."

"What do you mean? Am I losing you?"

She whipped her neck to face me. "No!"

I was aware of the attention we were drawing, and moved closer to her, taking her free hand in mine.

Anissa squeezed. "Of course you're not losing me, Mark. Why would you think that?"

"Because you can't keep your eyes off him. You disappeared. *He* disappeared. You were obviously together... I can't have been the only one to notice. Why? What happened? Where'd you go with him?"

Anissa stared at Sean, tugging her tongue at her lipstick, peeling away glistening sparkles.

"Anissa!"

"What?" she snapped.

"*Tell me* what happened."

She brought more wine to her mouth. Her pupils dilated. Glazed. "I..."

Sean headed for the exit with a cigarette pack in hand.

"Oh, Mark, please, you won't understand-"

"What the fuck are you talking about, Anissa?"

Sean slammed the office door behind him.

"What won't I under-"

"Sean caught me under the mistletoe again."

Turmoil twisted my insides. "Fucking hell, Anissa." Yet somewhere deep, deep within, unwilling to retreat, I felt fascination. It lay claim to the shackles of my shame, shaking them to their very core. "Just another peck on the lips?"

"No."

Perspiration stitched my shirt to my chest.

"I really wanted to wind him up..."

My hands were trembling.

"So, I just stood there letting him gape at me-"

My imagination exploded. "Christ, Anissa," I paused, gulping as Christmas lights twinkled above us, "did you flash him?" My mind's eye glimpsed her fingertips pull her nipples free from her top, and saw Sean bridge the gap between them, moulding his mouth to each in turn.

"No, baby, no."

"What?"

"Nothing like that... I... I..."

"Tell me what happened, Anissa."

"I... I sort of made out with him."

Excitement detonated in my chest, fizzling through anxiety, jealousy and fury.

"I'm only playing with him, Mark. It wasn't serious."

Do you think it's possible to want to fuck someone you don't even like?

"But he was *very* aroused."

Realism sliced fright through my fantasies. "How the fuck do you know that?"

"*Ba-by*," Anissa spoke slowly, so downright seductively, "I could see him grow in his trousers."

I felt a sickening bulge in my own. "You could *see* him?" I was shortening of breath. "Anissa, tell me the truth... Did you *feel* his cock?"

15

Festive lights flashed across her cheekbones. "No, baby, I promise. I wanted to. I *really* wanted to. I wish I was bolder... But I couldn't bring myself to do it."

My testicles tightened. Who did she think she was?

"But I did do something else, Mark."

"What?"

She squeezed my hand. "I told him to meet me in the storeroom in twenty minutes."

I tried to pull my palm away.

She wouldn't let me. "That was about fifteen minutes ago."

Had the cigarettes in Sean's hand been a decoy? His sign to Anissa he was on his way to meet her? "What were you planning to do with him? Were you going to kiss him again?" I looked down her outfit, resting my eyes on the brass buckle that fastened her belt around her tight waist. "Or did you plan on more?"

"He *is* leaving the country, Mark." Anissa drew her forefinger to her mouth and tantalisingly tongued the tip, as if pausing for thought. "I didn't know *that* when I suggested we meet in the storeroom."

The music played in the background. Tins of beer and bottles of wine flowed for the workforce. All seemingly paled into insignificance.

"I *could* get away with one fuck," she whispered.

"No!"

Sharon surveyed the storm between us.

"Come on, baby, you and I both know you'd love to watch me with someone else-"

"No, no, no!"

Tracey watched too.

"Putting on a little porno show for you," Anissa added, then drained the last of her wine from her cup.

"No!"

Nici noticed the kerfuffle, and drew the additional unwelcome attention of George, Billy and Dave.

"Not with Sean," I said. "No way. That cunt is right up his own massive arse."

"Then come with me," Anissa said. "Come with me downstairs to the storeroom."

"I don't want you to do anything with Sean." My hands were shaking. "I don't want to watch it happen." My true desires reddened my face. "Please, Anissa, enough is enough."

"It's not enough, Mark. *He* thinks he got the upper hand on me. I can't let this lie. Not now I know he's leaving. He called me a slut. He thinks he can have me." She shook her head vehemently. "I'm not having it." She squashed my hand in hers. "Come with me to the storeroom, Mark... We might still have time."

16

We stepped quietly down the steel steps which led to the reception. My eyes darted to the glass front, searching for Sean. It was difficult to see, as the interior lights reflected and masked the darkness outside.

"Come on," she said, and led me through the reception to a corridor behind the main desk. "I'm sorry, Mark, but you've got it all wrong." She stopped, turning into me.

I didn't lean in for a kiss.

"You'll understand one day. This is about control. His wealth versus my sex. And I'm going to win."

The corridor was cold and silent. "I *don't* understand," I admitted.

Anissa reached behind her, hit a switch and pushed open a door. One-by-one, fluorescent tubes lit up the room inside. "This is the storeroom, baby. Sean isn't here yet. *If* he even has the balls to come."

"What'd you tell him you'd meet him for?"

"I didn't, Mark. I just told him to be here. I left the rest dangling out there for his imagination." Anissa walked into the storeroom.

I shivered, the temperature inside was no warmer than the corridor. "Where'd you kiss him, Anissa?"

Her back remained to me. "Outside."

"Did anyone else see?"

"No."

"Are you sure, Anissa?"

"Yes."

I walked behind her, and caressed her lower arms, revealed from her elbows by frilly edges of her black top. "*How* did you kiss him?"

"Baby, don't. It was nothing." Goosebumps gave away the nature to her lies.

I spun her around, steadying her in her heels. "I don't fucking believe you. Do you want me to call you a slut?"

She shook her head.

"What about a whore?"

Anissa's eyes pleaded.

"Then show me what happened. You can't have long till he shows up anyway-"

"*If* he-"

I pulled her to within inches of my mouth. "I said show me."

She exhaled long and hard. "It started when Tracey fell, baby. He swooped his arm around me, and offered me a cigarette. While everyone piled to the middle of the room, he led me to the stairs-"

"He led you?" I asked, my ears pricking at the merest suggestion of sound from outside in the corridor.

"He had my hand. He... He *held* my hand. I pulled it away when someone looked."

"Who looked?"

Anissa blinked. Her eyelashes were sensational. "It doesn't matter."

"It *does* matter, Anissa. I want to know."

Her eyes fell to my chest. "George. The guy who danced with me last week. The one who dry-humped me in front of everyone."

The humiliation was staggering. "Continue."

"We walked down to the reception and outside. Sean lit a cigarette, passed it to me and lit another. We didn't really talk. I said something about the party being good, and he nodded. His eyes were all over me. He was staring at my breasts for ages. I joked he could get arrested. He said I should tell him not to do it if I didn't want him to. So I told him not to do it, Mark. I asked him to stop staring. He came closer... He slipped a hand down to my leg-"

"Where?"

"Just above my knee. He *grabbed* my flesh, Mark. I told him to be careful. If he marked my skin, someone would see. He was careful not to. He just ran his fingers around my skin, working his way higher, then lower when he'd get too close to my thighs. I smoked quicker, eager to finish and get away from him. He noticed and called me on it. I denied what I was doing, baby. I said it was his imagination. He smirked, a real knowing grin." Anissa looked over my shoulder.

I glanced to the doorway.

"It's nothing," Anissa insisted. "I'm just checking. I've a plan, baby, and I don't want anyone ruining it."

I cleared my throat.

"He played with the insides of both my legs. Not too far up. He wasn't *that* bold. I was getting excited. It *was* exciting. This big brute was doing things to me without even asking my permission. He took my cigarette out of my mouth before it was finished, and flicked it away. He spat his on the ground, looked into my eyes and leaned suddenly forward." Anissa grabbed my head, and pulled my mouth to hers.

I kissed her.

Her tongue was unfamiliarly reluctant.

I was allowed to take the lead. To seek out the corners of her mouth where sweet breath caught emotion. And lust. And fire.

There was a sudden spark inside her, as I touched her inner thighs. She looked lustfully into my eyes, then she broke away. "Meet me in the storeroom in twenty minutes... If you want more... If you want... To go... Further."

My cock was erect.

"That's what happened," Anissa said, stood with her legs parted.

17

"Come here," she said, and led me deeper into the storeroom. "I know what I'm doing." Anissa sat on the edge of a desk, and stroked the outline of my cock through my trousers. "Oh, baby, can I suck that?"

I flinched.

"What's wrong?"

I looked behind me to the door to the corridor. "What if Sean walks in?"

"I want him to." She spread her legs.

"Holy shit, Anissa," I said, my eyes snatched by her underwear.

"What, baby?"

I swallowed. "You... You've been dancing up there in that miniskirt... And underneath you were wearing... "

Anissa smiled, running her fingers through the red ruffles to either side of her pussy lips. "All day I've been airing my pussy in these crotchless panties, baby."

"Why?"

She leaned back on her elbows, dangling her boots in mid-air. "Hoping I'd get a chance to show them off."

"Jesus." I lowered my mouth towards her sex. "You *are* a fucking slut."

"Oh God, Mark." She drove her hips forward.

I took Anissa's clit in my mouth, nuzzling my nose against her shaven pubic hair. Her scent was glorious. Her taste strong, and moist.

She folded her knees on my shoulders, pulling me deeper. "That's it, baby, eat my pussy."

I kissed the soft 25-year-old skin between her inner thigh and the red lace of her panties. Anissa's miniskirt inched over her ass. Her tight frame rotated on the table, easing her sex against my mouth. I mauled her hood with my tongue. She was so fresh. So eager. So hungry. I placed my hands under her naked thighs and hauled her closer.

"Yes," she whispered. "Oh God... I *need* this."

I retreated from her clit and clenched her panties between my teeth, pulling one side away from her pussy. "Silence," I insisted.

She groaned, then ground herself against my stubble.

I lost myself in her moistness, teasing my tongue tantalisingly towards her opening, then back to her beautiful clitoris.

Anissa's body arched, attempting to drive her lips to mine.

I breathed warm air over her hood.

Anissa locked the underside of her knees on my shoulders.

I lapped at her clitoris.

She looked down, eyes glazed with lust and wine. "Mmmmmm," she moaned, and widened her thighs, shifting her miniskirt to her waist.

I circumnavigated Anissa's lips. She squirmed as I probed the sensitive area between her anus and vagina, nibbling as I went. Her opening pulsated before me. I inhaled her magnificence, then lowered my mouth onto her pussy.

Anissa wriggled on the table.

I chewed on her sex.

Her brown leather boots hung loosely over my back.

My cock strained in my trousers.

"Baby-"

I shushed her.

"Baby," she whispered, "you're the most amazing boyfriend. I kiss another guy and you reward me like this... By *eating* my pussy."

"Quiet, Anissa," I said, and turned her lips over in mine.

She giggled.

I broke from her sex, only to be drawn inextricably to her mouth, ravishing her adulterous tongue with my own. She was eager, animalistic even, clawing at my head and dragging me closer.

"Eat me again, baby," she whispered, her blonde hair falling back to the desk, her gold earrings tapping off the wood, and her eyes picking a spot on the ceiling.

I felt the vibrations of the speakers upstairs through the walls. How long would it take for someone to notice we were missing?

"Make me cum," she said.

18

I slithered down, kissing between Anissa's breasts. *Pink's Just Like A Pill* pumped above. I threw my eyes over my shoulder. The doorway was empty. My cock ached as I turned to Anissa again.

"I can't believe you kissed him," I said, watching her face for signs of regret. "You *actually* kissed another guy."

Her chest expanded, but she gave nothing away.

I noticed a dusty mirror propped in the corner of the storeroom, angled to face the door.

"Give me your fingers, Mark."

I slid my hands down the sides of her tight waist, over her hips and to her smooth, soft thighs. I studied her pussy, at once revealed and yet wrapped inside her crotchless panties. I placed my first two fingers over her clit, gently circling her for a few seconds.

She eased herself back along the desk, positioning the heels of each boot at either corner.

I spat on her sex.

"You bastard," she wheezed, knowing she needed no added lubrication.

I pressed on my erection through my trousers.

"Fingers," Anissa whimpered.

The ceiling above us creaked under someone's feet.

I yielded, switching my thumb to her clitoris and lovingly touching her with slow, rotational strokes. The fingernails of my first two fingers eased to her opening, grazing her glistening lips.

"Don't tease," she said, barely a decibel above silence.

I slid my fingers into her warm, wet slit.

Anissa moaned and grabbed at the edges of the desk, shaking its four legs. She panted, perspiring under the artificial lights.

I ploughed into her pussy, mauling her up to my knuckles. I ignored her growing movements and bent my fingers inside her, caressing her inner sponge. My thumb pressed down on her clit.

Her heels scuffed the surface of the desk.

My eyes made the mirror.

Anissa's right leg flailed high, mounting my shoulder and obscuring my view.

I thought of her tongue in Sean's mouth, then clenched her thigh between my front teeth and bit.

Her shriek was silenced only by her frantic breathing. She freed her hand from the edge of the table and swiped at my head.

I tightened my teeth for a moment.

"Mark!" she cried.

I released her, slid my tongue to her hood and manipulated her clit. Her labia leaked juices. I forced my fingers recklessly, carelessly in and out.

"Fuck!"

I added a third finger. My pace fastened, my hand blurring in motion. How could she kiss another man? Someone she claimed to despise? Allow him to touch her inner thighs? And finally to ask him to meet her in the storeroom? I wondered how she felt to have been stood up... To have been rejected.

I tore my tongue from her clit, and violently drove all four fingers inside her.

"Shit!"

I clawed at her sponge, squeezing her until her juices they were building towards orgasmic levels. Then I released her, and returned to fist-fucking her. "Your pussy's insatiable," I said, then licked her inner thigh, wondering if Sean's hands had roamed as far at the frilly edges of her crotchless panties. Was she hiding more? Had he touched her? Had he felt her? Had he pressed his fingers inside her?

Anissa suppressed an increasing murmur.

"Quiet," I said.

"I..."

I wondered if there was time to pull out my erection and stuff it into her.

"Like..."

I stared into Anissa's sex, unable to resist nature any longer.

"Being..."

I had to have her.

"Watched."

19

I dropped Anissa's right leg from my shoulder in the same moment I swore I heard movement from behind. She caught the top of my head, and hauled me down to her clit. My eyes met hers. She returned a stern, insisting stare.

I melted my mouth around her beautiful hood.

Anissa's eyes were over my shoulder.

I lanced my tongue from her clit, and started to crank my neck to check behind us-

She pressed hard on my head again.

I surrendered, licking her clit, rubbing my nose on her shaven pubes and ravishing her insides with my fingers.

Her stare was fixed on the door.

My heart pounded.

My cock ached.

I leaned slowly forward, losing her clit from my tongue's reach, and layered her abdomen in a succession of kisses.

Anissa's breasts heaved as she breathed. Her hands were locked on my skull, carefully restraining me from looking around.

I was certain even before I flicked my eyes to the mirror.

He was stood, leaning on the door frame, watching me devour my girlfriend. He didn't realise I knew he was there.

I was about to break away from her. To shut her legs. And to turn to confront the man who'd kissed and touched her.

"Oh God," she said, and pushed my head down from her belly.

I heard the slightest hint of exhalation from the door.

"Eat me, Mark." She drew up her right leg, obscuring my view of the mirror.

I withdrew my fingers from her pussy.

She was watching Sean, running her tongue over her lips.

I sucked her juices from my fingers, struggling to process what was happening.

Anissa's hand came to my forehead, leading me to the lips of her pussy. "Yes," she whispered.

What could Sean see? I didn't want him to glimpse my girlfriend's pussy. It was *mine*! I clamped my mouth down, lapping up flows of her current.

Anissa's moans were escalating. What'd happen if somebody walked through reception and overheard her? I was locked on my knees before her, my lust overpowering my conscience.

Her pussy kissed my lips. I licked the length of her, circling her clit and teasing it whole. I grabbed her right thigh and hauled her closer. Her flesh fell to the side of my face. I peered over her skin, to the mirror.

Sean had his fat cock in his hand. He was wanking it out of his fly.

The nerve!

Anissa pushed at my forehead, returning me to her luscious sex. "Oh my God," she said, her voice escaping her clenched teeth.

I heard Sean pull at his foreskin.

Anissa's eyes were ablaze with lust, staring at his groin.

I parted her pussy lips, and tongued deep inside her.

"Fuck!" she cried, shaking the desk with her buttocks.

Her first ejaculate littered my tonsils.

There was a footstep from behind.

Anissa bit at her lip as she watched him. "Shit."

I nestled my face in her crotchless panties, swallowing her juices.

Anissa reached under her miniskirt for the waistband of her underwear. She yanked her panties down her thighs.

Another footstep.

Anissa pushed me momentarily away. She drew her boots together to take down the red lace, then dropped her panties altogether to the floor.

I heard Sean breathe, deeper and faster.

Anissa spread her legs wide, exposing her shaven pussy.

His foreskin slapped back and forth on his fat cock.

She grabbed the back of my head, and pulled me down to her once more.

I lapped at her, eager for more of her juices as her skin shivered in the cold temperature. I threw my fingers inside her.

"Come," she said, fighting her rising grunts.

My ears reddened.

"Come closer." Anissa's eyes were on Sean. Her panting, breathless state for his stare. For his wanking. For his fat, erect cock. "It's okay... Sean."

20

He knew I knew he was there.

I closed my eyes, allowing the alcohol in my system to swim against my instincts. My morals were juxtaposed between maddening jealousy and a curious, sickening desire. My heart lurched in my chest. I *wanted* to see what'd happen next, and drove my fingers deeper into her.

"Come on," Anissa wheezed.

Embarrassment engulfed my every pore.

"It's okay."

I tugged on her clit with the forefinger and thumb of my other hand.

"Come."

There was no movement behind me.

"Please," she said.

The floor creaked under his foot.

I was instinctually drawn to lean further over her.

Anissa cried out, then clamped her lower lip with her upper teeth. "Do you like what you see?" she whispered, as the desk rattled under her ass.

He cast his bulky shadow over her. "Yeah," he replied, barely audibly.

"Come closer," Anissa insisted. "Really, it's okay."

Except she'd offered no consideration for my feelings.

She shoved her cunt against my fingers, bucking wildly for more.

Sean stepped by my side. He was pulling furiously on his cock.

Anissa pushed her boots to further extremes, revealing the beautiful, soft insides of her legs. "Mmmmmm," she moaned, licking her lips and looking to his member. "Baby, take your fingers out... Let Sean see my pussy."

My fingers slacked in her. My elbow arched. Shit. My forefinger and thumb pinched harder at her clitoris. Defiantly. Then my right hand eased slowly out from her, and her shaven pussy, lips gaping, oozed juices as I left.

Sean leaned closer. He was scrutinizing the most precious part of my girlfriend. He pulled harder at his cock.

"Eat me again, baby," Anissa whispered. "Your tongue is so good."

I smothered her sex with my face, licking the length of her lips to her clit. I replaced my hand at her entrance.

"Keep your fingers out." Her voice was hoarse. "They're not enough."

Sean groaned.

Anissa's eyes gazed longingly at his girth.

"Feck," he muttered, as he stood on Anissa's discarded panties.

She humped her cunt against my mouth. "Your cock is so-" Anissa whimpered as I redoubled my dashing on her labia. "Oh shit... Big and fat."

Sean graced her with the smallest of chuckles. He pulled rapidly on his dick.

"That's it," she said. "Masturbate hard for me."

I thought I heard the slightest of stirrings from the corridor. I sealed a parting kiss on her hood, then shushed her.

Anissa's eyes whipped to mine, cruelty and control defining her contours.

I submitted, serving my tongue to her delicious entrance. I was at once mesmerized.

"That's it," she said, watching Sean's cock. "Wank that fucking thing for me. Watch me. Tell me you like what you see."

Sean cleared his throat. "I like it." He slapped his foreskin.

More of her moisture slid between my lips. I was delirious.

"Come closer, *Sean*."

The room revolved in a magnificent, kaleidoscopic illusion. I was in a delayed state of horror. How much blame could we place on alcohol? These actions were committed knowingly. Willingly. Crushingly.

"Tell me you want me," Anissa said.

Sean stood awkwardly, his hand slowing around his cock.

"Don't stop... *Either* of you."

My tongue continued in subservient devotion.

"Yes," she whispered. "Do you like watching me get my pussy eaten, Sean?"

He was leaning forward, stealing a better view of my mouth mining her insides.

"Come *even* closer," Anissa said quietly. "Touch my leg as you wank yourself."

Sean placed his free hand on her lower leg, then apprehensively flicked his eyes to mine. The moment was minuscule, yet mammoth between us. There was understanding. Perhaps even agreement. We formed a treaty of trust that there was a border I would not permit him to cross.

"Oh yes," Anissa wheezed. "Grip me tighter."

The opening piano of *Train's Drops Of Jupiter* sounded out in the office above. The ceiling shook under a succession of footsteps. Dancing would distract the crowd for a while. But for how long?

"*Tighter*."

I could see Sean in the corner of my eye, wanking intently and gripping her calf. Sweat was sliding down the side of his face.

"Grip me so hard you mark me."

Sean's upper body stiffened. "Shit." He gargled, then started to convulse.

"That's it, Sean." Anissa arched her right leg. "Cum for me... Cum all over this fucking desk."

He shook his head.

"Cum, Seany, cum."

His face reddened. He clenched his teeth. A vein bulged by his temple. "Ugh," he mumbled, pulling violently at his girth.

"Cum!" Anissa bellowed, shaking the desk.

I reeled back from her pussy, exposing the pink depths of her insides to him.

His brow furrowed, Sean pumped his fat cock towards my girlfriend.

She gazed back with wide-eyed appreciation.

His knee creaked. His body tensed.

"Cum!"

My chest compressed in anxious agony.

She reached her fingertips to her clit.

I licked my lips, tasting her.

Sean grunted. He spurted his first shot of spunk over the desk.

"Yes!" Anissa said.

Feet thundered overhead.

A second spurt landed on the heel of her brown leather boot.

Perspiration poured from his face.

Another load landed inches from Anissa's thigh on the desk.

She turned her hips quickly, squeaking her ass cheeks on the surface. She aimed her sex at him.

The tussle between treachery and trust warred in my abdomen, only to be embraced with the demand for derision in my head.

Sean's final shot landed on the floor, missing Anissa completely.

Her pussy pulsated before him, motioning as if it was breathing desire itself in and out. She watched him, her legs still spread. She was grinning.

The power was hers.

Sean mumbled, then stuffed his spent cock in his trousers. He struggled through several attempts to do up his fly. "I... Er..." He turned swiftly, and scurried to the door.

I noticed severe red marks on Anissa's calf where he'd clasped her.

The sole of his shoe squeaked on the floor of the corridor outside. He hurried off towards reception.

21

"Fuck me, Mark," Anissa said, thrusting her pussy to the edge of the desk. "Fuck me right now."

I unbuttoned my trousers, grabbed her thighs and slammed into her.

Anissa's blonde hair flailed, her earrings swinging, as she seized my shirt and pulled my mouth to hers. We locked lips, swapping saliva. To have witnessed another man masturbate over her, was as disarming as it was disturbing. To have watched the necessity for control in her eyes. Heard the encouragement in her voice. *Cum all over this fucking desk.* Anissa had dictated his orgasm.

Do you think it's possible to want to fuck someone you don't even like?

I fucked up into her, determined to dissuade her attention from her memory of his fat, spunking cock.

"Oh, baby, I loved torturing that fucker. I *know* he was angry. He was humiliated. Full of rage. He had to watch me had by another man. It drove him nuts, baby. Drove him nuts that I'm had by you over and over again."

My hands clawed at her thighs.

Her warm breath thundered into my mouth.

My tongue wrestled with hers.

Her perfume was camouflage for her perspiration. For her juices. And his.

Anissa grunted, humping her hips and thrusting her cunt onto my cock. "Fuck, baby... Give it to me."

I pummelled her pussy with all my length, desperate to silence her scarlet need for promiscuity in the deadening aftermath of an incredible orgasm.

"I can't," she wheezed, whimpering beyond a whisper. "I can't... Believe he came... *Watching* me." Anissa's eyes shot shut. She was reliving the moment. Losing herself in a world of worship.

I momentarily saw Sean shoot his load over the desk. "Open your eyes," I said, seething between deep, hard strokes.

Anissa's eyelids retreated.

"Watch me," I stated forcefully.

Her front teeth nibbled her lower lip.

"*Feel* me."

She relaxed her pussy around my cock, taking me further inside.

"*I*'m your boyfriend, Anissa. *I*'m your future. Not cheap thrills with other men." I pulled my length out to her entrance. "Okay?"

Her silence masked her defiance under a thin veil.

I rammed myself into her again.

She clenched her teeth, widened her eyes and suppressed her voice in a series of explosive shrieks.

I relished her imposition and battered my groin against hers. My lips roughly careered to her ear, to her cheek and to her neck, driving her disposition further.

Anissa looked. Then she reached. Her fingertips falling suddenly upon distraction. "His cum," she said quietly.

I planted my teeth on her neck.

"Oh God... His cum."

I grabbed her blonde hair, yanked her head back to face the ceiling and devoured her throat, marking her for days to come. Christmas could conceal the evidence of her unruly lovemaking from her colleagues, though not from her family. My incisors would see to that.

She pried my face from hers, then smothered me in a succession of kisses. She circled my tongue, inhaled my breath and finally parted our lips. There was an inch between us. Anissa's eyes reading mine. Mimicking mine. Mastering mine. "Watch," she said, then leaned carefully to her right side.

I maintained my pace inside her, recognising the growing fire which boiled within my balls.

Anissa placed the forefinger of her right hand on the surface of the desk. She stretched her boot away, revealing more of the wood below her. Sean's cum languished in several drops.

"What are you...?"

Her forefinger snaked the surface.

Speakers blasted another infernal festive tune above the ceiling.

Her fingernail pressed onwards, closing the gap to his spunk.

"Don't," I insisted, stabbing my shaft into her.

Anissa halted, millimetres from his sperm. "It's just there."

"Anissa..."

Her body shivered as she lifted her finger slowly into the air. "Don't even-"

She deliberately, precisely lowered the underside of her fingertip into the centre of Sean's largest, most concentrated load. She moaned gently. "His spunk," she said huskily.

I slapped her naked ass, hauled at her midriff through her miniskirt and hammered into her, willing her to withdraw her touch from the remnants of his.

She was smiling, staring down at his sperm.

Sweat swished from my forehead. "Ugh," I growled.

Anissa grunted, pushing her left leg further away, opening herself further.

My fingers found her underarms, and clasped tightly.

"This is so sexy," she declared, lifting her finger. "So dirty." She caught his cum between her thumb and forefinger. "So wrong." She blinked, then stared.

My climax was approaching, wrought from an evolution of disgust for her debauchery and for my debasement.

Anissa's torso shook over mine. "Fuck."

A footstep fell on the steel stairs from above.

She rubbed his sperm from her first finger into her second. "Oh God."

"Anissa," I started, forcing my mutter through clenched teeth.

A second set of footsteps.

Her hand lowered again to the table.

My balls were tensing. "Anissa..."

Her third and fourth fingers dipped into his drying spurt.

A series of footsteps, echoing loudly through the reception, down the corridor and subtly into the storeroom.

"Anissa..." My yearning, burning moulded disgust and desire, seized my spunk in my testes.

Anissa positioned the first two fingers of her other hand over her clit, spreading her lips around my unstoppable cock. "I'd love to rub his cum into my clit... As you fuck me... Oh God-"

"Anissa-"

"What?"

Disembodied voices followed the footsteps.

"Someone's coming."

There was laughter.

"Oh, baby, cum for me. Cum now."

There was shouting.

"No." My insides emptied suddenly inside her. "Coming!" My sperm surged into her sanctum. "Someone's coming!" My balls slapped against the bottom of her ass.

Our eyes drew together in orgasmic, interrupted unison.

We heard Sharon, Nici, George and Billy. What if they found us?

Anissa's fingers slid over Sean's spunk as she abruptly withdrew from me. She pushed my chest with her left hand.

I fell out of her.

"I definitely did," insisted the distant sound of Sharon's voice.

I crouched, grabbing my trousers, as Anissa jumped to her feet and hauled her miniskirt down over her ass cheeks and her dripping, cum-drenched pussy. She shook her dishevelled hair, straightened her skirt and kicked her crotchless red panties under a filing cabinet.

Her left hand took my right. She squeezed. "You came in me again."

Then we ran towards the corridor.

Anissa stopped at the door of the storeroom. "Baby, I'm sorry. I love you. You're amazing." Her tongue invaded my mouth, kissing savagely.

The voices in reception grew louder. Animated.

I broke the kiss.

Sharon was staring. Billy pointing drunkenly. Nici suppressing a giggle. George was frozen to the spot.

As *Have Yourself a Merry Little Christmas* played from the office above, Anissa popped the forefinger of her right hand onto her lipstick-clad lower lip, slid it gently into her mouth and closed around it, sucking the drying sperm of another man onto her tongue.

She gulped.

22

I was thankful Sean was leaving the country. That episode in the storeroom of Anissa's work had been exciting – hell, it had been ground-breaking and exhilarating – but I couldn't come to terms with the possibility of it happening again, or escalating, without my presence. Despite Anissa's assertions that she despised him, I couldn't help feeling under threat from him.

We relived the events of the staff party several times over the Christmas holidays, and well into the new year as Sean became her fantasy fuck buddy for some time. Often she and I would fuck as she closed her eyes and imagined it was him pounding away at her. She squirmed, calling out at him/I to stop and erupting in an orgasmic fury as I ignored her protests. Anissa said she was never certain of her attraction to him, but confessed it came from a dark part of her personality. One she would never acknowledge in real life.

"Have you explored that part of yourself before?" I asked, post-coitus in bed one evening.

Anissa stared at the ceiling. There was a nervous ripple under her eye.

I propped myself on one elbow, leaning over her. "Have you?"

A deep, anxious exhalation left her body.

What part of her adventurous past was she reliving?

"I'm not saying," she whispered finally.

I pulled her negligee over her waist and reached down to cup her pussy, slipping my second and third fingers inside her.

"Oh fuck, Mark." Anissa turned her head. "Kiss me."

I licked the inside of her lips, fighting off the advances of her tongue.

"Don't tease," she wheezed.

"Tell me about your past, Anissa."

She whipped her neck away from mine. "No."

"What was it you said a few weeks ago?" I thought back for several seconds, pleasuring her pussy and hitting her clitoris with the heel of my hand. "You were trying to convince me not to go to your Christmas party. Jeez, Anissa, you were offering every outfit under your roof. I was having none of it, but you continued pulling out all the stops."

Her breath was a concoction of frustration and arousal.

My fingers danced across the outer lips of her labia. "You said you'd unlock your biggest secret..."

Anissa shut her eyes and sealed her front teeth on her lower lip.

"What was it you said, sweetheart?"

She shook her head. Moisture fell from one eye. "My master..."

I pressed my fingers deeper, and scratched the surface of her sponge.

Anissa took a sharp intake of breath. "Oh God... *Don't*... I can't take it." Her body relaxed. Her legs spread further. She surrendered to my touch.

"You said he used to make you wear a second skin body suit. You said it covered you from head to toe, Anissa." I cleared my throat. "You said it was in this house."

"I threw it away." Her pussy pushed outwards, allowing my fingers to delve deeper.

"You're lying, Anissa." I rotated my fingers on her sponge. "You said he was a man you'll never admit to seeing. You said he owned your pussy. *My* pussy. Who was he?"

Her eyelids tightened.

I pulled at her sponge.

Juice gently oozed over my palm.

"Go on, sweetheart." I kissed her beautiful forehead. "I can keep a secret... You *know* I can keep *all* your secrets."

"*He*..." Anissa's voice fell silent, her face contorting with the contagion of her anticipated confession. "I think..." She spoke at but a whisper. "I *know*... *He* was the instigator of... Wait... Do you remember I asked you if it was possible... If it was possible to want to fuck someone you didn't even like?"

"Yeah," I said, humping my heel harder against her vulva.

"*He* was the instigator of those impulses. The ones I experienced again for Sean."

"What age was *he*?"

"It doesn't matter, Mark."

"Tell me."

"Never."

I would find out. Someday. I was determined.

"I'll never tell."

The man who had possessed her cunt as his property. I would discover his identity. It was inevitable.

CHAPTER FIVE

1

"Anissa, where the fuck are you?" Gareth said into his mobile, as he stalked the hotel room floor. "Where the fuck am *I*? I'm in your fucking honeymoon suite, where I'm supposed to be."

To fuck her. Before I, her husband, even had.

"You're with Lee, aren't you?"

I wondered if he'd fucked her yet.

"You need to get back here and be with your husband."

I felt like a joke.

"Yes, Anissa, he's right here. I'm looking at him... No, of course he hasn't left you... Why?" Gareth looked at me.

"What?" I mouthed.

Gareth listened to whatever she was saying for several minutes. He grunted his only replies. Then he hung up.

"What is it?" I demanded. "Gareth, please, tell me."

He looked pale as he took a seat.

"What'd she say?"

"She... She'll tell you herself, Mark."

"What d'you mean? When? I don't even know where she is."

Gareth slid his phone in his pocket. "She's coming to see you." He stood up again. "I have to go."

To her? Not a chance! "You're staying right here where I can keep a fucking eye on you, Gareth."

He put his palm on my shoulder, then shook his head. "No, mate, you don't understand. Whatever this Lee guy, this master, has said to her... She never wants to see me again."

"Bullshit," I said, almost spitting.

"No, Mark. You and I both know Anissa. She wasn't bullshitting. She meant what she said." He walked to the door. "It's over between us."

I watched him in disbelief.

"She must be somewhere in the hotel, Mark. She said she'll be here in a few minutes. I really better go. She doesn't want to see me again." He opened the door. "But promise me one fucking thing, mate."

"What's that, Gareth?"

"Win."

"Win?"

"Win your wife, Mark. Don't let *him* take her away from you. Not after all you've been through... It's you she loves."

2

I sat alone in the honeymoon suite of the hotel. I was broken. And I was angry. And I was sad. And I was lost.

The job offer hadn't even sunk in.

It didn't even matter.

Nobody else knew about it.

All I truly wanted was not to exist. I didn't know if that made me suicidal. I didn't want to kill myself. I just wanted to no longer be around.

I loved Anissa. Despite all the fucking trouble and hurt she'd caused me, I still fucking loved her. I worshipped her. She was beyond beautiful. And there'd been a time when everything between us had been perfect.

Or so I thought.

But this hadn't started with cuckolding. Nor swinging. Nor even that first time she'd almost strayed with Sean, teasing him at the Christmas party. This had started earlier.

Before we'd even met.

When she'd been with her sister's husband.

When she'd been with Lee.

When my Anissa had been nothing more than a whore to another man.

A man she adoringly called master.

It'll all started one stupid night when I checked her mobile...

3

I was sat alone in the living room. Whiskey bottle in one hand. Anissa's mobile in the other.

The sound of her drunken snores snaked down the stairs, imploring me to capitulate to temptation. To navigate her text messages. To explore the secrets she might have dared share with her friends. To get to the bottom of how, when I'd voyeuristically watched her undress after her night out, her thong had been missing.

4

I'd watched my Anissa dress for her evening in town with her work colleagues. I'd lay on our bed masturbating, as she tried on a succession of revealing outfits. She picked her way through long skirts, miniskirts and microskirts, plunging dresses, backless dresses and scandalous dresses. Only her underwear had remained unchanged. A lacy black thong with pink ruffles and a ribbon, and a matching wonderbra.

"You're incredible, Anissa," I said, swallowing a lump of jealousy. "Stunning. Beautiful. Amazing."

She grinned, selecting the outfit she would finally settle on. "Thank you, baby."

I slapped my foreskin, yanked my scrotum and followed her fingers pulling on a sensational, seamless black dress, with spaghetti shoulder straps and cut out shredded sides, revealing her tight waist, her hips and her thighs.

"What do you think?" she asked, twirling in front of the wardrobe mirror.

"You'll break hearts in that, Anissa."

"Good... I'm in a mood to be horny."

I felt deflation detonate within my fantasies, then the fall-out scatter across my conscience. "With the girls from work, Anissa? Am I mad letting you out like that?"

She smiled. "Oh absolutely, baby. You're crazy!" Anissa tongued the corner of her mouth. "I really *do* feel in the mood to realise some of your fantasies tonight."

I gulped. "Some?"

As her mobile beeped loudly with the receipt of a text message downstairs, Anissa had turned on her six-inch stiletto heels and marched silently out of the room.

5

I downed whiskey from the bottle, then unlocked her mobile.

SHARON – "Hey. Taxi will be at yours at 9. Be ready. X"

ANISSA – "Okay. Just picked out my outfit. Mark nearly passed out. Will need your honest opinion on it later."

SHARON – "You slut."

ANISSA – "Shit. Really? Do you think the driver's disgusted with me?"

SHARON – "Just kidding. You look stunning, chum. I'm just jealous. You'll be beating them off tonight."

ANISSA – "I won't."

SHARON – "Oh yes, you will! The driver's gonna crash if you keep uncrossing your legs like that."

ANISSA - "No. Really. I won't."

6

There was a two hour gap until Sharon and Anissa messaged each other again.

SHARON – "Did you and Mark have a fight?"

ANISSA – "No, why?"

SHARON – "You kissed that guy."

ANISSA – "I did not!"

SHARON – "Pull the other one!"

ANISSA – "I will. If he comes back. I'll pull anything he

wants!"

SHARON – "Can you help me out? There's two guys nearby, but they seem more interested in Rosie the little temp bitch. Fancy a snog?"

SHARON – "I think I enjoyed that too much."

ANISSA – "My pleasure."

SHARON – "Do it."

SHARON – "Do it already!"

SHARON – "Thank God. You wiped the smile off her face. You're my hero!"

SHARON – "Hey, where are you?"

SHARON – "Where'd you go?"

SHARON – "Did you leave with that guy?"

SHARON – "Are you okay? Can't see you anywhere."

ANISSA – "I'm home. Don't think Mark noticed the obvious."

SHARON – "You're bad."

7

Noticed what? That her thong was missing? Or was there something else more obvious? Had I missed bite marks on her neck? Or a rip in her dress? And who was this guy she may have left with? *Had* she kissed him? Sharon certainly thought so.

I ignored my erection, and searched for more conversations.

NICI – "OMG! In case you forget this in the morning, you and

Sharon made out on the middle of the dance floor!"

ANISSA – "He he."

NICI – "And some guy dry-humped you."

NICI – "I can't get talking to you on your own. Just want to say, don't listen to you know who. You look fantastic. Every guy in here has his eyes on you. Your dress looks great on you. The thong is fine on show. Don't fall for that line. It's such a line. And there's jealousy behind some of those encouragements. Don't get more drunk. Don't do the dare!"

ANISSA – "Only saw this now. Too late."

NICI – "OMG! You're spoiled for choice now."

ANISSA – "Nobody at work hears of this!"

NICI – "My eyes have been truly opened!"

NICI – "Where are you? Taxi's waiting."

NICI – "Anissa, pick up. Taxi won't wait much longer."

NICI – "Did you leave with one of those guys? Are you okay? Tell me he hasn't got his hand up your dress."

NICI – "We had to leave without you. I feel terrible. Please tell me you're okay."

There was almost an hour between Nici's final text and Anissa's reply.

ANISSA – "Home safe. X"

8

So my Anissa had been busy, unable to answer her phone or reply to text messages, for quite some time. Why had she refused to explain her actions to Nici? Or had she, and then deleted the evidence? I doubted it, reasoning she'd have deleted all the evidence. What she'd left was more than enough to raise my suspicions. Then again, she'd been drunk.

What had Anissa done in that hour?

Who were these guys? How many had there been?

I closed my eyes, and recalled the image of her lithe form removing her shredded dress in the bedroom when she'd stumbled in, pulling it over her thighs, hips and chest. She still had her bra on. Just not her thong.

Her pussy had been exposed to the elements.

What elements?

Whose elements?

9

TRACEY – "It's a line. Don't fall for it."

TRACEY – "You're nuts, Anissa! She's a bitch."

TRACEY – "Your thong looked fine on you. I know you'll do what you want, but I have to say."

ANISSA – "You're right. I will."

TRACEY – "Nici's getting frantic. Sharon's convinced you're with some guy you kissed. I'll put them off the scent, if you want. You with him now?"

ANISSA – "Yes. Don't tell the other girls. I'll make my own way home."

My hand reached, inevitably, into my pyjamas, and tugged on my hard cock. I was distraught, and distressingly aroused. Her behaviour in the company of others was disgusting. These were others I'd met on several occasions. And whom I'd likely meet again.

I shuddered at the thoughts of their eyes on mine, knowing things about Anissa I didn't. Images in their minds I'd been denied. Had each of them witnessed my Anissa in a clinch, or clinches, with another man? With other *men*? Who had removed her underwear?

When?

Where?

How?

And why?

10

My mind was fuzzy as I hammered my hard on, imagining my Anissa leaning forward, bending her waist, while ensuring her legs and hips remained straight. Seeing her invite some man to raise her shredded dress over her thighs. Her ass. Revealing her cheeks in all their naked, bountiful glory. Then, turning her neck slowly, taking his tongue in her mouth. Forgetting what she had at home and her friends from work. Those girls who'd spend the next day piecing together their evening. Conspiring and rumouring her actions. Ruminating her behaviour. And coming to the conclusion that their beautiful, blonde colleague Anissa was nothing more than a promiscuous adulterer. A slut. A whore.

Anissa's mobile lit up.

My eyes locked on it.

And my balls bounced under my clenched fist.

Who the fuck was that at this hour?

I reached tentatively forward, gripped her mobile in my free palm and swiped it to unlock. There was one new text message, from an unknown number. One she did not have saved.

UNKNOWN – "I have your thong."

Resolve drained from my balls. Arguments resonated internally. Mental and physical manifestations which felt more like infestations. Of jealousy. Of angst. Of downright distrust.

Perhaps it was a friend, I reasoned. A helpful friend. A girl who'd been with them on their night out. Whoever she was, she was just trying to be helpful. Anissa had lost her underwear, and this girl had been kind enough to collect it from the club. Now she was just offering to return it. There was nothing suggestive, nor suspicious, about the message. Right?

Who was I kidding? Nici, Sharon and Tracey had all left without her. Anissa had confirmed to Tracey she was with some guy.

The message was from him. He was bragging.

I was a fool to assume otherwise.

Her mobile lit up again with another message.

UNKNOWN – "I'm sniffing it now."

I spunked uncontrollably over the floor, dropping her mobile loudly on the coffee table in the centre of the room.

Jesus.

He was sniffing them.

I spurted further ejaculations.

He'd kissed my woman.

Some spilled over one of the wooden legs.

He'd fondled her.

More trickled over my fingers.

And now he was reliving those moments with the scent of her sex languishing across his nostrils.

11

I drummed my clean fingers on her mobile.

No amount of deliberation was delivering me any closer to a decision.

I wanted to text back. To call. I needed to know who he was. Hear his voice. Make my disaster a reality.

Had Anissa cheated?

How far could she have gone before I'd call it a step too far?

I encouraged her. I *knew* I'd encouraged her. At every opportunity, in every conceivable fashion, I tried to persuade her to explore her sexuality with others. It was *my* fault she'd probably strayed. *My* responsibility. *My* actions to blame.

I read the messages again. He had her thong. He *actually* had her underwear in his possession.

I breathed loudly outwards.

Sharon, Nici and Tracey all knew more than I did. And I could never ask them.

I hit reply on Anissa's mobile, and struck a blank in my mind.

How could I reply? Anissa would certainly look through her phone the next day, trying to piece together her evening. Even if I deleted whatever I chose to send, he could reply at any time. One out of place message would expose my prying.

I downed more whiskey.

What if it was him? *Him*... Her man from her past... Her master.

I threw back another swig, and put my paranoia down to the alcohol.

He was a part of her past. Not her present.

My heart thumped. She'd kissed a guy. At least one guy. Been with him for an hour or so. Removed her underwear.

How was I to know it wasn't him? That he hadn't returned to reclaim his glorious prize? That part of her she so freely admittedly he possessed. Not her pussy. Not her sex.

Her cunt.

I spilled the sting of more whiskey down my throat.

It was true.

My Anissa's cunt was still another man's property.

12

I slapped myself in the honeymoon suite in the present.

She was with Lee now. Her master.

Yet still my mind was drifting back to the past.

Again to that time before she'd even been with Gareth...

CHAPTER SIX

1

I placed the ladders under the hatch to the attic, and sighed loudly. I'd collected *2000 AD* comics as a child – in particular, *Judge Dredd* was my favourite strip – but I couldn't find them anywhere in the house. If Anissa had thrown them out... I'd judge her!

I stepped onto the first metal step, and realised I was still shaky on my feet. I breathed out again, forcing a doomed attempt at exorcising my anxiety. I planted my second foot higher, and felt my muscles in my calf ache. The damage stress could inflict was incredible. Almost debilitating, leaving me restless and wrecked for days on end. Ever since Anissa had come home from a night's clubbing without her thong.

When someone had texted to inform her that they had it.

That they were sniffing it.

Then there'd been her subsequent explanation, insisting she'd removed her underwear as a dare. For a swap. That the office temp, a supposedly feisty girl called Rosie, had taken them, and that Anissa had taken hers.

"Let me see hers then," I'd snapped.

Anissa had casually unclasped her handbag, and removed another, unfamiliar thong. "These are Rosie's," she spat back. "Smell them, if you don't believe me."

"No, Anissa."

She'd thrown them at my face.

My bluff was broken, and I eagerly scented the fabric. The odour was obviously female, but immediately different from Anissa's. I reasoned the unknown number in her phone had also been Rosie's, and relented my accusations.

The look in my Anissa's eyes as I tested her was something I'd take to my grave. Those bold whites and piercing blue irises. The unspoken warning within.

"You see, baby," she'd said firmly. "I *did* kiss a guy when I was out, but nothing more happened. I stayed behind for a drink with him, but my attention waned and I decided to come home."

"Did you enjoy it?" I'd asked, afflicted by my addiction to

poking her fires.

"Yes."

"Really?"

"Yes, Mark. It was a kiss. That's all. An enjoyable kiss, with a good-looking guy. I'm allowed that. In the end, all I wanted was to come home and cuddle up to you."

I'd accepted her answers, although my mental tension prevented my usual enjoyment of her behaviour. There was only so much suspicion, paranoia and after effects I could defer to the whiskey. It *was* ridiculous to believe Anissa had met up with her master again. It'd been so many years since she'd last seen him. He was out of her life, and he was never coming back.

I climbed the final steps of the ladder, placed my arms through the hatch, and my elbows to either side, then propelled myself into the attic.

I picked a torch out of my back pocket, flicked the switch on and looked around. There were items all over the place. In bin bags, plastic bags, cardboard boxes and old wooden chests of drawers.

"Let the search begin," I joked aloud.

2

An hour later, I appeared no closer to locating my *2000 AD* collection. I had found many of Anissa's clothes. Skirts, jeans, dresses, jackets, shoes, stockings and lots more. She'd such an unbelievable collection of stockings. Someone in her past, if not necessarily Anissa herself, had spent a lot of time and money investing in such a vast number.

My mind wandered again. To her man from the past. That man who seemed to control her behaviour even to this day.

I shook my head, and dismissed the thoughts.

There was a couple of suitcases stacked one on top of the other. There was no way I would have ever placed my comics in there. As I turned away, I was struck by the possibility that Anissa may well have thrown them in to protect them from the elements. If I didn't check, I'd only keep myself awake that night wondering.

I sighed, and unbuckled the top case. Inside was a collection of old VHS video tapes. Many ex-rental. All pre-recorded. I found it both humorous and insightful, to peruse the changing interests of my Anissa's childhood. From *Ghostbusters, The Goonies* and *Look Who's Talking* to the more mature *Stand By Me, Sleepers* and *The Shawshank Redemption*. Then I stumbled upon *Elvira, Mistress of the Dark, In Bed With Madonna* and *Pretty Woman*. Did these latter movies reflect her developing tastes? Her first discovery of her inner sexuality? That darker side which was nurtured and unleashed by another?

Had he been the man she'd kissed in the club? The one who'd forced her to sidestep Tracey, Nici and Sharon?

I stooped on one knee, and swept sweat from my forehead. This was crazy! I had no evidence, concrete, suggestive or otherwise to support that theory. Why on earth would someone so much older have been in such a club in the first place? It was ludicrous! *I* was ludicrous! Her explanations had cleared the air. She'd danced with several other guys, and kissed just one. I had calmed.

It was time to embrace that calmness.

I lifted the top suitcase away, and set it beside the other.

Her master was her past.

I reached to the buckles of the second suitcase.

We all had a past.

I flicked open the buckles.

Even I. It was time to accept Anissa's, and believe the past was where those activities, that lifestyle, belonged.

I opened the suitcase.

"Oh, fuck... Oh, fucking fuck."

3

I was mesmerised. Shocked. Silenced. Stricken by awe, fear, fright and wonder. In one mental moment, riding the cusp of angst and anger. The next, catapulted from jealousy to joviality. I felt forced to swallow the shame of arousal. That inner acceptance that such a forbidden find had incited such wild stimulation within.

I turned the material over in my hands, then placed it precariously on the edge of the coffee table.

Oh, how I'd heard her juggle the facts of their relationship. Boast, brag and secrete the truth, never committing herself totally to one revelation.

She'd once offered to find this outfit, to wear it for me... Only to later claim she'd thrown it away.

But there it was... Before me.

I ran my hand over my scalp, and shook my head. This was inconceivable. Unfathomable. And yet incredible.

Exhilaration charged my veins, thumped my heart on my lungs and pounded my pulse in my head.

Suddenly... Every tale... Every tease... Every taunt... About him... About her... Together... Master... And... Slave... Was real.

"Fucking hell," I said, and poured myself a whiskey.

4

I touched the bright blue latex rubber in my fingertips, feeding it back and forth against my thumbs. The feeling was sensual. Inhibited. Taboo. Yet I was certain my Anissa's repression had been temporary when she was dressed in this outfit for her master.

How many years had passed, I wondered? How long since she had last donned the second skin body suit for her master?

Jack Daniels warmed my chest, and fuelled my suspicions. I was roasting a raging paranoia which coupled eagerly with an aching erection in my jeans.

I couldn't change her past. Nor could I control her present. If I could shape her future, would I swerve her towards the rubber suit, and indeed servitude, again?

I examined it further, bringing it to my nostrils and scenting the latex. The sense of forbidden behaviour was overwhelming. Foreboding actions committed between a mysterious, aggressive older man and his younger, obedient slut... His slave... His Anissa... And *His* cunt. I licked the rubber, and tasted the distinct flavour of domination. I imagined her tight, young body perspiring years earlier, leaving behind a trail of sweat, sex and submission. I ran my tongue higher, finding the metal zip where her crotch would have rested. It was cold, and callous, an invitation for the cruelty of another.

I dropped the body suit, and sat back, downing more whiskey from the bottle. I was overwhelmed. My Anissa, his Anissa, whoever she was... She had once belonged to this lifestyle. A daring, provocative role-playing world in which she had enacted the wildest fantasies of someone who fostered no interest in her well-being, short-term or long. I *knew* his treatment of her had inflicted damage. Her body was unmarked, but her mind was scarred and her soul soiled. For eternity. The core of her existence had been corrupted. That beautiful, wonderful smiling Anissa I proudly loved was a shell hiding a much darker, despicable interior.

The bourbon stung my throat.

Anissa was staying the night at her sister's. She wouldn't be back until morning. My recent accusations and distrust had wedged a gap between us, and I'd made little effort to repair the damage.

Now...

I lay the latex out on the wooden surface of the coffee table, and smoothed out the second skin rubber.

I needed to decide what I was going to do about my find.

Would I confront her?

Would I appease her?

Would I plead for her to reenact her past transgressions with me?

I slid more whiskey into my stomach. Jesus, this stuff was good. My head might well curse my behaviour tomorrow... But tonight was for the living.

For the enlivening.

For the enhancing.

Tomorrow I would suspire.

This was not tomorrow.

I rested my feet, tapped my fingers on the bottle and cast my eyes over the second skin body suit once more. Instinct and alcohol were dragging my weary mind in similar directions, insisting finally on identical conclusions.

I had stumbled upon the latex rubber remnant of her past.

I would leave it overnight for Anissa to do the same.

She could explain.

She could ignore.

Only one thing was certain... Where we went next was down to her discretion.

5

I listened to the car pull up in the driveway, watched the morning sun blaze through the windows at the front of the house, and stretched my arms and legs before I started my descent of the stairs. I heard Anissa's key in the lock, then saw her silhouette through the frosted glass of the front door. She pushed it open, as I reached the final step.

"Baby!" she said, smiling so brightly she melted my resolve.

I was kissing her before I realised, caressing the soft, bare skin of her arms and pulling her torso to mine.

Anissa broke the kiss. "I can taste alcohol on your breath. Did you have a late night?"

I was admiring her loose, white summer dress, how it hung over her breasts and dropped halfway between her thighs and her knees. Her legs were bronzed, bare. Her feet free in flat, white sandals. "Yeah," I muttered.

Anissa rolled her blue eyes, then elbowed the living room door open and strutted inside, her head turning in slow motion from mine and beginning to focus on the coffee table in the centre of the room.

My lungs sucked for breath.

Anissa's mouth opened. Her nostrils flared.

My chest expanded.

Anissa's jaw dropped. Her lips retreated to her gums.

I was caught between hesitation and regret, as elements of confusion and confrontation rained down on the room.

Anissa's reaction was unprecedented. She gasped, then fell suddenly to her knees before the table, leaning her forehead forward onto the wood, resting inches from the latex rubber of the second skin body suit. She reached behind her back, to her neck, and started to untie her dress. Anissa pulled the sheer fabric down the skin of her chest, over her belly and to her ass. She raised her thighs from the backs of her calves, slid the dress down her legs, her ankles and away from her feet, allowing her sandals to slip to the floor from her soles. Her thumbs clasped the waistband of her g-string, and slid off her underwear as well.

"Master," she whispered.

I paced the living room floor, surveying my naked Anissa knelt by the side of the table. The sound of my footsteps echoed off the walls, and I rubbed my hands behind my back. I'd drawn the blinds and the curtains. Anissa hadn't spoken for two full minutes. Her eyes remained down, refusing to blink. Nor did she dare glance to the body suit.

I stopped behind her, and felt power surge within me. There she was. Meek. Amenable. Susceptive. I felt consumed by the temptation to exploit her.

"Anissa, can you hear me?"

The movements of her breasts as she breathed were the only significant clues to her consciousness.

"Do you know where you are?"

Silence.

"Are you aware of what that is in front of you?"

Her tight ass tensed.

"So, you *are*," I said.

"Are *you*?" she replied.

I reached above her, and took a latex piece of the arm in my fingers.

"You have no idea the significance, Markus. That is the most profound, almighty symbol of the shackles I wore in my life for year after year."

"You *willingly* wore them, Anissa."

A momentary grin on her face grimaced, and her chin took to her chest. "You will *never* understand that most substantial part of my soul, Markus." Her blonde locks cloaked her eyes from my inspection. "Willingness was not a factor. Permission and pleasure were missing from my vocabulary. Consent and enjoyment casualties of my ascension into adulthood... I could become *lifeless*... In..." Her breath quickened. "*That*."

I walked around Anissa, then watched her forehead, coated with perspiration, lift lightly from the edge of the table. Her pupils pulled themselves higher. Her focus adjusted. She shivered, catching a glimpse of the body suit, yet her body appeared warm.

"It's... A... Amazing."

"Touch it," I stated firmly. "Reacquaint yourself with your past."

She was reluctant, her fingers floundering in mid-air. "I can't," Anissa said.

"You *can*," I insisted, making my hands into fists.

Anissa shook her head. "My compliance with another is forbidden without my master's presence. To touch *his* property would provoke *his* wrath."

"I thought he ordered you to embrace your opportunities with other men, Anissa," I said calmly, collected.

"He... Did."

I unrolled my fists, and wiped sweat from my palms on my jeans. "He wanted you to further your experiences." Determination was boiling in my veins. "Enhance your inner sexuality." Beguiling my senses. "Your promiscuity." Playing on my ego. "Your wanton way." Growing, crying and raging within.

Her escalating hesitation heckled my pride.

"Touch it, Anissa!"

Her hands trembled.

"Now!"

Her fingers stretched, lowered and snaked the wooden edge of the table. She wheezed. "I *can't*, Mark."

"You *can*, Anissa! Touch the rubber! Feel the latex!"

Emotion ravaged her face.

"Send your mind spiralling back to the wickedness of your past, *slut*!"

Her naked breasts were propelled upwards with her quickening breath. Her eyes switched to mine. Liquid welled in the corners. "Ba-by," she pleaded.

"You were trained *for* this moment, Anissa," I said, trampling her hope in hopelessness.

She blinked, and her pupils diverted to the outfit.

"Press your flesh on the fabric, Anissa. Make that fucking contact! Feed yourself! You *know* there's a darkness in your cunt that relishes the prospect... This opportunity... That chance has provided you."

"Mark," she whispered, saliva trailing from lip to lip. "Please... How did you find-"

"Never mind!" I blasted, and stepped next to her, placing the rim of my shoe against the edge of her toe. "Make that physical reconnection with your past, Anissa..." Cruelty contaminated my cranium. "... Or I'll break your fucking fingers."

Her back arched. Her body shuddered. "I..." Anissa's fingertips fell on the bright blue rubber. "Oh my God..." Her breathing racketed up another notch. "Fuck..." Faster, she was sucking for air. "I..." Her swift inhalations impoverished her body. "Shit..." Weakened her resolve for speech. "I..." And sent the panicking, recollecting slave within clambering worthlessly towards hyperventilation. "Ha..."

7

Anissa's fingers retreated from the latex. Her nails scraped the surface of the wooden table. She lifted her hands away, and her fingertips tingled. She sucked deeply and rapidly. Perspiration lavished her forehead, her breasts and her crotch. She turned, and looked up, her eyes desperately seeking sanctuary in mine. She panted, her body capitulating to the atrocity of panic.

"Anissa," I said casually.

Terror rumbled in the whites of her eyes.

"Anissa, I want you to listen to the sound of my voice."

Her chest vibrated. Her shoulders shook.

"Anissa!"

She concentrated her stare on my mouth. "Watch my lips, Anissa," I said slowly, exaggerating my every syllable. "Listen to me. Slow your breathing. Control yourself. You're only making it worse by fighting it. You cannot breath faster. You'll make yourself dizzy. You need to slow yourself. Prolong each breath."

She nodded, then ignored my orders with fastidious, swift inhalations.

"Anissa! You have to listen to me. You're having a panic attack."

I watched my words wash over her, scything the scares in her eyes.

"Take a long, deep breath."

She slowed, pushing her trust through her fantasies, her fears, her torment and her tears, and fell soothingly for my sense of command.

"Hold it for several seconds."

My declaration of dominance.

"Then release."

My dissertation of discipline.

"You'll be okay," I insisted.

Her blonde hair blazed forward. Her thighs stretched from her calves. And her hands wrapped longingly around my legs, pulling her face between my knees. She dragged another inhalation over the course of several seconds, paused, looked up to lock her blue irises on my pupils, and finally exhaled. Twin trickles of fluid fell from the corners of her eyes.

I stroked her cheek, and admired her naked body.

"Mark," Anissa croaked, clawing at my jeans, hauling herself higher.

"Yes... *Slut?*"

Her mascara took to her cheeks. "Do... Do you know who he was?"

"Your master?"

"Yes," she said.

I perused the possibility for several seconds, and cast my eyes to the blue body suit. Was there some significant clue to behold? A scent or a mark? An inkling in her behaviour? "No," I answered finally.

Anissa stared upwards, nuzzling the sides of her head between my knees. "I'm yours, Markus."

8

"Tell me what it was like to wear that," I announced slowly, pointing to the table.

Anissa laboured an illustrious, anxious breath as her eyes followed my finger to the second skin body suit. She stared for several seconds, as if allowing the realities of the outfit to invade her head, to evoke memories of long ago – she suppressed a gasp – and to instigate feelings of fright, fear and abject terror. "It brings claustrophobia back to me, Markus," she said, pacing a path through her apprehension.

I cleared my throat, realising I was instinctively flexing my fingers. I was glancing to Anissa's long, blonde hair. Intentions to grasp, to pull, to hurt, flowed through my mind.

"It was daunting to be slipped into it, Markus. Harrowing. To experience the act of being locked from head to toe inside rubber. To actually feel contained within a second skin. To have even my own nudity stripped away from me, as if my flesh was not enough... Not good enough..." She was hesitating again. "... For... *Him*."

I brought my hand in a slicing position to the back of her neck.

"But as it was finally secured, Markus, I felt a sense of liberation."

I gently massaged her skin.

"Having my entire body and face sheathed in latex... Then the realisation that I was at someone else's mercy... It... Was... Divine."

I flicked the ends of her hair from her shoulders. I felt dangerously close to succumbing to sickening urges, and composed myself in opposing concordance as I caressed her. My intentions thrived beneath, shaping into a crueller mould. I wanted to inflict pain upon her. Humiliate her. Destroy something beautiful which still resonated unbroken within her soul.

Anissa leaned her bare body backwards, swivelled her torso and returned her head faithfully between my knees. "Oh, Markus, I was transformed. My sight was limited, and my movement compromised." Her eyes searched despondently for tolerance in the roughshod whites of mine. "I was placed precariously close to untouched ecstasy. Can you imagine that, Markus? My body broken from within. Manipulated. Charged to yearn for a degradation a world full of promise should never divulge."

I bunched her locks within my palm.

"Sometimes he would dress me in this for hours on end, and leave me untouched. Ignored. Other times he would amuse himself by dishing out a barrage of verbal abuse. *Remaining chaste does not make you a virgin again, whore. You are a slut for life. Worthless. Just a cunt on two legs...* My *cunt on two legs*. Often, he'd take his pleasure from forcing me to forego sex for days on end. On rare occasions, even as long as a week. The more he could see me in that outfit, the less he'd return to me sexually. He was amazing, Markus. The manner in which he would incite desire within *me*. Have *me* need *him*... There's a fine line between love and hate."

I pulled violently.

"Fuck!" Anissa screamed.

I clamped her in place between my knees, and stretched strands of her hair from her scalp.

"Fuck! Markus, you're hurting me!"

I released her, and grinned. Power pumped and rippled like aftershocks in my veins.

Anissa stifled a sob, and wiped moisture from her cheeks on the insides of my jeans. "I..." She sniffed. "I didn't... Deserve that."

There was a sense of accomplishment to relish from such brutality. "Tell me more," I said, and drove my fingers through her long hair, finding her skull underneath.

"Sometimes he'd have me trussed up in that outfit for so long all my muscles would ache, Markus. He'd circle me. I couldn't properly see him, but I could hear him. Sense him. And then... *Feel* him. He would run his hands over my shape. The feeling of pressure through the second skin to mine was tantalising. Erotic, yet a lasting reminder that I alone was not enough for him. Not only did he have a wife, but he needed to cloak me in this incredible latex material. Perhaps I could've convinced myself it was to enhance my sexuality, but instinct continually told me it was to control it. Not necessarily to curb it. But to command it. Manipulate it. Use it in any and all manners he saw fit."

I felt demonic impulses itch within my arms and legs, urging me to act callously towards her.

"Frustration would filter from my every nerve ending and aching muscle, Markus. The recesses of my mind and the rhythm of my heart... Building... Growing... Gathering... Centring on my cunt."

I wanted to snake down her spine to her rump.

"I knew I should've spared my future this intensity, had a boyfriend my own age."

To pry her rectum open with both hands.

"I did have boyfriends my own age, they just didn't compare."

I wanted to twist the innards of her asshole inside out.

Anissa eased her neck upwards, channelling her eyes needfully to mine. "And when master would finally reach between my legs, take the zipper in his fingers and slowly, gradually slide it open to reveal my most sensitive parts, my ass, my pussy and my clitoris, the rush to my sex was phenomenal. The sense of release imminent. I was but a figure clad in second skin, Markus. But a figure with the focus entirely on my... On *his*... Cunt."

"Is it still his?" I demanded.

Anissa blinked.

"Answer the question, Anissa."

She slammed her eyelids shut, shoving moisture from the corners of her eyes. "I'm ye... He-"

"Is your pussy still his?"

"Not my pussy," she snapped. "My *cunt*."

"Anissa," I started, drawing deep breath, "if your master were to walk into this room right now, would your cunt still be his?"

She wheezed, whirling her cheeks wildly between my knees. "Yes," she admitted. "It will *always* be his! Even if I never see him again!" She looked up. "Regardless of what I myself want. Ownership of my pussy was given away. It's no longer my property. It's *his*, Markus. His *cunt*."

"You're mine, Anissa," I said, my tone calm but firm.

She tried but failed to shake her head.

"I am as trapped today as I was the first time I was stitched up in that body suit. It was a prison, Markus. A physical embodiment of control, designed to ensnare my mind. To strip me of my individuality. My independent thought. My downright human rights."

I inhaled her misery.

"I never want to be held captive in that bondage again, Markus." Her eyes implored sympathy to rouse behind mine. "Not in those airtight confines. The latex skin over mine... No... Never."

9

"Touch it again, Anissa," I ordered.

"I... I..."

"Touch it *again*, Anissa... Now!"

She took her head from between my legs, slid her knees slowly across the floor, and turned to the table. Anissa's eyes focused on the latex rubber. "Markus, I had such an affinity with this outfit... Please... *Please* don't make me touch it again."

"Anissa," I began, and walked one foot forward, "not only are you going to touch it again, but you're going to do everything I tell you. Whose are you, Anissa?"

She flicked her fringe from her eyes, and looked up. "I'm yours, Markus..." Her eyes rolled shut. "I am." Her forehead frowned. "I *really* am. It's you, Markus. You... I'm sure it is."

I took Anissa's chin in my hand, and turned her face towards the body suit. "Touch it."

She dragged a deep, long breath, held it and fed her fingers over the surface of the table. She exhaled, and her fingernails traced the beginnings of rubber. "Ohhhhh fuck, Markus." She was trembling. "I'm scared." She shuddered from the top of her spine to the bottom, where her perfect, little ass rested bountifully on the heels of her feet.

"Grip it in your hands, Anissa."

She fought a growing urge for increased respiration, shoved her wrists forward, over the latex, and curled her fingers and thumbs. "Oh shit... Shit... Shit."

"Take a firmer grip. Really grasp it."

Anissa's jaw shook. A piercing squeal started to escape from her lips. She slammed her teeth together. Tears, mascara and perspiration slid down her cheeks to the corners of her mouth. "Oh, fuck, Markus, are you going to hurt me?"

I rubbed the denim-clad calf of one leg over the bare skin of her behind. "Maybe," I whispered.

She clutched the rubber tighter.

"It depends how closely..." I lowered my mouth to her ear. "How *accurately* you can portray your past."

"I... I don't understand, Markus... What do you mean?"

"I'm going to make you relive your days with your master."

Trust unravelled in Anissa's eyes. "Markus, no! Please!" She threw her eyes desperately to the table. "This outfit... I was possessed by it. It's dangerous. It sucked life from my limbs." She scraped her fingernails over the rubber. "It was designed to be worn by a dominatrix... But when I wore it... It was to be used... Abused... Please, Markus... No."

I recalled her recent clubbing. Her unacceptable behaviour. Her dismissive attitude. And her rhetorical explanations. How she rotated accusation and blame, laying responsibility for her lies at my feet.

"Please," she pleaded, naked and pathetic between my legs.

"You're fucking wearing it... *Slut*."

I dragged my fingers through Anissa's long, blonde locks and pulled her to her feet.

She stumbled awkwardly, flailing her arms and suppressing a squeal.

"Silence!" I shouted.

Her chest rose and fell rapidly.

"Control your breathing, slut. I don't want you hyperventilating again."

She wheezed, panted and pressed her palm on her chest, holding her breath for several seconds. She exhaled. "Markus, I'm scared-"

"Good," I interrupted. "You've been due a lesson to learn for quite some time." I turned, yanked her wrist to follow and walked into the kitchen. "That time has now come." I pushed Anissa against the cold wall. "Stand there, slut. Legs apart. Cunt exposed. Push your tits higher. They're pert, Anissa. They're perfect. But for God's sake propel those nipples north!"

Her bottom lip quivered as she expediently obeyed my orders.

I twisted the cold water tap in the sink, and grabbed a pint glass. "I look at your pussy lips, Anissa, and I wonder how many men have seen you there, or touched you there, since we've been together-"

"Markus, I've nev-"

"Shut the fuck up, slut!"

Anissa slapped her lips together, and looked down. Her hands crossed demurely across her chest, cupping the sides of her breasts.

"Y'know, Anissa," I started, filling the pint glass with water, "you seem keen to cover yourself up." I gestured to the living room behind her. "That body suit will provide you with just what you want."

She shook her head. "Please, Mark-"

"Enough!" I halted the charging water. "Drink this."

Anissa took the glass in hand, and tipped a mouthful between her lips.

"Drink all of it, slut."

She returned a look of confusion.

"Hurry up, slut."

Anissa's hand shook as she swallowed more of the water. Some spilled down her chin, and dropped to her breasts. She winced upon contact with the cool liquid.

"Keep drinking," I said. "You've more to get through."

Her eyes narrowed on mine, and she lifted the glass higher, gulping down the contents.

"Did you and Tara touch alcohol last night?"

Anissa tilted the bottom of the glass. Her throat bulged as she took more. "Ahhhhh," she released finally, then sucked for breath. "Yes."

"What did you drink, slut? How much did you have?"

"Markus, please don't call me-"

I snatched the pint glass from her, and shoved it under the tap, refilling it quickly. "What'd you have last night?"

"We shared a bottle of white wine. I'd two glasses. Markus-"

"You're dehydrated. You need to drink more water."

Anissa shook her head. "Don't be silly, baby-"

"Enough!" I shoved the glass back into her hand. "Finish this. Quickly."

Anissa hesitated, flicking her stare from one eye to the other. "Okay," she said finally, and drank as fast as she could.

I tapped my foot on the tiled floor, and folded my arms. "Hurry up."

She stopped, then swallowed what she had in her mouth. Half a pint remained in the glass. "Markus, I can't drink anymore." She touched her stomach. "I can feel it bloating."

"I don't care, slut. You never obey me. You disrespect me at every opportunity. You make a fool of me. I bet every one of your work colleagues has a laugh at my expense. What must they think of you? The office tart? The slut? Or is it... The office whore?"

Defiance warred with compliance behind her eyes. Her cheekbones raised. Her lips pursed. Then her arm twitched. It was bending. Moving. Bringing her hand higher. The rim of the glass met with her lips. She opened her mouth. Raised the end of the glass. And water slid down her throat.

"Good girl," I said.

Anissa left her eyes locked on mine as she swallowed more.

"Give me your glass when you're done."

The fingers of her free hand drummed her bare belly. She held the last of the water in her mouth, breathed through her nose, and finally gulped it down. "Oh my God, Markus, you've no idea how hard that was. I thought I was gonna spew it up again."

"If you do, slut, you'll be licking it up."

Anissa held out her glass. "Why are you being so cruel to me?" she asked.

I took the glass.

"Markus, please tell me."

I set the pint glass in the sink.

"What have I done wrong?"

I turned the tap.

Anissa's attention drifted to the sink.

Cold water thundered into the glass.

"You're not going to make me drink another one, Markus, are you?"

The water tumbled loudly, climbing to the top of the glass.

"Why?" she demanded, and started forward.

I seized Anissa's shoulders and pushed her firmly against the wall. "To teach you a lesson, Anissa! You're always pushing me around, playing games with my mind and teasing my groin."

"I thought you liked it, baby!" she cried, and tried unsuccessfully to shrug off my palms.

I pinned her tighter to the wall, and surveyed the emotion in her eyes. Anticipation trumped trepidation. She wanted me to exercise my might. I could sense the disparaging desires behind her naked exterior. The need within her deception.

Anissa raised one foot from the floor, and caressed the inside of my leg with her knee. "Don't you like it, baby?" she whispered, puckering her lips together.

My heart hammered.

Her knee travelled higher.

My pulse thumped.

Her distraction detonated a minefield of arousal in my mind, and submerged subjugation in my loins.

I felt my face fluster. My strength struggle to muster. And indecisive thoughts suddenly cluster.

"Don't you long for the day when I acquiesce to your every command, Markus?" she asked, casting her sweet, warm breath over my face and the heat of her leg under my testicles. "When I'm naked, under your orders, in the company of another man? When my every action with him is dictated by whatever you bark at me? When I do nothing without your say so, and jump to immediately comply with your every instruction? For the day when you tell me to go down on him... To sit on him... To lie back and take him deep inside me?"

I released her wrists, turned and reached for the pint glass. "Down this, Anissa," I said. "Down it, then join me in the living room."

<h1 style="text-align:center">11</h1>

Anissa took slow steps from the kitchen to the living room. "Baby, I don't feel well," she said quietly, clutching her stomach.

"What you feel, slut," I began, stretching my denim-clad legs on one of the leather sofas, "is discomfort." I pointed to the second skin body suit. "What you are about to feel is... Distress."

She looked down to me.

I watched arguments form in her mind.

"But..." Protests pulled her lips over her gums. "I..." Resolve was conquered one thought at a time. "Okay," she whispered finally, all hope for quarrel drifting away into silence.

I stood. "Face me, slut."

Anissa turned her naked form to face mine, fully-clothed.

"Hands by your sides!"

She obeyed, slipping her palms to her hips.

I reached forward, and pressed my hand on her bulging abdomen. "Is that sore?"

Anissa sucked a succession of breaths as she answered. "It's uncomfortable, Markus."

"But *not* painful?"

She reluctantly shook her head.

"What about now?" I demanded, and snaked my free hand behind her back, crushing her belly in between.

Her legs instinctively crossed, clamping her cunt. "Shit. Markus, it's sore. My bladder's full. It's aching."

I laughed. "Nonsense! It's barely two minutes since you finished the third pint, Anissa. And I only have your word that you drank it. For all I know, you quietly dumped it into the sink."

"I drank it all, baby! I'm doing everything you tell me to!
*Every*thing!"

I nodded.

"Can I please go to the toilet, Markus?" she asked politely,
fluttering her eyelashes.

"No," I snapped.

"What?"

"Now, Anissa, put on the body suit. I want to see you fully
dressed in latex. Just as you were for him."

Her erect nipples pointed to the ceiling as her breath paced
suddenly faster. "Baby, I *need* the toilet."

"I don't care. Get dressed. Now."

Anissa uncrossed her legs, revealing the perfect lips of her
pussy, and turned to lean over the table. Her ass jutted outwards. Her
breasts dipped down. And her stomach uncharacteristically bloated.
"Will this make you feel more like a man, Markus?"

My palm flew through the air, and smacked her ass cheeks.

Her flesh rippled, and she stopped herself doubling over,
clutching her waist in one arm. "Fuck! I'm sorry, Markus. I'm sorry!"

I rubbed her flesh, soothing her sanctum. "You'd better be, slut."

"I am," she said swiftly, and took a deep breath as she lifted the
latex rubber in her hands. "I'll prove it to you." Anissa threw her
blue eyes over her shoulder. "Will you help me put this on? I want to
please you."

12

"Oooooh God, Markus, I'm so paranoid," Anissa said, struggling to
suppress the excess liquid in her lower abdomen and slip deeper into
her latex prison. "Do you think I've put weight on over the years?"

I grabbed her hair and pulled her mouth roughly to mine,
invading and eating at her tongue.

She was breathless when I broke contact between us.

"You're fucking beautiful, slut." I grabbed her ass in the confines
of the tight rubber, and squeezed. "Let's get you into the rest of this.
I want you fully covered."

Her eyes stared longingly into mine. "Even my head?"

"Your master had you covered from head to toe. That's how

you'll be for me. Understood, whore?"

"Yes, Markus," she insisted, and stretched her hand into an arm of the suit.

I enjoyed the onslaught of goosebumps which dotted her skin as she succumbed to the rubber brilliance.

She shuddered. "Jesus, baby, I'm fucking terrified." She forced her second hand inside.

"Become my whore, Anissa," I ordered. "Embrace your slave state. You were born to be a slut. Become mine."

"Yes, Markus," she whispered, closing her eyes and fastening her tiny frame within the fabric, enveloping her back and bringing the mask closer to her head.

I cast my eyes over her. Her calves sheathed within skin-tight, reflective rubber. The curves of her thighs, ass and unfortunate bladder bloating her stomach. Her petite, pert breasts squashed under latex supremacy.

She ran her cloaked fingers seductively over her hips, the tightness of her waist and her ribs to her shoulders. The rubber squeaked an extraordinary, erotic sound which evoked impressions of ownership. Of subjugation. Of one human soul belonging to another. "Baby," she whispered, "I have to admit... It *does* feel sexy... After all this time."

I studied the stunning features of her face. Her blue eyes meandering within the mental and physical remnants of her more experimental, youthful sexuality. Her cheekbones perfect and prominent. Her lips ravenous and rouge. "The mask, Anissa... You must wear the mask."

She scrunched her hair suddenly in her hands. "Help me, baby."

I stood against her, feeling the heat of her flesh pump through her second skin to the surface, and tugged my thumbs under the rubber hood, hauling it over her hands and head.

Anissa's pupils flashed upwards. "I," she started.

I cloaked her suddenly.

"... Love you..." She pulled her hands away.

I tucked the mask under her chin to her neck.

"... Master."

Fires blazed in my veins, and I stared at the hole. "I didn't realise it was open-mouthed," I said.

She nodded modestly, the entirety of her body covered from

sight but for her smile.

"How does it feel?"

"Sexy," she confessed, then a grimace on her lips betrayed her.

"What is it, slut?"

Her rubber-clad, gloved fingers traced her midriff. "You've no idea how much I *need* the toilet, Markus."

"Hold it, whore. You're forbidden from urinating for the foreseeable future."

Anissa released a long groan. "Am I to your pleasing?" she asked.

I stepped back, and admired my latex slave. She was so small. So vulnerable. "Did your master make you wear boots over it?"

"Yes. Tara's thigh-highs." Anissa slapped her lips suddenly together.

I inhaled the information. "So, he fucked you in your mother's house? Or did you take your sister's boots to his place?"

Her lips surrendered no explanation.

I placed my palm over her crotch, and tapped the zip. "You've gone all shy." I ran my fingers higher. "What could I do about that?" I pressured the heel of my hand on her bladder.

Anissa folded forward. "Baby, don't! Please!"

I grinned, then grabbed the rubber of her hood, pulling her face over my chest. "Unbutton my shirt, slut. I want to feel you over my skin."

Anissa placed her fingers on my shirt, then strived to find the buttons. Her grip was awkward, the latex and her lack of vision compromising her skills. Relentlessly, she struggled on and forced the first button free. The second came quicker. The rest followed.

I slipped my shirt over my shoulders and to the floor. "I'm going to sit down, slut. Then I want you to come rub yourself over me."

Anissa nodded, then followed me.

I sat.

She purred as she took to her knees between my legs, and rested her hooded head on my lap. Her hands explored my chest, the rubber squeaking loudly over my flesh. "Is this to your pleasing, Markus?"

My nipples were unfamiliarly tugged between her forefingers and thumbs. "It's different, slut."

"I want to please you, Markus. I'm... *Glad*... You made me face my fear. I want to share this experience with you. I... *Trust*... You...

With my life." She held herself.

"What is it, slut? What's wrong with you?"

Anissa's head faced mine. Her eyes cloaked in latex blindness. "I have terrible cramps, Markus." She squeezed her thighs together. "Please let me go to the toilet. I can just unzip my crotch. I won't need to undress. I'll be quick."

"No."

"Baby, please, I'm going to wet myself."

"I have forbidden you from urinating, slut. You will not wet yourself. You will not even think about pissing. If I scent a single hint of leakage, I will punish you in the most horrendous way. Do you understand?"

The rubber mask nodded in return, her quivering lips the only clue to her inner demeanour.

"Good girl," I said, and patted the top of her head. "Give me some examples of how your master treated you in this outfit. I wish to hear more of how my girl was once another man's slut-"

"*Am*," Anissa interrupted, daring to tread where my patience might break. "I *am... His... Property*."

13

"Excuse me?" I asked.

"I mean I'm *yours*, Markus... I'm confused... I was bred to be his... Forever." The latex hood mimicked her expressions beneath. "I'm *so* close to my past right now, baby... Please forgive me... It's overwhelming. I'm forgetting myself. Losing my mind "

I sighed loudly.

Her rubber fingers stroked my skin. Her mask caressed my belly. "I'm sorry, baby. I love *you*. I want you to manipulate my body... In the present. Will you?"

"Yes, Anissa."

"*Can* you?" she teased, tugging control swiftly to herself.

I hesitated. "Of course I can, slut!" I reached down to my jeans, and unbuttoned my fly. "I'll fucking show you, Anissa!"

The merest suggestion of shrewdness crossed her lips.

"Come here," I insisted, and pulled her hooded head over my crotch.

She slipped her mouth around my testicles. "Mmmmmm," she moaned, and licked in slow, deliberate circles. "I love sucking a man's balls."

"Did you love sucking your master's balls?"

She made an affirmative groan, then ground her latex-encased chin over my scrotum. "I used to drink his sweat, Markus. Oooooh, he loved a good work out, followed by me licking around his nether regions. I adored the natural masculinity of his musk. Then the taste of his genitals. Oh fuck... The memories... His sweat... His spunk... I still dream about it."

I watched the blue rubber fold around her body as she squirmed between my legs. "You *still* think of yourself as his property, don't you?"

Anissa placed her latex fingers around my cock.

"I bet you *still* fantasise about him, slut."

She wanked me forcefully.

"When you masturbate."

She squeezed my shaft, concentrating her thumb on a particular vein.

"When we fuck."

Anissa wheezed over my groin. "Yes... I do." She engulfed my cock in one swift swoop, sucking down to my base.

"Fuck," I gargled, riding the cusp of her commotion.

Her tongue and teeth racketed over my length. Her bright blue body suit creased as her back arched. She pulled her lips away, then stared her blank mask upwards. "I remember he told me he wanted to experience his most intense orgasm... Then he looked at me and said... *And you're going to make that happen, Anissa.*"

14

Anissa wrestled my cock in one rubber gloved hand, and attempted to comfort her belly in the other. "He was in a particularly good mood on this one day," she said. "His beloved Glentoran had just won the Cup." She sucked an inhalation of air above my crotch. "But he could've been in his worst for how he treated me."

I groaned, and thrust my shaft in and out of her blue palm.

"I'd been forced into a fourteen day period of celibacy," Anissa continued. "Some of that because we couldn't be together, but there'd also been a couple of occasions when he'd ordered me into *this* just so he could watch me squirm. He'd make me stand in front of him, sometimes for up to an hour, and often with my crotch unzipped. He said he loved having my three orifices exposed. *You're a whore, Anissa. A beautiful whore. But a whore all the same. And whores like you should make your holes available for men at all times.* Yes, master, I told him."

I crashed the bulbous head of my cock against her red lips.

The only visible part of her flesh moulded suddenly around my member, taking me down to my pubic hair. Her rubber fingers pressed between my testicles.

"Shit," I croaked, then pulled my dick away from her, opting to wank it instead over her latex face. "Keep talking."

"We found a two-hour window where we could be alone that day, a Saturday. He wanted to celebrate his team's win, and that included depriving me of my individuality in this second skin body suit. My cunt ached for his cock, baby. I *needed* to be fucked. He'd refused my requests for masturbation, for a long cucumber to slide in and out of my pussy-"

"Your master controlled your masturbating frequency?" I snapped.

Her tight, bright blue mask nodded. "He did at that time in our relationship. He controlled so many things. His tastes would change. Sometimes he'd grow tired of me. Other times his interests would return. So there I was, stood fully clothed in my body suit before him. We'd two hours to ourselves. Two hours where we were guaranteed privacy. Two hours where no one knew what debauchery he was committing on me... *In* me."

I slapped my palm down my shaft to the base.

"He interrogated me, Markus. *Did you wank* my *cunt this week, whore?* No. *I don't believe you.* Please, master, I swear to you, your cunt is eternally faithful to you. I would never, ever risk your wrath by betraying your bidding. *Fucking slut. I bet you've been sucking off all the young guys you meet.* No, master, I haven't! I spurn their advances." She licked her lips. "*You've probably been passed back and forth between them, Anissa. I know your body.* He started to tug on the zip at my groin. *I'm going to inspect you.* Seconds later, his fingers were fondling me all over. He pulled roughly at my pubes, chastising me for not conserving my youth with a wax. He squeezed my clit between his forefinger and thumb. *I bet boys have licked you here.* Not during my celibacy, master! *So, there have been boys, then?* Yes, I admitted. But not for weeks. *This is* my *cunt, Anissa,* he said, and fired his fingers inside me. I stumbled suddenly on Tara's boots, and he barked at me for disrespecting my sister. Oh, fuck, he rubbed it in. *You're a disgrace, Anissa. A cheap bag of meat on stilts. Are you fit to wear those boots?* I shook my head. No, master. I'm a shameful excuse for a human being."

I pulled Anissa's hand to my cock, and explored the heat her second skin flesh was exerting.

"*I bet they fucked your pussy, and your ass. It's* my *cunt, Anissa! Mine!* I know, master! I'd never share it with anyone! And you know my ass is virginal. He laughed. Oh, fuck, baby, he laughed so very, very hard, and his fingers slipped slowly out of my moist pussy. I felt my body freeze as those fingers moved under my cunt. My anus tensed. Please, I whimpered, I don't want you to. *I have to know if boys your own age have been having you there, Anissa.* I shook my head. I couldn't see him. His face was hidden from me by my mask, but I was sure he looked heartless... Cruel."

I grunted, my cock caught harshly in her tightening grasp.

"Baby," Anissa whined, "please let me go to the toilet."

"No."

"Can I at least unzip my crotch? Try to ease some of the pressure."

"Absolutely not, slut." I gripped the rubber latex of her lower arm, and encouraged her into renewed action. "Continue your fucking story. Do it justice. Don't rush it... Or you'll be punished."

"He pulled his hand away, and wiped my juices into the rubber over my chest. *No lubricant,* he said. *No pussy juice. I need to know how tight you are.* Let me suck my fingers dry for you, master. *No, whore, you're just trying to placate me. You only wish to wet my fingers.* He put his hand between my legs again, Markus. Past my pussy. And onto my ass. He pushed my cheeks aside, held me open and tried to exploit my insecurities. *Do you think your breasts are disproportionately small, Anissa? Do you look at the other girls and feel inadequate in comparison to their fuller figures? Do you glance at their breasts and feel a deep envy growing within? Does it start in your head and end in your cunt... In* my *cunt?* I thought you liked my titties, I cried. I was vulnerable, Markus. I was weak. And he plunged two fingers violently into my anus!"

"Will you ever fuck him again, Anissa?" I demanded suddenly.

Her lips locked together.

"Well, slut? Will your master ever return to reclaim his property?"

Her mouth trembled.

"To take back *his* cunt," I added.

"I... I... I can't answer that, Markus."

Rage rumbled in my throat. I grabbed the back of her head, and hauled her masked face to my length, tearing between her lips.

Her response was a muffled moan. Her face bobbed up and down, her tongue swiftly acquiescing to my needs.

"Yes, Anissa," I said. "That's it, slut. Suck your man's cock. Take it down your fucking throat. And remember the taste. The smell. Get it through your fucking skull who the fuck you belong to now!"

I could've sworn her mouth curled into an insidious, power provocative grin around my member.

I hammered her to the hilt, slapping my balls off her rubber chin. "Choke on it!"

She gargled, tongued the underside and somehow sucked it deeper.

"Fuck!"

Anissa stretched her jaw, wriggled her lower lip over my testicles and wheezed as the last of her airway surrendered to my shaft.

"Shit, Anissa," I spluttered.

Her body contorted within her second skin prison.

My abdomen tensed. Waves of lust rushed in my bulging balls. I gripped the sides of Anissa's head in her mask, and pried her mouth from my length.

She gasped for breath. Saliva and precum spilled from her lips. She ran her tongue outwards, collecting ample samples, and swallowed. "Oh, baby, it tastes so good."

"Tell me about his fingers in your ass, slut," I barked.

Anissa grimaced.

"What is it, slut?"

"My bladder, baby... Please... I'm bursting."

"No!"

"Markus, I'm going to wet myself."

"Continue your fucking story, Anissa," I insisted. "Your needs don't matter. I'm sure your master was wise enough to make that one of your first fucking lessons."

"Yes," she conceded meekly. "I'm nothing. I know I'm nothing-"

I seized her blue latex throat in my palm. "Don't look for sympathy, slut. It doesn't become you." I tossed her neck aside, and grabbed her hand. "Masturbate me, slut. You ought to be qualified in the arts of using rubber for pleasure. Demonstrate it to me, and tell me what your master did to you."

"I was wailing, Markus. He had these two big fingers jammed right up my virgin asshole. *You're tight, whore. Maybe you weren't lying.* I wasn't, I screamed! *I bet you've had something up there, Anissa.* Never! Oh fuck, Markus, his wrist was rubbing against my pussy lips, but no pleasure would counter the agony in my anus. It felt like there was a fucking tree up there. And then he kissed me, catching me completely unaware. His tongue probed dominantly over mine. His fingers pushed deeper in my ass. I couldn't fight him, Markus. I couldn't control the situation, or dissuade his cruelty in any fashion. Fuck, I could barely stand in my sister's fucking thigh-highs!"

"Your sister's thigh-highs," I muttered, fucking her fist.

"He broke the kiss, baby. *What've you had up your asshole before, Anissa?* Nothing, master, I pleaded. *I don't believe a little slut like you has never experimented on your own. Have you?* Shit, Markus, I wasn't thinking straight. I'd lied to him. I *never* lied to him. There was no height I could scale to ease the excruciating pain in my asshole. What the fuck could I do? *I can't see your fucking eyes, whore, but I can read the hesitation on your lips. Answer me. Now!* I remember my head darting left, then right." She mimicked the movement in her mask. "He squeezed his thumb on the flesh outside my ass, and his fingers inside. *How much anal play have you indulged in your life, Anissa?* My pulse pounded. My breath fastened. Master, I've played with my ass. He shoved his fingers further. Please, please, please! Please, master, don't! *Details, whore. Give me details. I want to know how rough I can be.* How rough, master? *Yes, Anissa. I need knowledge of your past experiences... Prior to the act of robbing you of your anal virginity.* I whimpered."

15

I glided my foreskin over her red lips, and coaxed her into a returning a warm, wet kiss.

"Mmmmmm," she moaned, submitting herself willingly to my shaft.

I pulled out, and placed my cock back within her latex fingers. "Keep talking, slut."

"I promised master none of the boys I'd been with had ever had my ass- *Yet*, he interrupted, and slid his fingers slowly to the edge of my anus, then darted forcefully back inside. I started to tell him what I actually *had* done."

"Tell *me*," I said, and caressed her rubber mask with the back of my hand, pressing my knuckles into a cheekbone.

"It'd all started in the bath, Markus, months before master fingered my ass. I'd just masturbated myself to a lovely climax, rubbing my clit and stroking my nipples. I'd avoided penetrating my pussy. My fingers didn't compare to the real thing, and I *so* enjoyed toying with my clit. But I was continually drawn to stroking myself between my legs, below my pussy. As I relaxed post-orgasm, and allowed the warm water to wash over my body, I gently grazed my anus with my long fingernails. I bent my knees and stretched my thighs, opening my hole up. I just circled the outside of it, Markus... Ran my nails over those little folds you adore so much-"

"Enough about what *I* love, Anissa. You're reliving your past. There'll be no relief for your bladder if you disappoint me in this."

She hesitated. "I'm not sure I-"

"Just get on with it," I snapped, and gyrated my cock in her palm. "And wank me properly. It shouldn't be me doing all the work."

Her rubber-clad thumb stroked up and down the underside, her fingers slowly drumming the top. "Each time I played with myself in the bath, I took it a little further. And that first time I finally slipped a finger inside myself- Fuck, Markus, when I told master this, he twisted his fingers inside my virgin ass. I thought he was going to rip me open. Visions of blood flooded my mind. My eyes blinded within *this* mask. My body captured, at his mercy. I kept talking, hoping to pacify his perversion. I described how I'd pushed my forefinger into my ass for the first time, how I'd gasped, struggled and strived to relax the tenseness in my muscles. Slowly, my confidence and curiosity grew. I pushed deeper. The water rushed around my hand. Bubbles floated to the surface. I was inside my own ass, and my lone finger felt huge. Master reminded me what huge was with his two fingers. *Continue, whore*, he commanded. Yes, master. I was tempted to turn my ass in slight rotations over him."

"I bet you did, slut," I said.

A smile flicked on Anissa's face. Her fingers gripped my member tighter, then slid the foreskin back from the head. "I wish I could see your huge erection, Markus."

"Your past, slut. Bring your past to life, or your punishment will be worse. *Feel* that agony in your bladder, Anissa. Imagine being forced to down *another* pint of water."

"Oh, Markus!" she screamed. "I couldn't! Please! No!"

"Then talk faster, slut."

"That first time with my finger in my ass, I slowly curled my finger. I prodded deeper in myself. I was even late for a New Year's party because I was having so much fun on my own. It was different, and fed a forbidden fire inside me. I wanted to finger-fuck my anus, I really did, but as I slid my finger slowly outwards, I felt an unfamiliar, and very unwelcome, pain. I didn't like the sensation of retreat at all. I didn't penetrate myself again on that occasion. Upon hearing this, master suddenly yanked his two fingers out of me. Fuck! The pain was horrendous! I felt he was plucking out my innards. Then he forced them back in. Out. In. Out. In. *I'm opening you up to become an anal slut, Anissa.* I was fighting for breath. *Well, say thank you then! Don't be so ungrateful!* I was panting. Thank- Thank you, master."

My nostrils flared.

"I soon took my anal fondling further, slipping pens inside myself. Yes, pens. I liked them because they were thin, and long... And... Ohhhhh... There were times when I tried it in public, and I *loved* that. There were ways I could position a pen so it would penetrate my asshole, and the people around me would've no idea. I'd be slowly, so slowly, slightly humping up and down, and they'd never know. A long pen under my little skirt... Such fun."

My resolve for administering control over her was floundering into desire. An overwhelming urge which dictated I should unzip her crotch. Expose her tight snatch. And shove my raging hard on into her. I shook my head, and dismissed the thoughts in lieu of her confession.

"But my playing with my ass didn't end there, Markus. As master relaxed his pressure on my ass, I raised my hooded head to face him and told him how I'd located one of my stepfather's discarded beer bottles. It was the final chapter in my anal masturbation. I'd lie back on my bed at night, and slide the neck of the bottle into my anus. I'd be able to slap my pussy at the same time, and rub my clit. Oh, it was tight, and it was exciting. I could almost imagine it being a real cock. Would a man ever be content just to hold his shaft inside me? Not to fuck me. Not to hurt me. Just to hold his erection still in my ass, as I played with myself to climax?" Anissa panted, and her free hand lightly touched her waist. "My diaphragm aches, Markus." She clenched her rubber-skinned legs together. "*Please* let me to go to the toilet."

"Your master wouldn't have spared such a consideration for you. Why should I?"

Anissa's masked face slipped despondently downwards. But her palm yanked onwards. Obediently. Assuming her place well known. "*It's time, Anissa*, he said. Time, master, I asked? My body was trembling from head to toe. *Turn around, bend over, and pull your ass cheeks apart... I'm going to make you realise that pussy sex is just foreplay... And that my cock will* never *be just a tool to rest inside you, while you bring yourself to orgasm.* He laughed. *Never.*"

16

"Foreplay, Markus," Anissa continued, taking a deep breath, "except he wasn't in the mood for foreplay. He was going straight for my ass... My ass*hole*." Her mouth grimaced. "Master warned me there was still much of our window together remaining." Her hand strained on her midriff. "Oh fuck, Markus, I'm going to burst-"

"No, you fucking won't," I interrupted, and squeezed her hand around my cock. "Concentrate."

"I was bent over the sofa, holding my anus open for him. *I intend to really use your ass, whore. I'll prolong your suffering, if you struggle.* He pressed on my lower back, and caressed the second skin latex. I was desensitized to his touch. The sensations secondary in my senses, rendered so by a combination of the rubber and his massive cockhead being pushed against my opening. It's so big, master. Please don't fuck my ass. I'll do anything you want. Please. I'll lick *your* ass, master. I'll tongue *your* hole. Please don't shove that huge- And the breath was blasted suddenly out of my body, Markus! Master swiftly shafted the bulbous head of his dick inside my anus. Oh God, baby, the temperature of a furnace boiled throughout my body! Perspiration gathered between my flesh and the latex, stitching the layers of skin together as one."

I wanted her mouth, wet, wonderful and worshipping, on my balls.

"*Just think,* he whispered, *what everyone would think of you, if they could see you now. Covered from head to toe in blue latex rubber. Your three holes exposed. And* me *taking your anal virginity.* He eased himself deeper, and I wailed out. Saliva spilled from my mouth, and tears fell from my eyes. My rubber fingers squeaked on the leather sofa, as I searched for solace. He laughed, and launched himself at least another inch into my rectum. *I sure hope for your sake, Anissa, no one comes home early. How would you ever explain it?* I don't know, I cried out. *You wouldn't,* he stated clearly. *If anyone ever discovers the truth, that you're my secret whore... My property... You are to take outright responsibility.* Yes, master. I chased you. I seduced you. You fell for the charms of my younger pussy. *No, Anissa,* and he slammed himself balls deep in my aching asshole, stretching me many times further than I'd ever experimented before, *I fell for* MY *cunt.*"

I yanked her head to my length, and fucked her worthless, slut mouth for more than half a minute.

"Mmmmmm, mmmmmm," she moaned, muffled by that which she'd been born to feed and breed upon.

I pulled away, and slapped my rod on her latex hood. "Talk, slut."

She sucked air to her lungs, and squirmed in her abdomen.

I spared a facetious laugh. "You're *really* uncomfortable, aren't you, slut?"

Anissa struggled to nod, and her palm slackened on my schlong. "Please, baby, enough. I've played the part well, but I need to pee."

She started to stand.

I grabbed the back of her head.

Anissa tried to shake my hand away. "I said enough, Markus!"

I seized her tighter. "We're not playing today, Anissa. This is not my fucking fantasy. This is *your* fucking reality. Finish the fucking story. Piss yourself, and I'll treat you like the nasty, fucking piece of shit you'll have proven yourself to be."

The sheathed sockets of her eyes stared at mine.

How much could she see?

Her lips slapped together. Parted. Her tongue ran under her lower lip, pushing her mouth out in her tip. "Yes, Markus... I'll continue... For you..." She paused. "Master's long, hard cock tore dryly into my asshole. He spared no spittle, nothing, to ease the agony. I yelled out, and all he told me was *Haul your ass open wider, if it's sore, you slut!* Yes, master, I wheezed, clenching my teeth together. My sister's heels were pointed out. My head buried in the sofa, masked throughout it all. My mouth freed only so my wails could escape. Master loved my suffering. I'd been denied his cock for so long. Begged for it. And now I was getting it. *You lied to me, whore. You told me you'd never had anything up here. Then you admit to your fingers! Pens! Beer bottles! What kind of perverse slut, are you?* Your kind, master! I'm your kind! He grunted, pushed my face into the sofa, and shoved his cock deeper into my asshole. I was filled to the brim, baby, and perspiring at a phenomenal rate. My pulse was thumping. My lungs filling and spilling, wheezing. My mouth compromised in the sofa."

"You loved it, Anissa," I said.

She shook her head. "It was excruciating, Markus... At least at first. He wasn't interested in pleasuring me. As much as he loved the sexual deviant within me, he preferred to administer his power over mine. Hearing me confess to a succession of clandestine solo sessions with my ass only stoked his fires. And he blazed those fires into my asshole, Markus. Further, he kept finding differing angles he could drive himself in. He wasn't fucking me, so much as he was staking me. And no amount of tears, cries and pleas from me were going to convince him to ease off."

My cock twitched in her hand.

Anissa's lips lassoed into a lascivious smile. "You like the idea of me being force-fucked in my ass by my older lover, don't you,

Markus?"

I growled.

Anissa threw her second hand to my balls, and squeezed her rubber fingers lustfully over my bulges. "You do, baby, don't you? You can see me fucked royally in your head, can't you?"

"Yes," I croaked.

"Oh, baby, you've no idea. He could see the fear his stabbing evoked in me. Fuck, he could *feel* my innards shriek, my little asshole tensing so timidly. *Enough, Anissa. Time for a new lesson. That feeling you feared when you first touched yourself here*, and he emphasised his point with a brutal buck forward, *will become the one you learn to embrace*." Her legs crossed at the knees. "I was momentarily confused, my senses lost in his brutality. Slowly at first, then suddenly faster, he slid his cock all the way out. *Pull your anus open, slut!* I obeyed, and he placed himself back inside me, then buried himself to the hilt." She tensed her latex ass, hips and thighs, visibly fighting the stress in her bladder. "Oh fuck, Markus, he repeated the process several times over, until I started to relax. Until my wails became quails. My groans moans. And my cries highs. He was cursing me with adoration for sodomy's forbidden lust. Ensuring I would crave, for the rest of my life, the outrageous sensation of a huge cock being pulled slowly from my ass, then assertively slid back in."

"My anal slut," I said.

Anissa let go of my balls, and held herself between her legs, folding her thighs over the back of her hand. "Markus, I'm going to wet myself."

"I don't care," I said.

"Please, baby, let me go to the toilet. I'm gonna piss myself."

"So be it... But you'll be punished."

"Fuck!" she squealed. "You bastard."

I pried her fingers from my penis, and slapped it across her lips.

Anissa's teeth clenched, and she fought the feelings of savagery in her cunt. She puckered her lips, and forced her softness across my length. "I'll let you do anything to me, Markus. Please just let me go."

I sighed loudly, and placed her hand on my length again. "If you can make me cum, slut, I'll excuse you to the toilet."

She struggled within the second skin body suit, and adjusted her position several times over as she shifted her fingers back and forth on my shaft. "Oh, master, I cried out in painful passion, overjoyed at this discovery that my asshole could receive a cock with such beautiful disdain."

I laughed.

"To be speared across the line between contempt and craving," Anissa continued. "But master was more than just a teacher. He was a cruel, brilliant dom, and he had his needs which ought to be met. He yanked his cock out of me, and I swear my anus was spluttering for several seconds afterwards. He sat himself on the sofa, pointed his mammoth cock upwards and told me to straddle him. Yes, baby, with me on top, cowgirl, he impaled my asshole again. He held me under my arms, lifting and dropping me on his dick. I was probably no more than a blur of blue latex bouncing on his cock. Robbed of individuality, just a tight hole to fuck and tear."

"Did... He... Rupture you?" I asked tentatively.

Anissa grinned.

My face reddened, emasculated by her silence. I refused to beg her for the further information I so desired.

Anissa's stomach rumbled, and her smile vanished. She clamped her hand beneath her cunt, and a strain streaked across the visible flesh of her face. "His naked body powered upwards into my ass, Markus. I'd *never* been fucked there before. Honestly. The agony was excruciating. My small breasts were tight on my chest in the rubber. I was gasping for breath, searching for respite from the torture he was inflicting on me. *Promise me, Anissa, that someday you'll become an anal slut.* I promise, master, I said, desperate to declare anything that'd bring him over the edge. *Promise me you'll give your asshole away to any man who dares show the guts to take it. Who has the courage. The cruelty.* I promise, master. My ass will be for all mankind!"

My pulse thumped in faster rhythm. My balls bloated with familiar brazenness. It was approaching.

"But my tight, virgin ass was not to be how master would achieve his most intense orgasm..."

17

"Not strictly," Anissa added.

My eyebrows narrowed.

Anissa's discomfort was obvious as she reached one hand between my feet, to my bunched jeans, and yanked my belt free. "As I sat my ass on his big dick, Markus, he pulled out his belt, and wrapped it around my neck." Anissa mimicked the motion on her throat, taking both hands and tightening the strap like a noose. "He pounded upwards, relishing the fact he was hurting me. My pussy exposed, and ignored. My erect, little clit crying out for the attention which would've reduced the pain. He wasn't interested, and choked me suddenly." Anissa coughed as she repeated the process before me, her saliva spluttering onto my bare chest.

"He choked you as he came?" I asked, wanking.

"No," she croaked, struggling for air.

"No?"

"He... Made... Me..." Anissa jerked the belt suddenly free from her throat, and leapt forward, wrapping it around my neck. "Choke *him*!"

She fastened the leather strap, cutting off the air to my lungs. "Anissa," I struggled, seething through clenched teeth.

Anissa pulled it tighter. "Wank yourself faster, Markus. You'll love it. I promise you!"

My heart battered my chest. Terror reigned through my veins. Yet my erection soared in my palm, my balls bouncing beneath.

"I pulled that belt as hard as I could on his throat. The fucker had tortured me for so long. This was my pay back! And I fucked down *so* hard on his cock, riding him cowgirl for all I was worth. There was a numbness- Oh fuck, my bladder! I'm gonna burst, Markus-"

My eyes bulged, raging with command through my disorder.

"Fuck!" Anissa cried. "A numbness in my anus, pushing the pain aside. I used it, driving myself down harder on his mammoth cock. *I* was fucking *him*, sacrificing my insides in search of his orgasm."

The belt tightened, and I felt my mind tugged to another state. I was light-headed and woozy, whirling through a whirlwind of deprivation. My hand pulled my length towards utopia.

"Master taught me later," Anissa gasped, leaning herself backwards, maximising the pressure on my belt, "that there are arteries at the sides of your neck, which carry blood to the brain. When they're cut off, you can experience a whole range of various feelings, emotions. They can vary, Markus, so relax."

I tried to go limp, though my lower arm was tensed. My balls bloated. My erection raging.

"You feel your heart pumping?" she asked. "You should. That's blood trying to pump to the brain. But where's it going to now? Don't panic, Markus, you'll ruin the experience. Embrace it. I'm denying you oxygen, feeding you carbon dioxide. It'll fuel your orgasm with a feeling so addictive it's likened to cocaine."

I felt a tremendous rush from my retina to my rectum. A vibrating suppression from my pecs to my penis. A twisting tornado which delaminated from my torso to my testicles.

"Wank, Markus! Wank! Cum! The second you start to shoot, I'm gonna release you."

I gargled, grabbing my balls in my free hand.

"Because when master came up fucking hard in my asshole, I didn't know when to stop. I kept pulling on his belt, choking him. I felt his balls slapping and emptying beneath me. I fucked down harder on him, splaying my ass open for his spunk. More shot up. It was incredible. Disgusting, and yet divine at the same time."

I jacked myself faster, as weightlessness carried my conscious onto another plane.

"My anus all gooey, creamy and glued to his amazing cock. I hauled his belt harder. His eyes were out of this world! His chest and face bright red. Veins bulging, as if ready to pop. He couldn't communicate with me. His body was convulsing. His mouth gaping open. His tongue wilting. Then his eyelids rolled forward."

Clouds of black crawled swiftly around the edge of my vision.

"Master'd stopped pumping beneath me. But his erection wouldn't die. With a huge spear in my anus, I was sat atop him, on a pedestal. I didn't realise the dangers. The risk. The fast approaching point of no return. I couldn't even see him! It was only because of what he told me afterwards that I ever knew what really happened."

My hand hammered harder. My vision swayed with blurs of bright blue and purple, bulbous red. Breathlessness reigned. Arousal, rage and relaxation marred and scarred as one, teetering my loins over the consummation of climax.

"He'd passed out before I realised!" Anissa yelled, and let go of the belt.

My sperm flew through the air.

"Oh fuck, baby!"

My shoulders stretched. My back arched. My lungs racketed through a succession of almighty inhalations and petty exhalations.

"Shit! No! Fuck! I can't..." Anissa's masked face found mine.

I stared back at her, wheezing, clawing and emptying ejaculations over my legs, the leather sofa and the latex rubber second skin of her arms.

Anissa's mouth rounded into a shameful O. "Ohhhhh fuck, Markus, I can't... I'm... Shiiiii-"

I felt bizarrely out of body, and yet contrarily, confidently within the confines of a most extraordinary orgasm.

"Oooooh yes," she breathed, in relief.

I watched in woeful exuberance, overcome with realisation, as Anissa committed a most wretched, miserable sin. Her body recoiled, reverberations of rubber pervaded by liquid. A series of squelches from her lower ends, particularly her legs and her crotch. The zip between her thighs locking her ignominious secret within.

"You," I struggled. "You... Fucking pissed yourself?"

Anissa was gasping, unable to stifle her incontinence.

"Didn't you?"

Her mouth trembled as she nodded.

"You filthy, fucking bitch," I said, and shook my head in disgust.

Anissa fell forward, her masked face rubbing into the sperm on my leg. "Oh fuck, Markus, I feel pathetic," she confessed. "Like nothing. Like shit."

I groaned.

"A dirty, fucking piece of nothing... Saturated in my own urine." She licked several hairs on my leg. "All my pride, my spirit, my humility... It lies in tatters!" Her rubber hood shot up, placing her face in line of vision with mine. "I never thought *you* could help me achieve that feeling, baby... But... Oh fuck, you have... I... Fuck... I fucking love you!"

I grabbed the back of Anissa's head, as more cum leaked from my erection. "Come with me, slut." I wrestled my stiffened legs, unbent my knees and staggered to my feet, hauling Anissa upwards with me. "Didn't I warn you you'd be punished, if you wet yourself?"

"Yes, Markus," she said, and moisture crunched in the rubber of her feet.

I shoved her through the kitchen door.

"What are you going to do with me, baby?" she pleaded.

"I'm throwing you outside, slut."

"In *this*?" Her hands gestured inwardly to her blue body suit.

"It's where you fucking belong, piss whore."

18

"Go on," I said, and pushed her into the conservatory.

"Baby!" Anissa screamed, as her latex made contact with the wooden flooring and caused a sickening squelch. She spun around. "I'm not going out there!"

I seized her elbow, carefully between forefinger and thumb, in disgust at her urine. In my other hand, I twisted the handle of the door which led outdoors. "Yes, you are." I yanked her through the door, and tossed her to the ground.

"Fuck," she cried, as her hands and knees sent stones scattering in several directions.

I kicked my jeans from my ankles. I was naked, and somehow gloriously still erect. I stepped outside, and felt immediate discomfort from the loose stones on the soles of my feet. Anissa was bent over before me, her blue ass in the air. "Hold still," I said.

Her head flicked left, then right. Her vision robbed of the high fences to either side.

I fell to my knees behind her, took the zipper dangling between her crotch in hand, and hastily unzipped her.

"Markus," she said quietly. "Someone will see us."

Urine dripped from between her legs to the ground, as I took my hard cock in my hand. "I don't care, slut. You've had this coming."

She struggled on the stones, trying to claw herself forward.

I slapped my hand on her lower back, and pushed her body into the ground.

Her bare pussy and ass stared back between her unzipped crotch. "But Jenkins... Sebastian... Francesca... What if they see?"

"I don't care," I said, keeping her clamped in place. "I really don't give a fuck." I edged forward, ignoring the irritation on my knees, and slammed my shaft into her soaking cunt.

"Fuck," she quipped.

I hauled her hips backwards, and fired my phallus recklessly in and out of her.

Anissa's torso vibrated. "Shit." Her fingers fought the stones for balance. Her knees and thighs trembled, as she realised the impossibility of deterring my onslaught.

I controlled my grunts, and powered through the vile stench emanating from her insidious sex.

"They'll only see *you*, baby," she spat quietly.

My hips slapped her latex thighs.

"They'll not recognise *me*."

I shoved her hooded head into the ground, and leaned over her back, finding my mouth by her sheathed ear. "They'll hear *you*," I whispered, and welted her ass with my palm.

"Fuck!" Anissa's knees scuffed the stones. Her back arched under me. And her ass powered backwards, swallowing my member deep in her cunt.

I failed to suppress a growl, then surrendered to my lust and tunnelled her innards.

Anissa screamed out, and splayed her legs farther apart.

I grabbed her masked skull, and held her into the stones.

"Shit," Anissa gasped.

Moisture slid between our sexes. A foul, noxious concoction of cum, juice, sweat and urine.

She twisted her head, and tongued at my fingers.

I pushed her face harder into the stones, and ripped my cock at her gaping hole. My mind dismissed the pain slicing across my kneecaps, and concentrated instead on my balls slapping beneath her. This was my woman. My slut. My piece of shit piss whore whose body had once belonged to another. She was mine to take. To punish. And to debase. I wanted to humiliate her in the eyes of our neighbours. To let them in on the secret that she was this piece of sexual meat to be mauled. I was confident in my muscles. My mastery. My technique. I was capable of propelling my Anissa higher. To ascend that spectacular standard set by the man before me who she refused to identify.

Anissa coughed, then shrugged my hand from her head, and leapt onto my fingers, clenching her teeth on the bones between.

I ravaged her whore's cunt, squishing wetness from her lips and saturating my pubic hairs.

She slackened her incisors on my digits, and spat over them. "Fuck," she panted. "You fucker."

Blue skies overhead offered elements which would only encourage other people outdoors. Someone would hear her.

"You're fucking me so good."

Sooner or later.

She sucked her saliva from my fingers.

Savagely, I fucked into her and grabbed at her hips, twisting her tiny torso to meet my rampant strokes. My balls banged together. Sweat spilled from my cheeks and shoulders. The drained state of my loins were destined to prolong the orgasm I sought so ferociously to find.

"What?" Anissa spluttered. "What's wrong with you?"

"You stink of piss," I growled back, recognising her taunting tone all too well.

"Can't you cum?" she snapped.

A trio of birds squawked as they soared above us. A heavy, articulated lorry thundered along the nearby main road. I tunnelled onwards into her, hidden behind the horizontal wood of our high fences.

Anissa elicited a mocking laugh. "You can't cum-"

"Soon you'll stink of cum, slut," I stated, and slammed my palm on the back of her head, forcing her face into the stones. I slaughtered her insides, and abandoned restraint on my throat. My grunts escalated. My hips oscillated. "Fuck!" I yelled, fury tearing from my lungs.

"Markus," she muttered, mounting pressure muffling her voice.

I snarled as I stabbed deeper inside her, determined to impale the sensitive edges of her sponge. Frustration was boiling in my veins, overcoming my spirit. I smacked Anissa's ass, attempting to release the restraints on my aggression. To drown my inadequacies. And exorcise my inability to climax.

"Markus, stop this."

I clawed through one layer of her skin to the other, pressing fingertips through latex into flesh.

"You're making me a scapegoat for your own jealousies!"

Her mocking words ravished my mind. I launched myself

aggressively through her, slamming her body downwards into the stones.

"Your own anxieties!"

Her insults incited arousal in my brain.

"Your own failings!"

She was blowing apart my inhibitions.

"This isn't you!"

My breathing snagged on ragged.

"You're not him!"

My lower abdomen tensed.

"You'll *never* be him!"

My balls bloated.

"I don't want you to be!"

Avalanches of cum raged through my shaft.

"Do you hear me?" she demanded.

I roared as my bulbous, red slit emptied into the treacherous insides of her cunt.

Anissa swept her masked head from the ground. "Oh, baby."

I pounded several more swooping shots into her.

Her bright blue, latex fingers reached for my thighs, and stroked my matted, sweaty hairs. "Baby... Oh, baby... That was crazy. *Good* crazy. Gorgeous. But crazy."

My head was dizzy. The surroundings suddenly coming into focus. I felt awareness. We were outside. I was naked. And Anissa was in a second skin rubber body suit! I retreated from her insides, and suffered pain in both knees. My skin was cut to either side.

Old Man Jenkins' back door slammed loudly behind us, shielded from view by the fence.

I grabbed Anissa's arm in my palm, and hauled her upwards.

Her hooded head looked warily to mine. Her mouth was still, open. Her tongue and teeth frozen in frame.

I turned, and we sprinted hand in hand together into the conservatory.

19

The sun shone through the conservatory roof onto Anissa's golden locks. Her mask was pulled back from her head, and hung loose on her neck. She was sat on one wooden chair. I on another.

I watched as she took a latex blue finger and brushed a strand of hair away from her eye.

"I don't know what to make of what just happened, Mark," she said, sitting with her knees around six inches apart, leaving her pussy unguarded. "You said whether you'd hurt me depended on how accurately I portrayed my past." She crossed her legs. "Didn't I do a good job?"

She'd performed wonderfully, in truth, unlocking a door to her past which I was both somewhat pleased and somewhat enraged to have entered. Through her willingness to re-enact those days, I was proud yet pained. However, in my plying her with those multiple pints of water, I felt a sense of redemption. A retaking of my masculinity. A physical stamping of my authority.

"Never try to be like him, baby," Anissa snapped, as the rubber creased noisily around her chest. "I didn't fall in love with you because you remind me of him. You couldn't be more different, and that's what-"

"Have I ever met your master, Anissa?"

She hesitated, her pupils darting between both my eyes. "I'm not answering that."

"What?" I rubbed my temples.

She shrugged.

I adjusted my deflated cock between my thighs. It was thick with moisture. "Okay... Then tell me this, have *you* seen him since we met?"

Anissa sighed. "Markus, you know how discussing the realities, especially the present realities, of this man's existence disturbs me. I've just relived my past with you, and then we took it to another level." She placed her latex hand over the flesh of mine. "It was exciting. Let's just leave it at that." Her cheekbones raised, and she forced a smile. "Okay?"

"Anissa, you make him sound like some kind of manifestation." I pulled my hand away from her. "Just fucking tell me, have your paths crossed since we got together?"

She was staring at me. "Okay, you want the truth? Yes."

"What, Anissa?"

"You asked me a question, Markus!" She twisted her wrist, jabbing her finger into her own chest. "I've answered it! Don't turn it on me now! I've been honest!" Her finger pointed suddenly to me. "How dare you think of trying to manipulate my sincerity against me!"

I felt confusion cascade within, crashing down the charm of charade. The realisation of my foolishness. My naivety. My stupidity. "When, Anissa?" Paranoia nodded knowingly. "When did you see him?" I felt myself mocked from the inside out.

"I'm not answering that, Markus. You don't know who he is. You wouldn't understand the... Consequences of discussing him with you. It's not something I can do... *Ever*... Accept this... Please. And move past it."

My fingers took to the seat of the chair, between my legs, and drummed loudly. I looked up to Anissa. She was watching me. Then I flicked my eyes down. I was disgusted within. Had I been betrayed? Had I spared her too much freedom? Too much sympathy? For her lifestyle before we met? For her scars? Her ruptures? Was her own behaviour now, and her secrets, somehow a responsibility I had to assume?

The sun cast silhouettes of our silence over the wooden floor.

Did I spare her further blushes, and endure the indignity of her actions myself? I glanced to her long legs wrapped in latex rubber, and inhaled. Was the pungent mix of our madness a damning, insightful indictment of the core of our relationship? Was human waste and reproductive matter all which we held dear... Which we held in common?

Anissa rustled her dishevelled hair in her hands, offering no solace from the ensuing silence.

I felt alienated in my nudity before her.

Her eyes strayed to my flaccid penis. An almost vindictive sleight of victory crossed her lips.

My lower abdomen tensed. "So," I began, striving to summon calmness to my tone, "you've met up with him-"

"You asked me if our paths have crossed, Markus. They have! I didn't say I'd met up with him. You make it sound like I-"

"Fucked him," I interrupted.

Her feet squelched on the floor. "Fuck you." Her rubber squeaked as she stood up straight. "*Fuck... You.*" Anissa shook her head vehemently, then stormed out of the conservatory.

I sat back on my chair, and wondered... Well, had she?

CHAPTER SEVEN

1

I'd been harsh with her. And it'd worked for a matter of minutes. But it'd been nothing more than role-play. The years that followed that day had only served to prove who truly wore the trousers in our relationship.

And she never, in all those years, explained if she had or hadn't ever fucked Lee while we were together.

"Lee," I said aloud, mocking myself. "Not Lee..."

I was still in the honeymoon suite. Still in the present. And still fucking married to another man's whore.

"Master."

I just knew he was inside her in that moment.

2

I broke the law and smoked a cigarette indoors.

Rebel without a fuck.

My heart truly hurt though. I'd been cuckolded before. I'd swung with her. I'd known her to fool around with God knew how many different guys. Even Gareth had apparently made love to her that very morning. But it'd been with my understanding. Hell, even my permission. Of course there'd been things I hadn't been totally onboard with. That was part of the thrill.

This hurt.

This was killing me.

My wife had ran off to be in the arms of another man after we'd got married.

"She's coming to see you," Gareth had told me before he left.

How long ago had that been? Fifteen minutes? Twenty? Thirty? An hour?

Master would probably fuck her all night long and forbid her from seeing me ever again.

I'd lost.

I flicked my ash out the window.

I'd lost her.

I took another drag.

She'd never truly been mine to lose.

I almost forced a grin as I thought about how quickly Gareth had conceded defeat. Even he knew he was no match for her master.

I felt an invisible stake drove through my heart.

I swallowed.

Those thoughts I'd earlier dismissed as not being particularly suicidal were very rapidly rising to a will to die...

I thought of my service issue revolver.

A wish to die-

I heard something outside. Something subtle. Quiet. Then a beep. Followed by a click. The handle turned on the door.

"Baby," she said, appearing in her white wedding dress, her make-up still absolutely flawless and her smile as beautiful as ever.

I doubted I'd ever get over her.

3

Anissa closed the door behind her.

I tossed my cigarette out the window.

She didn't come running to me.

I didn't have the words to change her mind. Nor my own.

This wasn't our Hollywood moment. Nor our happy ending. Just our it's all over. I lost. He won. Goodbye.

Anissa walked a few steps into the room, looking around her, as if somewhat mesmerised by her surroundings. "I'm sorry I'm late."

What?

She looked at the clock. "Sorry, *so* late."

I waited for something.

"This room's beautiful."

I noticed she still had her wedding ring on her finger. I felt mocked. Yet I still wore my own.

She lifted the rear of her dress, to prevent it from ruffling, and sat herself on the grand honeymoon bed.

"I don't think we'd have to get divorced," I said, matter-of-factly, as I noticed the garter still wrapped around her white stocking.

"No, Mark, I don't want that either," she said swiftly.

I gestured to my mobile. "I looked it up. We can get the marriage annulled. It was never consummated..." At least not by her and I.

Anissa narrowed her eyebrows. "What're you talking about?" She yawned.

I knew how she'd got tired.

"Baby, what d'you mean?"

I felt anger over my humiliation. "Anissa, you married me today... Then you ran off with..." I almost said master. "Jesus, Anissa, Tara's husband? Your *sister's* husband?"

"I didn't *run* off with him, baby. We needed to talk."

I peeled my eyes from her cleavage and focused instead on her bare shoulders. Why the fuck did she have to look so damn stunning in that dress? How the fuck was she my wife? I told myself to concentrate, and had to pick a spot to stare at on the wall. "But he was the one who manipulated you like that and treated you like that when you were still so impressionable?"

She nodded.

"And you just disappeared off with him today?"

Anissa made a sympathetic smile.

I felt only pathetic.

"Mark, relax. It isn't what you think. We don't need an annulment-"

"The hell we don't!" My eyes were on her again.

She looked surprised. Not quite shocked. But certainly a little taken aback.

I started to pace the room, channelling my breathing. "I understood the deal. *You* understood the deal. I agreed to it. You were allowed to sleep with Gareth this morning, and again this evening."

"Yes," she whispered.

"Did you have sex with him this morning?" I demanded.

Anissa was so composed as she tilted her head to follow my walking back and forth. "You know I did, baby."

I was gazing at her fingernails. So professionally varnished. The expensive jewellery on her wrists. The rings on her finger. "He said you made love."

She blew out air. "It was a quick fuck. I didn't have time for anything else. I'd so much to do today. I was glad when he came."

I stopped in front of her. "Have you slept with him since we got married?"

"Baby," she started, reaching out her hand, "you already know I haven't."

"Do I?"

"Mark, you know me better than anyone on this planet-"

I feigned loud laughter.

"You *do*, baby."

I rejected her hand, and began pacing the room again.

"It's over between Gareth and I. You can believe me when I say that. You can trust me. It's over. We're not even going to be friends."

I stopped. "Why, what'd he do?"

"He didn't do anything. Not anything wrong. I've just come to realise I need to trust my instincts." She uncrossed one leg, then recrossed the other. "He isn't right for me."

My heart was in turmoil. I knew the reason. It was because he was back. Her master. Why the hell would she need Gareth when he was around again?

"Do you trust me?" she asked.

I said nothing.

"Do you trust me when I say Gareth and I are over? That chapter in my life is finished. It was fun. I enjoyed it. *You* enjoyed it too. But it's done. This is a fresh new start for us-"

"Anissa, can you hear yourself?"

"Yes, Mark, I hear myself perfectly clear. Now, please, answer the question... Do you trust me?"

No. "About you and Gareth being finished?"

Anissa nodded.

Yes. "I'm looking you right in your eyes, Anissa..." And oh fuck were they not the most beautiful eyes in the world. "And I believe you."

She took a deep breath, yet it was not one of anxiety but of composure. "I didn't ask if you believe me. I asked if you *trust* me. Because I'm not playing a game here. I'm not lying to you. This is our wedding night, Mark, and I'm being deadly serious... Do you trust me?"

I was stood right before her. "I trust you, Anissa... When it comes to Gareth."

She touched a diamond earring in her left ear. "Meaning *what* exactly, Mark?"

"It's not Gareth you've been with all these hours since the wedding." I had my hands behind my back. I didn't want her to see they were shaking.

Anissa smiled at me. "I love you so much," she said. "You need to meet him."

"Who?!?"

"Lee."

"What, Anissa?"

"Baby, please, I'm begging you..."

I made my hands into fists.

"Just be cool."

"Be cool?" I demanded. "Are you fucking crazy, Anissa? You want me to meet your master, and you tell me to be cool?"

She shifted forward on the bed, and seized my upper arm, rubbing my muscles through my suit.

I let the moment bring back a million familiar feelings for just a split-second.

"No, Mark, wait." Anissa squeezed my arm so tight. "Not me." She momentarily slipped the tip of her tongue out from between her lips. "*He* wants to meet you." She smiled, and for the first time since she'd entered the room she looked nervous. "And it's not master." Her smile faded. "It's Lee."

"Lee?"

"Just Lee, Mark."

I unclenched my fists. "I'm confused."

"About?"

I let my arms go slack by my sides. "Lee and master are the same person?"

"They were," Anissa said, sliding her palm from my upper arm to my hand and taking hold of it in hers.

I fed my fingertips to her wrist.

She mimicked my motion.

I felt her pulse thud.

"Lee!" she called out, turning her face towards the door. "You can come in now!"

My jaw dropped.

Anissa tightened her grip on my wrist.

I felt my own pulse thunder within her grasp.

4

"He's here?" I mouthed.

My wife smiled up at me. "He wants to meet you, Mark."

And what? What master wants, master gets?

The handle turned.

I watched hopelessly as the door to the honeymoon suite began to open. It seemed to take an age to move only a few inches, and then he came into sight.

His eyes were piercing. Intimidating. As if instructing my instincts to look away from him.

Anissa rubbed her thumb on my wrist.

I'd better trained instincts than this.

"Lee," Anissa began.

Master.

"I'd like you to meet Mark. Mark, this is Lee."

He closed the door behind him, then held out his hand long before he'd yet to reach me.

I made my right hand into a fist. I didn't even think about it.

Anissa knew me. She'd never seen me like that. But my wife knew me. She held my other wrist tighter. "No, Mark!"

Lee stopped in his tracks.

"Let go of me, Anissa!" I yelled.

"Baby, don't do this!"

I hated she still had a hold over me – emotionally. Physically, I could've hauled her off the bed with me if I tried. But emotionally I froze.

"Settle down, soldier boy," Lee said, holding both his palms up. "I didn't come for trouble."

"What the fuck did he call me?" I snapped, throwing my eyes to my wife.

She gently shushed me.

"Who the fuck d'you think you are, Lee?"

Her master.

"You took advantage of her when she was in her late teens. You were married to her sister. And now you turn up on the day of her wedding to fuck up the rest of her life as well?"

"Baby," Anissa said, and stood in front of me. "Look at me."

I stared through her.

"Mark!" she cried.

I wanted to kill him.

"This isn't what you think it is, baby."

I dragged my wrist free from her, then turned around and paced a path to the window.

"The past is the past, Mark," Lee said. "I'm not here to apologise for it." He was standing alongside my wife.

I wouldn't let him dare lay a hand on her in front of me, never mind fuck her again.

There was inches between them.

"You fucking should," I said. "Her mother, her stepfather, Tara, your ex-wife, they now all know. Everything makes sense to them. She's lost her family because of what you did all those years ago. No, because of what you did today-"

"You're my fucking family, Mark!" Anissa screamed.

The room reverberated from the boom of her voice, then fell into a sudden, prolonged silence.

"May I fucking speak and be listened to?"

I ignored her and pulled out another cigarette.

"Spot me one, Mark?" Lee said.

"Fuck off."

"Sorry, Lee," she said. "He's usually more understanding than this."

I lit up.

"No worries, 'Nissa, I'm sure it's been a long day..."

I was shaking my head. The audacity of this cunt.

"It got off to a pretty bad start..."

Yeah, because he'd shown up after all this time.

"But you've seen the light when it comes to Gareth..."

What?

"At long, fucking last."

I flicked ash out the window. "I'm sorry, Lee, what?"

Master and sub stared back at me.

I looked at my wife. "You told him about you and Gareth?"

"She's told me everything, Mark."

I looked out at the night sky. "This is unbelievable."

"Allow me," Lee said, and squeezed past Anissa. "If I come any nearer, are you going to try to hit me?"

"I can't promise anything," I said, then nodded him over.

He gestured to my cigarette pack.

"Fuck it, go ahead." I must've been losing my mind.

Lee lit up. "Look at that woman, Mark. Go on, look at her. Take a good, long look at her."

I gazed at Anissa. She looked stunning, yet vulnerable. Even afraid. Was this the hold he had over her? Was she already imagining what sordid things he'd do to her every hole when I inevitably walked out of here in a few minutes and out of her life for good?

"She's not the young girl who was in something with me, Mark. She's a grown woman. A beautiful woman, if I may say so, and she's your wife."

I heard him.

"She's with you, Mark. Not me. You."

I couldn't take my eyes off her, even though I wanted to demand answers from him.

"I've been around lately. Not in your house. Not in your lives. But I've been watching things, keeping my eyes peeled. I knew something was going on with that Gareth guy. I knew Anissa very well. I reckoned they were fucking. I was right. But one thing I can tell more than anything, Mark, is that that grown woman fucking adores you. She's *in* love with you. She was never in love with me. And certainly not that deadbeat, Gareth. It's you."

I sighed. I wanted to see it.

"Tell him, 'Nissa."

She put her hands together. "It's true, baby. Mark, I love you so much it hurts. I know I've lost sight of a lot of things and I've taken you for granted. I've hurt you. I know I have. I'm sorry. If I could go back and do it all again, I'd do it differently. But if you give me a chance, I can prove myself to you-"

"Anissa," I interrupted, "save it. Lee, you too." I dragged on my cigarette, then ignored the wafting smoke which started to sting my eye. "You two have spent hours together today. On *our* wedding day. How do I forget that? I know you were fucking. How do I forgive that?" I threw my cigarette away. "I can't."

"I didn't fuck her, Mark."

"That's true, baby, he didn't fuck me."

"There was no physical contact between us," he insisted. "Well, of course I hugged her and kissed her on the cheek. Maybe even once or twice on the lips. But it meant nothing."

"Mark, that's true. He's telling you the truth."

I gazed at my wife. "The problem here, Anissa, is whether you're telling me what I want to hear, or what he's telling you to say. I can't decide. But he's your master, after all. You'll always do what you're told."

"That's not true," she said, her voice shaky.

I started to move.

Lee put his hand out to my chest to stop me. "I know you could break every bone in my hand, soldier boy, but Anissa trusts you with her life. And that's good enough for me. Besides, I'm a pretty good judge of character and I think you're a very, very decent guy. A gentleman. Am I wrong?"

Rage was building within, inflating my chest.

"Am I wrong?" he asked again.

I breathed out. "You're not wrong."

"He's the best," Anissa said, and a tear ran down one cheek. She wiped it away. "Please don't spoil my make-up. I've done so good all day to keep it perfect for you, baby."

"Mark, can I just say one thing to you? Let me say what I came here to say. Then you can beat me to a pulp or you can let me leave in one piece. Either way, I'm going to allow you both to get on with the rest of your lives."

I looked at him, smoking my cigarette. "Make it quick." I glanced to my suitcase beside the bed. "I've got somewhere I need to be." I didn't.

Anissa nearly choked when she realised.

"Okay, I'll make it quick. Son, I had to be here today. I owe you nothing, but I owe Anissa everything. I don't know how much she's told you, but she told me today she's told you enough. You know the hold I held over her. I felt it too. I knew it was still there after all this time. But yet it wasn't really. It just needed closure. Emotional closure, so to speak. The air to be cleared."

I just wanted to know if I could believe they really hadn't fucked. I looked at my wife's tight torso in her wedding dress. Was this man's sperm inside her? In her stomach? In her vagina? In her anus?

"The spell has been broken," Lee continued. "I came here to break the spell today. And it's broken. I've no hold over Anissa anymore, I hope you believe that. It's the truth. She's told me of your lifestyle, especially in recent months. That's over. Your wife will no longer need another man. She'll no longer be promiscuous. She can be a faithful, loving wife, if you'll let her. Look at her, Mark. I can see it. Can you?"

I wanted to. I wanted desperately to believe it was true.

She took a couple of steps forward.

I did too.

"The spell *is* broken, Mark." She started to lift the front of her dress, revealing white lace panties. "See this. This is *my* cunt. Not Lee's. Not master's... Mine." She wiped under her eyes, as if she was forcing herself to hold back a real flood of tears. "Or it's *yours*... Forever... If you'll take it."

I faked another laugh.

"I married *you* today, Mark. Yes, I saw Lee and it threw me. But I turned around and I walked back down that aisle and I said *I do* to you... That means everything to me." She inhaled through her nose. "I pray it means everything to you too."

"I didn't understand that," I said. "Why you came back and married me when you'd just seen him. It made no sense. I've sat here for ages, trying to work it out."

"I'm in love with you!" she cried.

Lee moved behind me to throw his cigarette out the window. "Mark, good luck." He held out his hand.

I wouldn't shake it.

"Understood." He turned and approached Anissa. "Good luck to you too." He leaned into her and kissed her gently on one cheek.

She never took her eyes off me.

He whispered something in her ear.

I heard it.

He loves you too.

"I hope so," she whispered back.

I couldn't control the subtlest of reassuring smiles just cracking on my lips.

Anissa had the slightest hint of relief across a face full of distress.

Lee marched silently on through the honeymoon suite to the

door. "Goodbye, you two. I wanted to do a great thing today. Don't let my motivations be in vein." He took one last look over his shoulder. "Grab your happiness with both hands. You only get one life. Live it." Then he walked out the door, closing it firmly behind him.

5

I took a deep breath as Anissa stared at me. "Well," I started, "he's a barrel of fucking laughs, isn't he?"

Anissa laughed, then tried to compose herself. "I'm sorry, none of this is funny."

I shook my head. "No, no it's not."

"Baby... Never mind, I've no right." She looked down.

"What is it, 'Nissa?"

"Will you hold me?"

I hesitated.

She ran her palm over the sheets. "Even just lie on this bed with me? Talk to me? You don't have to touch me. I just need to be close to you."

I rubbed my stubble. "I don't know, 'Nissa, I really think I should just go home and think things over."

She tugged a quick intake of breath. "You're going to leave me alone on our wedding night?"

Why, was she thinking there was still time to run after Lee or send a quick text to Gareth? I knew that wasn't where her mind was, yet it'd been on the tip of my tongue to say so through spite. Through jealousy. And anger. "Anissa, you left me alone on our wedding day."

She nodded. "Okay, I deserved that. I was stupid. I'm sorry. I lost track of time."

"Yes, Anissa, you were stupid. Very stupid. You were unforgivably stupid. And how stupid do you think you made me look? Made your family look?" I walked towards the bed. "Lie down."

She shifted backwards on the bed, making room beside herself for me.

I remained standing. "I've a lot of questions."

"I'll answer them, Mark, I promise."

"Have you spoken to anyone in your family?"

"Just my stepdad. He said everyone's furious."

"Yeah."

She ran the sexy fingernail of her forefinger over her wedding dress. "They each suspected it all along, my mother and Tara, but he knew for certain and he lied to them for me throughout these years. I've probably lost them all, and I deserve to. But I can't lose you, Mark. I'd rather die than lose you."

I sat on the edge of the bed.

"Hey," she said gently, "husband."

"Hey."

Her breasts were heaving in her dress as her every breath was deep. "I love you so much, Mark."

My head was spinning.

"Do you love me?"

"I wouldn't have married you if I didn't."

Anissa reached her hand out to mine. "Lie with me."

I let her lead me down on the bed. "I'll lie next to you," I insisted, and lay on my side to face her on hers.

"Just lie? You won't hold me."

"Just lie, Anissa, and talk, okay?"

She smiled. "Yes, baby. I love when you talk to me." She squeezed my hand. "Is this okay?"

I nodded.

"You're so fucking handsome, Mark. I don't tell you that enough."

I sighed.

"You are. You're sexy. You're muscular. You're so much more physically attractive than those other men ever were, and you're the sweetest, kindest man in the world to boot."

"I'm not kind, 'Nissa."

"You are, baby. You don't even realise it."

I found myself falling into the trap of looking longingly at those luscious lips of hers. And those cheekbones. Her beautiful blonde hair. Jesus, she was so fucking stunning. Why wouldn't she make walking away easy?

"I can't read your mind, Mark, you're going to have to tell me what you're thinking... It's okay, I'm a big girl... I can take it... Even if it breaks my heart."

"Did you really not have one final fuck with Lee?"

"No, Mark. I swear on my mother's life. I swear on my own life. What he told you was the truth. Even when he kissed me on my lips it wasn't romantic. There was no chemistry-"

"You felt nothing?"

Anissa shook her head. "Not, nothing. Just a huge difference." She gave a little laugh. "We weren't lovers, as such, Mark. Kissing wasn't a big thing in what we had. It's not like when I'm with you. You've taught me so much about love. My heart's pounding just looking at you right now."

I scratched my head.

"Say it, baby. Whatever it is you have to ask me, I'll tell you the truth. I've no reason to lie to you. I don't *want* to lie to you."

"Were you tempted when you saw him?" I asked. "Honestly."

"Baby, I'm not going to lie. The moment I saw him at the church I was back in that place I was all those years ago. I was his. I was waiting for him to tell me to go with him. And in that very moment I might've. No, no games. No bullshit. I would've left you for him. I would've humiliated you on our wedding day. Much, much worse than I have. I'd have marched out of there hand-in-hand with him, if he'd wanted me to. I'd have lost you and my entire family for his beck and call... But."

"But, Anissa?"

She took an eternity of deep breaths. "It's different now," she whispered, staring into the distance. "He is. I am. Everything is. I'd have known that tonight even if I'd spent our wedding day being his slave all over again. I'd have woken up tomorrow and felt the biggest regret of my life."

I was so confused.

My wife placed one hand on her heart. "He was never here."

I swallowed saliva, as she let go of my hand.

"Only here." She rested her other hand between her legs. "This was supposed to belong to him forever."

"You really mean it doesn't now?"

Anissa shook her head. "Definitely not. I didn't have that throbbing. That need. That pull. His hold over me has worn off. I only really realised that for sure after I went to see him." She gently rubbed one hand on her chest. "Baby, I'm crystal clear about this. I have absolute clarity this evening. Lee, and it's so good to finally be able to call him just that, is my past. A past I should be ashamed of. A past I know I will be ashamed of. Immensely. I can already feel that shame growing with my realisation."

I couldn't peel my eyes from the piercing stare she returned me. "Our guests think we had a fight. Your side all blamed me. I don't want them to know the truth, Anissa. Please."

"Slip your hands under mine, Mark," she said. "I'm not telling you to, I'm asking you to."

I reluctantly slid my hands beneath hers to feel her crotch and her breast.

"These are yours. My heart and my pussy. They're yours. You have them. You'll always have them. I feel like such a fool for ever behaving otherwise."

I almost looked away.

"I'm so in love with you, Mark... My husband."

I hesitated.

"Are you sorry you married me? You must've been in shock at the time."

I swallowed again. "I was in shock... I still am."

She gripped my hands, pushing them tighter on her body.

"Anissa," I began slowly, "I'm in love with you too. *So* in love. *So* ridiculously, explosively in love..."

She closed her eyes. "I feel a but coming... It's okay... I deserve it."

"No but." I shook my head. "I promise." I was almost bewildering myself with the truth. "I was just going to call you... My wife."

6

"Are you tired, Mark?" she asked, rolling onto her front. "It's been a long day."

"No, and yes. My head's still spinning and I'm beat, but I'm not in the mood to sleep."

"Me neither, baby." She gestured to her back. "Can you help me out of this dress? It's so tight."

I reached to the back of her corset-like dress and began to

unfasten the ivory buckles. "You looked beautiful today, 'Nissa."

"Thank you." She exhaled as the corset slackened around her body. "I can breathe again at last." She giggled.

I instinctively touched the bare skin of her back.

She raised herself to let the corset fall away, then shimmied herself out of the entire dress. "What do you think?" she asked, lying on her side in just her white wedding lingerie and garter.

I smiled.

Anissa cupped her bare breasts. "I have a slip I can put on."

I gently removed her hands from her chest. "That won't be necessary."

She was lying in a lacy, white suspender belt and stockings, a matching thong and stiletto heels.

"Did you pick this lingerie for Gareth?"

She closed her eyes.

I knew what she was thinking... Was this the sort of question she'd have to endure for the rest of our lives?

"Don't, baby."

"It's okay, Anissa. I'm not having a go. The plan was he was to make love to you tonight. I'm just asking if you picked your lingerie with him in mind or me?"

"Both," she whispered, then opened her eyes. "Are you mad?"

I shook my head.

"It's *really* over between me and him, Mark, you have to believe that. I knew this morning when we had sex I wouldn't be doing it again. Yes, the original plan was to have sex with him in front of you after the wedding. But I'd already changed my mind before the wedding. I don't think I could've done it, even if you'd begged me. We need a fresh start. I want that so much, Mark-"

"Did you show Lee your lingerie?"

"No, Mark. I promise you. He didn't even ask to see."

I ran the back of my fingers between her breasts. "And if he had asked?"

She bit her lower lip. "Maybe, at first. When I first went to see him. But not as the day went on. And certainly not now." She rubbed my hand. "All of me belongs *only* to you now. I'm your wife, Mark. I'm proud to be your wife. I'm going to live to be your-"

I slid my tongue into my wife's mouth.

Anissa returned my kiss with a fiery passion, pulling me closer by the back of my head.

My fingers strayed to her wonderful sides, seizing hold of her tiny body and enjoying the feel of what was mine.

"Husband," she rasped into my mouth, then slipped off my blazer. Her fingers undid my tie, then unbuttoned my waistcoat.

I shrugged it off.

Anissa took her time to unbutton my white shirt, running her fingertips over the flesh of my chest.

I hungrily kissed her, pulling her on top of me as I rolled onto my back. My cock was so hard in my trousers underneath her.

She paused.

"What is it?" I asked gently.

She looked suddenly sad.

"Anissa? Tell me." My hands froze on her ass. "Did I do something wrong?"

She shook her head. "No, you didn't. You're perfect. I'm so sorry." She carefully ran her fingernails around my nipples. "I wish I'd danced with you tonight at the reception. I should've been there. I owed you that first dance. I'm so sorry I fucked everything up-"

I kissed my wife again.

She kissed me back.

"I love you, Anissa."

"I love you too, Mark... More than you'll ever know... But I'll show you. I'll prove it to you." She yanked my shirt open, sending the remaining buttons flying. "I promise."

I felt her grind her crotch down on mine, as she removed my shirt. I slipped my fingertips into the rear of her thong and crazed her anus.

My wife didn't flinch.

Anissa explored my upper body, caressing every toned curvature and muscle. "My Adonis," she whispered.

I rotated my fingertips around the edges of her rectum.

"I'm yours, Mark."

All of her?

She drove her groin down hard on mine and moaned as she felt my erection through my clothing.

I tried to kiss her again.

Anissa stopped me momentarily, only to lick around my lips. "I want to worship you, baby." She tongued my upper lip. "Fuck, you're beautiful." She was dry-humping me. "I've never wanted you so much."

I raised my hands from her rear to under her arms, and lifted her just above me enough so I could plant my mouth on her nipples in quick succession, swapping adoringly between the two.

Anissa threw one hand beneath herself and fondled the outline of my cock through my trousers. "Oh, Mark, I'm so lucky to have you."

I tasted her areola so fresh on my tongue, as my heart beat faster. The desire I felt for this woman was incredible. I believed her. I somehow knew I could. My trust in her would rebuild again over time. I knew when she was deceiving me, and I detected nothing of the kind in her anymore.

"Oh, baby, that's so good." She began to unbuckle my belt. "Are you okay?"

"Yes, honey."

"Are you sure?"

I kissed both her breasts, then her chest, shoulders and neck. "I'm sure, Anissa."

Our mouths entwined.

She unzipped my fly and slipped her hand into my trousers.

I groaned as she rubbed my cock through my underwear.

She smiled as she kissed me back, ever the tease.

"I *need* your touch," I stated.

She grinned further. "Don't beg," she warned.

"I'm not."

Anissa stared into my eyes for several seconds, squeezing my cock so hard.

I felt my vein throb in her palm.

"You're not begging, Mark?"

"I'm your husband, Anissa." I raised my left hand to show her my wedding ring. "This gives me power..."

She raised one eyebrow.

"Over you."

I felt her groin vibrate on my abdomen. "Oh fuck, Mark, you turn me on so much being my husband." She threw herself back onto the bed, then snaked herself around my body, positioning her crotch over my head and her face above my cock. "This is the first and only cock I'm going to have in my mouth while I'm married to you." She dragged down my underwear, then took hold of my hard on, wanking it at the base. "I can't resist you." Anissa engulfed my sex in one go.

"Fuck!"

My wife sucked my cock like never before, running her mouth up and down it at a phenomenal pace, all whilst still holding the base. Her grip tightened and the movement of her hand stilled. She was determined to prevent me climaxing too soon.

I held her by her thighs, one wrist gliding against her garter.

Her white lace clothed pussy was right above my face.

I stared at her sanctuary.

She fed my dick deeper into her mouth.

Her sex was really all mine now.

Anissa tried to take me down to her throat.

I loved how she'd deliberately dressed her thong last, so I could slide it down the outside of her suspenders without having to remove them. She knew that's how I liked her to wear them. I raised my neck to propel my face into her crotch and inhaled. The sweet scent of my wife's pussy was all I found.

Gareth fucked her there this morning.

I tried not to think about it.

Gareth probably came inside her there this morning.

My erection pulsated between her glorious lips.

His sperm is probably still swimming inside her.

I pinched hold of the waistband of her thong.

It's probably ready to leak right out of her.

I gently slid her panties down to her thighs, resting them nicely next to her garter.

You can't seriously be considering a cream pie.

I'd given her everything else before our marriage.

You'll never change if you do.

I ignored my wife's clitoris, and shoved my tongue straight inside her cunt without hesitation.

Anissa grunted around my member, stuffing it down to her tonsils.

I pried her buttocks apart, then slid my fingers deeper towards her crack.

She licked the underside of my sex.

I parted her cheeks again, then moved my fingertips to the edges of her rectum.

She aggressively squeezed my cock, as if threatening to respond to my actions if I even fucking dared.

I wanted to penetrate my wife's ass. I was desperate to. I'd wanted to for years.

You know the rules, cucky, that ass will never be for you again. You lost that right. You forfeited it the night you went too far. You know the one. The one you can't even describe out loud. The night she never forgot. Nor forgave you for. She'll never let you take her there again.

I rubbed the rosebud of my wife's anus.

She moaned amorously around my sex, releasing her grip on the base and taking it whole, reaching her throat.

I gently slipped the tip of my forefinger into her ass, whilst earnestly eating the insides of her pussy. I couldn't taste Gareth. I didn't want to. But I was hungry for my wife's juices. And she was so fucking wet. I could barely believe it.

She gyrated her rear to meet the mild strokes of my forefinger.

Was I imagining this? Was Anissa actually striving for more?

She thrust her cunt against my face.

I dared push my finger past the fingernail into her asshole.

"Oh my God!" she cried out, as if spitting my cock all the way out from her throat.

My heart pounded. What if I'd gone too far?

She pushed herself up by her palms.

My finger dropped out of her.

She slammed her sex down hard on my mouth.

I tried to gasp.

She stuffed her anus against my nose, as if trying to suffocate me.

I couldn't put my finger back inside her.

She ground her pussy on my lips. "Give me your tongue, Mark! Give me your fucking tongue! Eat my pussy, baby! Now!"

I was obedient without thought, striving to delve deeper than before. I let my hands fall back on the bed. I needed to concentrate my everything on pleasing her cunt. On proving I wasn't afraid. Not of Gareth. Not of Lee. Not of anything.

Her juices slid into my mouth.

I swallowed.

She groaned.

I knew something was different.

"That's it, Mark, eat me!"

Something was very different.

"Eat my cunt, baby! Taste every part of your wife's pussy!"

My hands fired forward, grabbing her ass, and hauled her down harder on my face. I stretched my tongue as far as I could and swirled it around inside her, tasting every corner I could find.

Anissa was frantic atop me.

My cock throbbed, untouched, before her.

She grabbed hold of it and started to wank it furiously. "Yes, baby, you're so fucking good to me." She flew her hand up and down it. "I need to be good to you too."

I slurped at her puffy lips, swallowed, then sucked every ounce of moisture from her I could find.

She found my scalp with her free hand, running her fingernails over it. "Oh my God, Mark, you're the most amazing husband in the world!"

I inhaled her anus.

"Every part of me is yours."

I lapped at her lips.

"Can you taste me?"

I returned an affirmative muffle.

"Can you really?" she asked. "Can you taste *it*?"

I probed my tongue deep into her vulva.

Anissa threw herself down on my cock, taking it whole.

8

Anissa tongued her juices from every part of my face she could find them.

"Thank you, thank you, thank you, Mark," she whined, holding my head in her hands. "Oh my God, that was earth-shattering."

I stared at her, then stood up and out of my trousers. I looked down naked over her.

Anissa slipped off her thong panties. "Get on your knees," she said, pinching hold of her garter. "You're supposed to remove this with your teeth... Hubby."

I seized her leg and hauled her forward.

Anissa gasped. "Gentle, baby!"

I gave out an evil laugh.

Her breasts rose and fell in unison with her breath. "Please."

I grinned. It'd been so long since I'd been dominant with her.

Her pussy was splayed open, yet I'd only penetrated her with my tongue.

Master fucked her. He split her in two.

I ignored the audacity of my anxious thoughts, then kissed her stockinged leg from her shin to her knee, then onwards to the garter on her thigh.

"Do it, lover," she said, smiling down to me.

I clamped her garter between my upper and lower teeth, then growled.

"Look, baby." Anissa gestured to her pussy. "She wants you so bad she's throbbing for you. Look!"

I watched the vibrations in her lips, then saw the stain leak out within her juices. I dragged the garter down her leg like I was a rabid dog.

"Claim me, baby."

I dragged the garter off her foot, then spat it out across the floor. "Claim you, 'Nissa?"

"*Re*claim me, Mark."

I pushed her legs wide apart. "You know, 'Nissa..." I shoved her head back on the bed. "You might well be my wife..." I guided my cock to her pussy and ran my head up and down her puffy lips. "But tonight..." I shoved myself to the hilt inside her. "You're my whore."

Anissa grabbed my shoulders, digging her fingernails into my muscles. "Yes, baby, make me your whore wife."

I grabbed her chin in my hands.

"Make love to me."

I kissed her lips.

"Fuck me."

I pinned her down by her throat.

"Use me."

I speared her deep.

"Spoil me."

I felt her legs wrap around my waist, pulling me further into her.

Anissa's mouth met mine, twisting me into a passionate embrace. Her hips met my every vicious stroke with equal intensity. Her wedding ring dug into my flesh as she gripped me tighter.

"I can't imagine life with you," I said.

"You don't have to. I'll only ever be a slut for you. Nobody else. I'm *your* whore."

I felt her nipples brush against my own as I fucked my wife.

She locked her legs tighter around my body, dragging me faster into her. She was crying out with lust, rocking the honeymoon suite with her rasps.

I was determined to make her the loudest bride the hotel had ever heard.

"Kiss me," she yelled. "I want to taste my insides from you again."

I knew what she wanted to taste from me, but I yielded nevertheless.

My whore wife sucked on my tongue, moaning as she relished those forbidden remnants.

I tunnelled her cunt, pulsating shamefully faster and harder.

Anissa broke the kiss and gasped for air. "You fuck me so fucking good, Mark!"

I grabbed her arms and pinned them above her head, crushing her torso with the whole weight of my own.

She nodded vociferously. "Yes! Fuck, yes! I need this! I fucking need this!"

I lowered my mouth close to hers.

Anissa tried to kiss me.

I pulled deliberately away.

She wheezed.

I let my lips linger nearer hers.

She tried again to kiss me.

I pulled away.

Her body trembled beneath me, and she tried in vein to pull me down with her legs. "Baby, please kiss me."

I smiled.

"Make love to me, fuck me, it's both with you, just fucking kiss me."

I released her arms.

Anissa grabbed my head, forcing my lips to hers.

I kissed her wildly.

She returned the same, doubling her efforts in desperation.

I fucked her slippy, sloppy pussy.

Her hips bucked back.

I felt her lips squelch around me.

She tried to suppress a giggle when she heard them.

I stared into her eyes.

"You turn me on so much, Mark."

I doubted she truly believed I bought her excuses for the saturated state of her cunt, yet I pummelled onwards into her regardless.

"I can't get enough of you."

I volley myself to the base inside her.

"I need more of you."

I felt my face redden. There was no more of me to give.

"Take me from behind," she said. "Fuck me like a bitch."

"A bitch?"

"*Your* bitch, baby." She started to turn underneath me.

I couldn't slow myself, and kept fucking her as she rotated her sex on my shaft.

"Oh yes, Mark," she cried, pausing her movements as she reached her side. "Oh yes, that hits the spot." She reached her fingernails for my chest and ruffled my hairs. "Oh, baby, you make love to me unlike anyone else."

I growled between grunts.

She looked up to me. "Sorry."

My balls slapped her ass as I slammed into her.

Her eyes rolled back in her head.

"It's okay, honey."

One of Anissa's suspenders pinged free from her stocking. "Oh my God, Mark!"

"It's okay."

She was screaming out wantonly.

"I promise."

"What, baby? What's okay?"

I looked at her.

She returned a momentary look of innocence, then a devilish

realisation crossed her face. She clutched her own breasts in her hands. "I'm sorry."

"Don't be."

She panted.

"You always wanted it," I insisted.

She shook her head.

"No?"

"No, baby... I always wanted *you* to have it."

My face began to redden.

"I always wanted *you* to taste it..."

My entire upper body flushed red.

"Taste *him*."

Anissa didn't even acknowledge my embarrassment, instead turning herself onto all fours and forcing her cunt back to the very base of my erection. "Oh yes, Mark, that's it! Now I've got you. Now I've got every amazing inch of you."

I planted my palms beneath her lacy white suspender belt. The image of my wedding ring wasn't lost on me.

"Make love to me, darling," she said. "Don't stop now."

I realised my shock had startled me. I wasn't even moving.

Anissa was doing all the work. "Baby, your cock's great. But it's never as great as when you really give it to me."

I started to move in and out of her again.

"Harder, Mark, please. I'm too turned on to feel that."

I strove to drive myself harder, concentrating on her amazing body again.

"Please, Mark, try."

I was fucking trying!

Anissa said nothing.

Yet all I sensed from her was disappointment. My length hardened.

She said nothing.

I drilled deliriously deeper into her.

Nothing.

Faster.

She slowed her own pace.

"You're so wet," I said.

Anissa ignored me.

I was sweating as I slapped my shaft swiftly in and out of her soaking cunt.

She propped her arms on her elbows and her chin on the heel of her palms.

What the fuck? Was I actually boring my wife on our wedding night?

"It's not your fault, baby," she whispered.

I was fucking her even unlike the pace of before, yet she seemed oblivious to it all.

"It's mine."

I slapped her ass.

Nothing.

I slapped both cheeks, then grabbed her flesh hard, squeezing it until I could see it redden.

"My pussy's too wet to feel you."

Maybe if I could just fuck her for a couple more minutes and quickly cum this charade could be over.

"I thought I'd saved myself for you."

I grunted.

"With Gareth."

What if she truly had been with Lee?

"It was practically a quickie."

I didn't want to know.

"But I think he sensed my feelings had changed."

This wasn't the time.

"I think he knew."

"Knew what?" I asked, grimacing as my testicles started to tense.

"That it was over, thank God."

I hesitated. I knew there was more.

"Because, baby, when he came inside me it was like never before."

I couldn't stop now. My climax was so close.

"Didn't you notice how tight I kept my legs together when we stood at the altar?"

No!

"It was all I could do to stop his sperm running out of me."

My adrenaline was rushing.

"I wanted to save it..."

My heart pounding.

"For you."

My balls ready to unleash.

Anissa hauled herself off my cock.

"What the fuck?" I yelled. Was she going to finish me off with her mouth?

She threw her body face down on the bed, then reached behind and stretched her ass cheeks apart. "Take me there, baby."

"What?"

"Take me in my tighter hole."

"Your ass, Anissa?"

"Yes, baby, fuck me in my fucking ass."

"But-"

"I deserve it after I let Gareth stretch my pussy out too much for you."

I was seeing stars.

"Come on, baby! Fuck my ass!"

I moved reluctantly forward. "But, Anissa, don't you remember what you said?"

"Just fuck it, Mark!"

"You said I'd never have you there again after what happened the last time."

"I know."

"I haven't fucked your asshole in years, babe."

She let go of one cheek, and seized my shaft, wanking it as she dragged it towards her rectum. "That was different."

"Different, 'Nissa?"

She threw a look that could kill over her shoulder. "I wasn't your wife then." She narrowed her eyes. "Husband privileges, baby... My ass belongs to you now."

My face flushed redder, but not through humiliation or debasement. It was purely through desire. A sick and twisted desire to debauch her anal sanctum.

9

Anissa guided my erection to her asshole. "You can fuck my ass, Mark, or you can make love to it. Whatever you want. It's yours now."

I nodded profusely.

"But promise me you won't cum in it."

"Why?" I demanded.

"Not on our wedding night, baby. I want this to be special. I want you to cum inside my pussy. I don't care if I don't physically feel it." She rubbed her juices from the head of my cock over her rosebud entrance. "I'll feel it emotionally... I *need* to feel that emotional completeness from you tonight. D'you understand, husband?"

"Yes, Anissa."

She rotated her rump on my slit. "Promise?"

My balls felt they were already so close to emptying. "I promise," I said hoarsely, hoping I wasn't lying.

She smiled, then looked forward and released her grip on my rod. "It's all yours, baby... Do whatever you want with it..."

I aimed my hard on at her hole.

"Except cum in it."

I paused, then angrily tried to shove my cock all the way into her ass in one stroke.

Her rectum resisted, forcing my length to slide beneath it towards her pussy. "Try again," she said, somewhat impatiently.

I rolled my foreskin back in my palm.

"Just take your time, baby. Be patient. You've the rest of our lives to spend together, doing this night after night if you please."

I pushed the head gently against her entrance.

Anissa grabbed her butt cheeks, prising them apart.

Her hole started to open up, taking the beginnings of my cock.

"It's been so long since I've been here," I said.

"I've missed you there so much, Mark."

Anissa's rectum stretched around my bulbous head. I groaned with pleasure, both physical and mental. I was taking my wife back from the men who'd had her. Who'd not appreciated her. Who'd downright abused her. Especially here.

She moaned aloud as I entered her further. "Oh, baby, it feels perfect." She let go of one cheek, and slid her fingers between her legs to fondle her clit. "OMG, Mark! It's so good!"

I was only an inch or so inside my wife's ass.

Her body was trembling beneath me. "This is where I need you, baby. I can really feel you here. I just couldn't in my pussy, I'm sorry."

I shoved myself a second inch deeper.

Anissa gasped.

I removed her other hand from her buttock. "Let your ass do all the work," I told her.

She wheezed as she nodded.

I felt her tight sphincter resist as I eased more of my cock into her.

She gently rubbed her clit. "You're amazing, Mark."

I leaned my torso down on her back.

Anissa raised her hips to hold my length inside her.

I kissed the back of her neck.

She moaned her approval and smiled.

I eased more of my shaft into her, feeling the folds of her inner sanctum surrender.

"Oh, baby," she whispered, turning her head.

I kissed the soft skin of her jaw, her cheek and finally her lips.

Anissa massaged my tongue with her own.

I drove the final inches of my member into her, towards her bowels. "I don't know the last time you were penetrated here, and I don't want to."

She stared at me for several seconds, then she blinked, moisture thick in her eyes. "It wasn't today-"

"I said I don't want to know!"

She nodded.

My naked body engulfed hers, clothed only in the last of her virgin white wedding lingerie. I carefully withdrew my cock until only the head was still inside her, then I slowly slid deep inside her again.

Anissa toyed with her clit in one hand, and found my lower arm with the other. She grasped me so tight. "I love you so much, Mark."

I kissed her shoulder as I began to exit and enter her faster.

She slid her hand down my arm to my hand, entwining her fingers with mine.

I felt her wedding ring over mine.

"You make me so happy," she said quietly.

I pulsated as I ploughed deep into her.

"Fuck!"

I relished the rush of taking my wife in her most precious hole.

That special place she'd vowed, years ago, I'd never have again.

"I *do* forgive you, Mark."

"What for, 'Nissa?"

"Hurting me there the last time."

I felt humbled, yet still I increased my velocity, hurtling my hard on in and out of her.

Her face contorted, as if struck by sudden pain.

"Am I hurting you?" I asked desperately. "Again?"

She almost nodded, then hesitated. "It's just *very* intense." She squeezed my hand. "But it's a good intense, baby... An amazing intense." She plunged her free fingers into her pussy. "I need you to be able to do this right."

I listened to the squelches of my wife's beautiful cunt, and felt the fine, tight ridges of her anus as I admired her incredible, slim body beneath me.

She slapped her pussy lips, then played with her clit again.

"You're mine," I said in her ear.

"Yes!"

"Your ass is mine."

"Forever, baby."

I was hammering her harder, slapping my balls against her with every downward stroke.

She squealed with delight.

I tried to kiss her.

Anissa tried in vein to give me her all, propelling her thighs back to meet my strokes and attempting to stake my tongue with her own. "Turn me over, Mark. I want to see you as you make love to my ass. I want to kiss you."

I hadn't had enough of her in this position, knowing from memory just how deep I could take her from behind.

"Please, baby, it'd make me so happy."

I growled as I grabbed hold of her body in both hands and turned her on my cock.

She flicked her fingertips over her clit to try to control the agony in her anus.

I turned her roughly on her side first, then spun her to face me and dropped her on her back.

Her rectum stretched around the thick base of my cock. "You're fucking cruel," she rasped. "But I fucking love it."

I pinned her down by her wrists.

"Just don't cum in me yet."

I aggressively fucked her ass, feeling the wetness of her cunt on my lower abdomen, her breasts against my chest and finally her lips on my own.

Anissa tried her best to match my movements.

I stabbed her sphincter.

She cried into my mouth.

I suppressed her lips with mine.

Fear was abundant within the whites of her beautiful eyes.

I let my length fall free from her asshole.

Anissa took the moment to steal a couple of quick breaths.

I easily slid my cock into her pussy, wetting it with everything she had for me.

She groaned.

"I thought you couldn't feel anything."

"I lied... I just want you to make love to me... In my ass."

I smiled as I withdrew again then, whilst still holding her wrists down, forced my cock back into her anus.

Anissa heaved. "I love that I'm building bridges with you, Mark."

I made my member the storm in her rear.

"I can never give up on your love, Mark."

I tunnelled relentlessly into her.

"You're the only person who's ever truly believed in me."

Recklessly, I even tried to hurt her insides.

"Ever truly been in love with me."

I knew all too well the punishment for taking her anus too far.

"I see and feel it all so clearly."

I felt the familiar rushes within my loins.

"I love you so much."

I let go of her wrists.

Anissa threw her arms around my neck, dragging me into another explosive kiss.

I was so fucking close.

Don't cum in her ass.

But I so fucking wanted to.

Anissa's legs splayed wide. She funnelled the fingers of one hand to her clit. And those of the other straight into her cunt.

I reaped the benefits in her tongue.

Her asshole tightened on my shaft. "I know you're close, baby."

I couldn't answer her, as I rode her ass for all its worth.

"You know where I want you to shoot your load."

I grunted.

"I hope you know why."

Why?

"I hope you want it too, Mark."

Want what?

Anissa broke the kiss, then dragged her fingers out from her cunt and stuffed them into my mouth.

I dutifully sucked the moisture from them.

"Fuck me, baby. Then spunk in my cunt."

I grimaced. My stomach muscles tightened. I yanked my cock out from her rectum. Then stuffed it between her soft, pink folds and into her wet vulva.

"Oh God, yes! I feel it, Mark!"

My balls bulged.

Anissa's eyes lit up. "I can feel you about to cum!"

My face flushed.

"Baby!"

My sweat spilled.

"Yes!"

My heart pounded.

"Mark, I want your..."

My foreskin stretched back from my head.

"Baby."

My slit parted.

Anissa smiled as she watched me, stroking my skin with her fingers and the stockinged parts of her legs.

I roared as I shot my first, hot volley inside her.

Her body vibrated against my own.

I came again, ferociously, determined to outdo he who'd been inside her before me.

"Oh, Mark, you are incredible!"

Determined to outdo *all* who'd been there before me. I emptied load after load into her shaven trench.

Anissa's eyes told it all.

I kept cumming. It was as if I couldn't stop. So many months of pent-up frustration just fuelled my fires.

"Don't you dare stop," she cried, trying to encourage my hips with her calves to keep fucking, dragging me deeper. "I want your cum all the way up inside me, swimming, searching... Fertilizing."

I crashed on top of her, spent.

Anissa rubbed my back. "You're done?"

I panted.

"You sure, baby?"

"I'm done-" I felt yet a little more trickle out from my slit.

"You're *not* done," Anissa said, laughing, then patted the back of my head, holding me closer. "I love you so much, Mark."

10

We'd laid still on the bed in each other's arms for almost half an hour after we'd made love. My cock was soft, but it was still inside her.

Anissa looked so beautiful and vulnerable, just staring back at me, occasionally blinking, with moisture clear in her eyes under the light of the room.

"I guess the annulment's off the table now," I said, jesting.

"You can still divorce me, Mark... If you want to?"

I said nothing.

Anissa grabbed my shoulders, forcing me first onto my side, then pinning me down on my back and mounting me. "*Do* you want to divorce me, Mark?"

I stayed silent. Then felt my sperm and her juices leak from her pussy onto my crotch.

Her eyes widened. "Mark, please answer me."

I grinned.

"I promise you, Mark, I'll be the most loyal, faithful and loving wife you could ever imagine. I'll take good care of you. I've waited all my life to be a wife to a man like you. No, sorry, not someone like you. There's no one like you. You're a great man. The greatest man I've ever known. I only want to be *your* wife... But do you want to divorce me?"

I looked straight up into her eyes. "No fucking way, Anissa."

She eased her grip on my shoulders, stroking my skin.

"I haven't really asked you," I said.

"Asked me what?"

I clicked my tongue. "How do *you* feel?"

"Me? Baby, I'm happy. So happy. I couldn't be happier."

I inadvertently narrowed my eyebrows.

"What, Mark?"

I hesitated.

"Say it, please. Whatever it is. We need to be honest with each other from here on out."

"Well, Anissa, it's just... Your family. What the fuck are we going to do now they know about you and Lee?"

She took a long, deep breath.

I couldn't help gazing at her breasts.

"I don't know, Mark. I don't think Tara will ever speak to me again. Why should she? I betrayed her in the most horrible, despicable way. It doesn't matter that it was more than ten years ago, or that I was still in my late teens. What I did was wrong, and whether I was under Lee's spell or not there's no acceptable excuse. I always knew if the truth came out, I'd lose her. I made no effort to hide the truth today."

"And what about your mother and your stepdad?"

She ran her hand through her long, blonde hair. "My stepdad will treat me the same. I just might see less of him because my mother is going to take a long time to get over this... If she ever does."

I stroked between her thighs and her buttocks. "Nissa, I'm not going to lie to you... This is fucking terrible."

She bit her lower lip. "I know, Mark. It's new to them and to you. A shock, I'm sure. But I've had more than a decade to prepare myself emotionally and mentally for this day... I just didn't expect it on my wedding day. But *you* are my family now. You and..."

"I've news, honey," I said, realising I'd almost forgotten all about it.

"Oh yeah? Shoot, cowboy."

I exhaled. "Soldier boy."

Anissa placed her right palm on my chest, over my heart. "What's your news, baby?"

"I got a job offer. I've accepted it."

Anissa's face lit up with the most amazing joy.

"I'm going back to the army."

The colour was draining from her face, masked only by her excessive wedding make-up.

"Don't worry, honey, it'll be a desk job. I'll be home every night."

She smiled again. "Oh, Mark, really?"

I nodded.

"Baby, you need this. You've been out of work too long. I'm so happy for you. For us. This is music to my ears. All my worries are going out the window!"

"And they're going to get me the help I need for my PTSD, if indeed that's what I have-"

"You do, Mark." She threw herself down on top of me, kissing my chest. "Oh, baby, this is amazing. Everything feels like it's falling into place."

"Are you sure, Anissa?"

"Yes, definitely." She cuddled me closer. "There's only one more thing I want from the rest of my life with you, Mark."

"And what's that?"

She kissed my cheek. "Baby."

"Yes?"

"No, baby, I want to have your baby."

"Okay."

She threw one stockinged leg over my midriff. "I want to be the mother of your child."

I felt the stickiness of her sex on my skin. "I want that too, Anissa. I do. I feel the time's right. We're in our thirties now. Hopefully, we've learnt from all our stupid, fucking mistakes. We can put the past behind us and focus on our future."

"On our family," she whispered. "That really is why I wanted you to cum in my pussy tonight. I'm ovulating, Mark. I already have Gareth's sperm inside me from this morning. I'm sorry. I couldn't tell him not to cum in me. He's used to it. Sorry, he *was* used to it. Past tense. He's had the snip, but there's still a slim chance one could get through. I don't want to bear his children, Mark. I want yours. I know your sperm's superior. You're younger, stronger, healthier. Yours should eliminate his."

I felt shocked to the core.

"Survival of the fittest... And you are so fit, baby." She was stroking my face and kissing my forehead, the corner of my eye and my cheekbone.

I was staring at the ceiling, as she rubbed more of her wetness against my body.

"Just promise me if I do get pregnant and we can trace the date of conception to our wedding day, you'll never take a DNA test to see who the father is, Mark."

I couldn't promise.

"Anything that's of me you should automatically love..."

"Of course," I lied, through steeled, seething teeth.

"Even if it is another man's child."

THE END

THE GARDEN CENTRE GUY, PART SEVEN

1

I'd maintained my silence on the subject for several days, enduring the burning bite of curiosity. When would Anissa tell me all that'd happened with Jackson? How far had he taken her? How deep had she taken him? I was desperate to know, despairing that a single question out of place would seal her lips forever.

"Morning, my sweet, patient man."

"Morning," I said, eyeing her familiar yellow bikini.

"Shush, Mark. I don't want you to talk. I want you to wank yourself off, while you watch me in my bikini. I'm finally ready to tell you about the rest of my night with Jackson... What happened after he came in the wine glass...

"I hadn't got off, and I was so horny. But the idea of masturbating in front of a guy I didn't know very well... While he watched... The appeal was wearing off, as was the wine.

"I stared at his cock, watching it pulsate and slowly, surely deflate from its massive erectness. Mark, my goodness, what I'd do to see that big thing again. Just to imagine reaching out and touching it. To stroke it. To milk it. My pussy lips were squirming together, squelching without being probed. I was in such need of relief.

"He'd growled as he smiled, dumping the last loads of his spunk into the wine glass. I'd teased him, swirling it around and threatening to drink it down. He just panted. The beautiful whites of his eyes growing wider.

"After a couple of minutes, I reached for my bikini bottoms. It seemed like it was time to get dressed. But Jackson grabbed my wrist. *What are you doing?* I told him I was getting dressed. He shook his head. *No, you're not.* He shot his eyes to my breasts, as I took a deep, nervous breath. They were expanding, betraying my inkling to leave... To come home, and be dutiful and loyal to you... But as his grasp tightened on my arm, it became obvious you were no longer in the equation. I was his now. Until he was done, and ready to kick me out.

"Jackson stood up. Oh, Mark, the way his big, black cock swung between his thighs... I was staring, unable to function for anything else. He pulled me up to join him, yanking my wrist. I stumbled on my five and a half inch heels, and he caught me in his other arm, snaking my waist to my back. I yielded to his superior strength. He let go of my wrist, pushed my hair out of my eyes and kissed me deeply, slipping his tongue over mine, massaging the insides of my cheeks, and making me his own.

"I was dripping down the insides of my thighs. Oh God, Mark, I'm sorry, but I already knew what was going to happen if he dared touch me down there... Down *here*... My pussy would submit... Without question... A cunt like mine was built for a ferocious monster cock such as his... If his fingers happened to stray... If only they would've... I leaned my knee out, and grazed his leg. He kissed me harder. I rubbed his skin. But still his hands stayed away from my sex.

"Did he want me to plead? To beg? I was prepared to, Mark. Honestly, I was ready to fall to my knees, and worship him back to full hardness. I was ready to implore him to give it to me... But it wasn't what he had in mind.

"*I want to shower, Anissa. Come shower with me.*"

2

"He led me naked through his apartment, hand-in-hand, to his bathroom. The way he stood, leaning into the shower to switch it on. His muscles rippled. His skin stretched. His cock looked so gorgeous, baby, just glistening with his spunk on his foreskin. I was standing with my thighs together, squeezing the lips of my pussy. I took a deep breath, as he turned towards me and eyed up my tits. He wanted to touch them. I think he needed to. But my earlier warnings seemed to control him. His cock slapped his thigh as he moved, grabbing a towel from the radiator and placing it beside the shower. *For when we're finished*, he said.

"I crouched down to undo the straps on my stiletto heels. He just stood in front of me. His cock lingering down his leg. Oh, Mark, it was mere inches from my face. The strap was stuck. I couldn't concentrate on it. There was this massive blur of black on the edge of my vision. Even semi-erect it seemed solid. It was long, just not as long as it'd been when he wanked it beside me.

"*Are you all right down there*?

"I looked up, expecting to find him looking down at me, perhaps laughing, definitely smiling. Instead he was taking his sexy, white palm and wrapping it around his member. He pulled it gently back and forth. His foreskin slapped over and away from his massive, bulbous head. His slit stared back at me. A little of his cum leaked from inside. It was just crying out for a mouth to engulf it. To suck it. To swallow it down.

"*Come on*, he said, and gestured with his mammoth tool to my stilettos.

"Sorry, I gasped. Oh fuck, Mark, wank that little white cock for me. I'll close my eyes and listen to it, imagining it's something much more than it is. Like Jackson's was. As he pulled himself over my face, while chastising me for taking to long to take off my shoes. Sorry, I told him again. God, Mark, I was wheezing. The hot water was hitting the floor of the shower only feet away, and the steam was rising. I was finding it difficult to breathe. But it was my desires for him... To... Overpower me... Which were overwhelming my words on my tongue.

"He exhaled so loudly, Mark, as if to show his displeasure. He shook his cock at me. His foreskin closed over his massive head. The remnants of his sperm leaked out the front, and fell onto the floor by my foot. I scooted my heel over it, as I finally undid the strap.

"Jackson laughed, then turned to enter the shower. *I'm usually a gentleman*, he said. *It should be a case of ladies first, even I did just want to walk behind you to watch your ass*. He stepped into the shower, and the hot jets of water hit his magnificent body. Fresh steam resonated off him. My God, Mark, he was an Adonis.

"I slipped off my second strap. I'd been crouched on the floor for over a minute, struggling. Then I was suddenly niggled by doubt as I stood. I thought of you, alone and wondering where I'd be. I craved more wine. Fuck, I probably needed it. I didn't think I could do anything more with him, not like that. My head was turning to the door... I was going to leave... I could dress quickly, while he washed himself... I could get out of there- Then he grabbed my arm, and hauled me into the shower after him.

"He kissed me, Mark, dismissing my doubts. He stroked my

hair, my neck, my shoulders and my back. The way he held me and caressed me, he made *me* feel beautiful. So desirable and wanted... And all I could do was steal glances of his big cock left unattended and large. Oh, how I wanted to experience that... *Thing*. My pussy ached, needing relief... Needing cock... Needing fucked.

"Jackson poured shower gel over my chest, squeezing extra amounts on my tits and in particular on my nipples. *Can I wash you, Anissa?* I bit my lower lip, then nodded. I said please, Mark. I actually said please.

"He placed his big fingertips on my shoulders. He kneaded my skin. For a split-second, he actually made me wince as he pressed on my bones. Then he relaxed his grip, and smiled reassuringly. Oh, Jackson, I said, and fell into another kiss with him. I was so hungry. So horny. I just wanted him to reach an arm under one of my thighs, to lift my leg high up to his shoulder and fuck his monster cock into my pussy!

"But he was so much smoother than that, Markus. *So* much...

"He controlled the kiss, slowing me down to his level. It only made me want him more. I breathed into him, and he swallowed my breath. Then he tugged my tongue into his mouth, making my pussy yearn for him all the more. I needed it. Him. His dick.

"His fingers were rubbing the gel into my skin, massaging my upper arms to my elbow. The hot water of the shower was lashing into his back. I was cool, robbed of the heat and held against the door. Jackson was in control. There was nothing I could do to break his stranglehold on power. I was nothing more than a lamb... A horny, little lamb lusting after his slaughter.

"The gel on my breasts was cooling too, swirling over my projecting nipples and slipping down to my tummy. He *had* to touch me there. He just *had* to... Right?

"He broke the kiss, and looked into my eyes. *I've never been this close to someone so beautiful, Anissa. I know you didn't cum out there. I want you to make sure you* do *get off... In here.*

"What do you mean, I asked?

"He just smiled, and placed a sponge in my hand. Then he poured a load of gel over it... And over his big, big cock. *Will you wash me?*

"My mouth fell open. I couldn't speak. He... He wanted me... To rub the sponge... All over his... His... Specimen. Oooooh, Mark... I

was delighted. It was such an excuse to touch it, to really feel it up...
And yet somehow not to feel it...

"I left it a reasonable three or four seconds before I moved the
sponge in my hand. I twisted my wrist to aim it at his crotch. Then I
reached forward and grazed it. Fuck, the way it twitched. It looked
perfect. His head was back. He didn't want to kiss. He was just
enjoying the moment. And so I decided to make the most of it. I
squeezed the sponge within my palm, and wrapped it around his
length. I moved up and down on his massive, black cock. It was like
I was wanking him, yet I couldn't quite feel him properly. I could
feel his girth. I could *really* get to grips with him, but still somehow
it maintained a layer of innocence... Because of the sponge.

"He groaned. I wasn't just washing him. I was pleasuring him.

"Oh God, Mark, he was huge, and he was growing under my
touch. What if he *was* going to fuck me? My heart skipped a beat...
He'd rip my pussy to pieces... Mmmmmm... I had to cross my legs,
squashing my lips together... I *wanted* him to rip me to pieces.

"I asked him if he'd like me to wash his balls.

"*Yes, Anissa*, he said. *Please.*

"I had to move my other arm. I gently caressed his groin as I
brought it down, stroking his black pubic hairs. They were so long,
but so perfect given his immense length. I had to lift his member up
in my hand, away from the sponge. He breathed out loudly. He liked
it, even though I didn't pleasure him in my palm. I just held his cock
out of the way, then softly, sensually massaged his massive balls
with the sponge in my other hand. He was groaning, Mark. He had
me naked in his shower, tending to his tender regions. He sounded so
self-assured... So confident... Like he was in heaven.

"Then he brought his hands down from my shoulders to my
chest. He started to rub the gel into me. He was so close... So
dangerously close to breaking my forbidden barrier.

"I ran the sponge under and behind his huge balls, Mark. I
inadvertently squeezed his cock in my other hand as I held it. He
groaned, then pressed his fingertips into me with growing boldness.
He was touching the top of my breasts, then in between to the
defined beginnings of my cleavage. I released his cock, and it
dropped over my wrist, as I pulled the sponge along his scrotum.

"It was so intimate, Mark. I... I didn't know what I could bring
myself to tell him to do... But I found my voice to tell him to touch

my tits.

"*Are you sure?*

"Yes, Jackson, I said. I want you to rub the gel into my breasts... In particular, to my nipples.

"*Okay*, he said, as I shyly moved the sponge up to his torso. His cock was clean. I had to wash around it, or I would lose my mind for him.

"Jackson had his fingers and thumbs on my tits. He was dragging the tips from my outer edges to my nipples. *They're like bullets, Anissa,* he said.

"Oh, baby, I wanted him to suck on them. That would have sent shock waves to my clit, and to my cunt. I would've leapt on him, stuffing his solid, semi-erect member inside myself.

"He let go of my boobs, turned around and asked me to wash his ass. Oh, Mark, it was such a beautiful, black ass. I was rubbing the sponge over it, gasping, then grinding my teeth to silence myself. I was gagging for him. Absolutely gagging. Even my nips needed mauling. I was *actually* naked in the shower with this sexy, handsome man. You've no idea how many reality checks came and went in my head.

"And none more powerful than when Jackson turned around again. He placed his palms on my arms, pulled me into the path of the water, to wash the last of the shower gel from my skin, and told me *I feel bad I came before you, Anissa. I want you to finger yourself. Here. Now. I want you to bring yourself off in my shower.*

"Baby, what was I supposed to do?"

3

"I... I said okay... I'd said it before I'd even had a chance to think it through.

"So I stood before him, and slipped my fingers to my groin. I parted my thighs, and slowly inserted my fingers in my pussy.

"*Yes*, he said. *That's it, Anissa. Show me how you masturbate at home.*

"It was awkward, standing there in his shower, baby. I couldn't get the right angle I needed to hit my spot. I was frustrated... And he was watching me. I just needed to change my position... So I did. I squatted down low, putting my weight on my toes and spreading my legs wide. I was able to get my fingers deeper inside myself. Oh, baby, it was amazing. I was fucking myself hard beneath him. The water was splashing off my arms, my tits and my fingers... I was slapping my pussy lips, sprinkling them with warm water. Oh, I was losing myself in my lust. To be watched as I played with myself, when I so desperately needed relief, was so arousing.

"And then I opened my eyes, Mark. Oh God, Jackson's cock was level with my vision. Its incredible length lingering down to within touching distance of my mouth. It was so tempting. And I was so desperate. So needy. I had to do something with it.

"Jackson, I said, my voice hoarse with desire, bring your big cock to me. Please. Rub it against my cheek.

"*Are you sure?*

"Fucking hell, Mark, I thought he was going to make me beg... And I was fucking sure I was going to!

"Yes, I cried, fucking myself senseless under him, rub it over my whole face! All over it, Jackson!

"And he did, Mark, he rubbed his big, black cock over me. From one cheek to the other, over my lips and my nose. It was more than the length of my whole head, and he was massaging it into my skin. Oh, baby, I started to pant, as I fucked myself. You could hear the water thundering off both our bodies. My heart was pounding. My pulse thudding in my head. His huge, beautiful member all over me. I opened my mouth. I let him graze the inside of my lips. He didn't push it in. He was too careful for that... But I couldn't help clasping onto it between my lips, as if I was puckering up to kiss it, or bite it, and my orgasm came racing into my cunt. Holy shit, Mark, I shook like a leaf. Buckled like a bitch. And flowed my juices onto the floor of his shower like a whore in heat.

"I let my tongue hang out, against his length, as I gasped for breath... I was high on him, baby... Imprisoned in my pleasure... Shoving aside the shame of my naughtiness... If only he'd forced his cock into my mouth... I'd have... Oh, baby, I'd have willingly... Suck-

"Oh yes, Mark, that's it! Come on! Wank it! Oh shit, yes! Baby, yes! Fucking hell! Look at that pulsing, white cock! Your spunk must be ready to- Oh yes, baby, there it is! Spunk all over the place! Shoot it, baby! Oh God, that cum could've been in my pussy. Oh, Mark, you are a bad, little wanker, tugging on your white cock until you shoot on the floor.

"Mmmmmm, baby, watch me... Watch me... As I... Lick... It... All... Up."